A **BLOOD** RED MORNING

ALSO BY MARK PRYOR

^ABLOOD RED MORNING

A HENRI LEFORT
MYSTERY

Mark Pryor

MINOTAUR
BOOKS
NEW YORK

First published in the United States by Minotaur Books, an imprint of St. Martin's Publishing Group

www.minotaurbooks.com

Designed by Omar Chapa

Library of Congress Cataloging-in-Publication Data

Names: Pryor, Mark, 1967- author.
Title: A blood red morning / Mark Pryor.
Description: First edition. | New York : Minotaur Books, 2024. |
    Series: Henri Lefort mystery ; 3
Identifiers: LCCN 2024005556 | ISBN 9781250330604 (hardback) |
    ISBN 9781250330611 (ebook)
Subjects: LCSH: Murder—Investigation—Fiction. | World War, 1939-1945—
    France—Paris—Fiction. | France—History—German occupation,
    1940-1945—Fiction. | LCGFT: Detective and mystery fiction. | Historical
    fiction. | Novels.
Classification: LCC PS3616.R976 B57 2024 | DDC 813/.6—dc23/eng/20240209
LC record available at https://lccn.loc.gov/2024005556

Our books may be purchased in bulk for promotional, educational, or business use. Please contact your local bookseller or the Macmillan Corporate and Premium Sales Department at 1-800-221-7945, extension 5442, or by email at MacmillanSpecialMarkets@macmillan.com.

First Edition: 2024

10 9 8 7 6 5 4 3 2 1

To my wonderful Mum. Thank you for your love, support,
and our shared knowledge that I'm your favorite child.
I love you.

A BLOOD RED MORNING

CHAPTER ONE

Paris, France
December 31, 1940
5:17 A.M.

The tall man turned onto rue Jacob and moved silently along the sidewalk toward the building, and the specific apartment, detailed in the letter tucked into the breast pocket of his heavy wool coat. He clicked a flashlight on every few seconds to illuminate his path in the darkness; he didn't want to trip and thereby make noise to alert people he was coming.

He didn't mind the blackout, though; in fact, quite the opposite. Flitting around Paris doing a dirty job for the Germans was a despised but lucrative endeavor, so the fewer people who saw him the better. That was the best reason to do this at night, or early before the sun rose, but he'd discovered another good reason to go first thing in the morning: to catch his suspects unaware, to surprise them when they were too groggy or hungover to lie. Or to lie well, anyway.

It wasn't that he liked his new job, not that exactly. But he'd lost his old one at the bank when the Germans took over the city, and he had no other way to provide for himself and his aging mother.

And it was challenging in a way his bank job wasn't, he had to admit that, because he'd never thought of himself as an intimidating man, despite his height. He was too thin, and his mother had always described him as baby-faced. She still did even though he was almost fifty. He wasn't scary-looking, no, but he had the sandy hair and blue eyes that the Germans liked.

Of course, the gun and black leather wallet with official credentials dosed him up with a lot more confidence to knock on doors, to ask questions. To get aggressive. One aspect of the job he did enjoy was the look of respect in the eyes of the people he visited. Or maybe it was fear, which was even better.

These people deserved to be afraid. They looked down on him, but those he talked to were the worst of the worst. Writing letters to the police and to the Germans, snitching on their neighbors, their friends. Even their own family members sometimes.

He's violating curfew every night.
She's having sex for money.
That illegitimate child is Jewish.
They're both buying and selling on the black market.

In school they called it tattling. On the streets it was called snitching. In Paris these days it was at a new level, people taking out their petty jealousies, exorcising resentments that had built up for years. People were using the strict German regime to get their neighbors fined, beaten, or jailed for years of grievances, real or imagined.

That's why he was stalking down rue Jacob before dawn, to investigate one such claim. A neighbor had written to the authorities about a woman buying food and clothing over and above her allotted rations. The snitch claimed she was some kind of princess, which could make it interesting, the man thought.

He'd never met a princess.

He wondered if she'd be intimidated when he confronted her. He needed a few more details from the snitch, but then he'd go straight to her—

Ah, wait, here's the building, he thought. He was there already. *And who is this coming toward me? It's still curfew, so I will make a note of that!*

"Do you live in this building?" the tall man demanded of the stranger, in his most authoritative tone.

"Who are you?" the stranger replied.

"My name is Guy Remillon, and I'm asking the questions." He adjusted his new hat, which was still a little tight. "Do you live here?"

"None of your business."

"If I'm the police it is."

Remillon didn't like the look of disdain he was getting, and liked even less the rude response he got.

"You're not police, of that I'm sure. Now leave me alone."

He was about to reply, and forcefully, when the door swung open and a man stepped out.

"Who are you, and what are you doing at this hour?" Remillon asked.

"I would like to know the same from you," the other man re-plied. "Don't tell me you're here on official business."

"Oh yes, most definitely." Remillon straightened to his full height. "A very serious allegation against a woman in this building."

"Is that so? What allegation?"

"Black marketeering. She could be transported for that."

"Yes. She could."

Remillon looked past the other man and into the lobby of the building, which was why he didn't see the gun until the last second. Didn't see it until it was too late. Remillon's eyes opened wide, then his mouth did the same, and he felt a punch to the chest before staggering backward into the middle of the street. He was confused for no more than a second, then his already-dead body crumpled to the cobbles. The new hat that he'd bought with his first paycheck from the Germans rolled away as his head hit the ground, making three wobbly revolutions before coming to rest upside down in the gutter.

CHAPTER TWO

December 31, 1940
10:17 A.M.

Chief Louis Proulx barged into my office without so much as a knock on the door, which would have given me a moment to swing my feet off my desk and maybe even open my eyes.

"Detective Lefort?" he said, emphasizing the word "detective." "It is Homicide Detective Henri Lefort, isn't it?"

"You know perfectly well—"

"Are you seriously telling me you didn't hear a thing this morning?" He slapped my report, which was a blank piece of paper jammed into a manila folder, onto the desk where my feet had just been. "No shouting, no screaming? How about the shot itself, for God's sake?"

"I'm a heavy sleeper."

"You were drunk."

"Someone can be both drunk *and* asleep," I pointed out. "But either way I was off duty, and when I'm off duty, my liver is none of your business."

He shook his head, apparently not wishing to debate either philosophy or my off-duty prerogatives. "What are you working on?"

"A bottle of Irish whiskey."

"Here, Henri, for Christ's sake. At your job."

"Ah. Not so much, as it happens. When the Germans corralled most of our young men for war or work, they also removed the majority of our criminal population. I hope that's going terribly for them, by the way. They should employ their own criminals."

"Their own criminals are wearing military uniforms and are busy stinking up our city," he said, but I noticed he lowered his voice. Sensible, too; it was starting to seem like you couldn't trust the people that you used to.

"The truest words you've ever spoken."

"Right, then." He perched himself on the edge of my desk. "Since you didn't see or hear a damn thing, you're not any kind of witness."

"Oh, is that how that works?"

"Funny. How it works is that if you're not a witness, you can be the lead detective."

"And by *lead* you mean *only*, right?" He started to speak but I cut him off, knowing what he was going to say. "Resources don't allow for more than one . . . I get it."

"Correct." He stood and smiled. "At least you won't have to travel far to the crime scene."

"Who was the *mec*?"

"The dead man? No idea. But he had a gun and some German

credentials on him, so either a thief, an informer, or . . . something else."

"Any idea why he was at my building?"

"Did you just want me to solve the whole thing so you can sit here with your feet on your desk snoozing?"

"Can't say I'd mind, honestly. Cold and dangerous out there, much nicer in here."

"Sorry to disappoint, but I'll be the one staying warm and dry. Maybe our dead man had something more on him that will tell his story." He opened the door and flashed that insincere smile at me again. "If not, I'm sure you'll figure it all out. Have fun at the morgue."

"And by morgue, you mean . . . ?"

I was asking because the authorities had taken to using the jail cells in our building, the Préfecture, as the morgue. The combination of a high death rate since they'd come to town and some faulty ancient plumbing at the actual morgue had required the sausage-eaters to find extra space. They'd settled on the dank, cold jail beneath us, figuring that we'd want victims of murder close by for our investigations. I didn't see the logic, myself, since in my experience the absolute worst witnesses were dead people.

He pointed downward. "I do, yes."

"So no autopsy, or are they doing those here now, too?"

"They are not, but he was shot once in the heart. We don't need a medical professional to tell us that."

"Did someone at least dig the bullet out for me to look at?"

"You're assuming there's one inside him."

I couldn't tell if he was irritating me on purpose. "Well now, I wouldn't have to assume if someone had done a goddamn autopsy, would I?"

"Very true."

"Well, maybe next time." But my sarcasm was lost on him.

"Probably not, if the cause of death is obvious."

"Great. Back to my bullet, can you get someone to have a look at least?"

"I suppose we could arrange that, if they didn't find one at the scene."

"Well, did they?"

"There you go again, asking me to do your job. Have fun in the morgue." He gave me a cheery wave and didn't wait for my reply before shutting the door.

"You already said that," I muttered, for no one's benefit but my own.

•   •   •

I stood next to the naked body of a tall, sandy-haired, and slightly emaciated man who had been shot once, right through the heart.

"Here you are, sir." A uniformed officer who looked to be in his late teens handed me a folder, which I opened and quickly scanned. "Also, someone from the German High Command is here, wanting to see the body. I don't know why."

"Paperwork."

"I'm sorry, sir?"

"Paperwork. The Germans are all about papering everything, and that includes documenting each and every murder of their new subjects. You can show him in."

"Yes, sir. He said he doesn't speak French, but I can translate."

"German speaker, eh? Probably one of the reasons you got this job."

"Yes, sir. Lucky me."

The officer disappeared and came back a moment later with a nasty-looking piece of work. He was as tall and emaciated as our victim, but also had the misfortune to be bald, gaunt, and appeared not to have been exposed to the sun for the past decade.

"Good God, man," I said. "Did you come to see the body or check in as a corpse?"

The German fixed his eyes on me, and they were brimming with contempt. "*Quoi?*" he said, establishing that he knew at least one word in French, even if that word was only "what."

"I was merely wondering, how long since you yourself died?" I looked him up and down. "A couple of weeks, I'd guess. Maybe a month?"

The *flic* declined to translate word-for-word, I noticed, probably because he was busy turning bright red with the effort of not laughing.

The Kraut decided to ignore my question and instead grabbed the file from my hands. He perused it for maybe five seconds and then spent a moment looking from it to the corpse. He finally handed the file back to the officer and asked something in German. He nodded at the response, and turned on his heel and left.

"What did he say to you?" I asked.

"He thanked me for my time and professionalism, and said you would be arranging for me to do some real policing based on my excellent work assisting with this matter."

"I can only assume from your glib attitude and baseless optimism you've not been with the Paris police for very long?"

"Six weeks, sir. It was either the police or some Kraut factory in the Rhineland." He looked around the dank room with a grimace. "And I'm still not sure if I made the right choice."

"You did, son. What's your name?"

"Renaud. Paul Renaud."

"How old are you?"

"Twenty."

"I could use an impertinent *flic* from time to time."

"Impertinent?"

"It was a compliment. You remind me of me, when I was young and stupid." He bristled and opened his mouth, but I clapped him on the shoulder and grinned. "Also a compliment. You're gonna need a thicker skin, though."

"I'm guessing you can help with that," he said with a smile.

"Oh, most definitely." I turned to the body. "Flip him onto his side for me. Facing away."

Renaud grimaced again but did as I asked. The dead man had a few large moles and more hair than I expected on his back, but no holes in it.

"What are you looking for?" Renaud asked, and let the body fall back to supine when I nodded for him to do so.

"An exit wound."

"And since there wasn't one, the bullet is still inside him?"

"*Exactement.*"

"And that means . . . ?"

I liked his eagerness to learn, so I didn't mind the questions in the slightest. He really did remind me of me at that age: equal parts ignorant, curious, and appropriately disrespectful of authority.

"Whether or not the bullet is still inside him only matters because it means it's still retrievable. If we can get it, we might be able to tell what kind of gun he was shot with."

"And if we find a suspect who has the same gun . . ."

"Right."

He leaned over the body, peering at the neat hole in Remillon's chest. "Where inside do you think it is?"

"No clue. Bullets bounce around inside a human body like a rubber ball. Could be anywhere above the waist. I've seen someone get shot in the chest and cough the bullet up as he died."

"*Merde.*"

"Not pleasant. Even less so for him, of course. Anyway, I'll arrange for a doctor to come by and have a look. In the meantime, where are his things?"

"In my office." He jerked a thumb over his shoulder toward a desk that was bare save for a pile of clothes and some other bits and pieces. I walked over to inspect everything.

"Ration cards, identification," I murmured, mostly to myself, "ah, and look at this, a Luger P08."

"Technically a Mauser."

"I'm sorry?"

"It was a Luger P08, but Mauser took over production after the last war." He shrugged. "Same weapon though."

"You're a firearms expert, are you?"

"Just a hobby."

"Good one to have for wartime. You happen to know whether the gun was found on him?"

"Where else would it have been?"

"If it was tucked into his pants or in a pocket, that tells a different story than if it was found on the ground beside him."

"How so?" I didn't answer, wanting him to figure it out, and after a few seconds a look of understanding seemed to wash over him. "Ah, yes, if it was on the ground, he'd have been holding it. Maybe pointing it."

"Right. Maybe he started whatever ended him."

"Whereas if it was in his pocket or waistband . . . got it." He nodded, then looked down, as if disappointed with himself. "I'm afraid I don't know where it was found. I wasn't here when he was brought in."

"No way for you to know then."

He looked up quickly. "Wait a second. I probably should have mentioned this before, but that Nazi who was here just now."

"What about him?"

"He looked through the dead *mec*'s things, too. Only, he found something, a piece of paper, and kept it."

"Kept it?"

"I saw him put it into his coat pocket."

"Interesting. And inappropriate. Any idea what it was?"

"No, I didn't really pay attention to this stuff, sorry. Just looked like a piece of paper folded in half."

"Just a plain piece of white paper? And did you see any writing on it?"

"Actually, it was blue. And no, no writing that I saw, but it was a quick look so there might well have been, and I just didn't see it."

"Anything else you can think of?"

"No, sir."

"Well, I best track down that piece of paper. I don't like it when someone hides something from me like that. Then again, it tells me it's important information, and I do like that. Especially if I'm not supposed to see it."

"You're talking about the Gestapo thug who was just here."

"I was, not this poor fellow." I looked down at the body of Guy Remillon. "Although you have to agree, that Nazi didn't look much better than this *mec*."

"True, sir." Renaud grinned. "Perhaps you'd best hurry."

"Indeed." I returned the smile. "Did you catch his name, by any chance?"

"No, sir, I didn't."

"No, me neither." I clapped him on the shoulder. "Maybe I'll try the real morgue. Someone there is bound to know him."

CHAPTER THREE

My first trip was back upstairs to look for Nicola Prehn, who'd not been at her desk when I rolled into work. Nicola was an early bird and the smartest person in the murder squad. If they ever allowed women to become cops, and given the way the world was turned upside down I could see it happen, well, she'd be running the entire force within a week. She'd be good at it, too, and I knew that for a fact: She ran the operations in the apartment we shared like a major general. Always food for breakfast, even these days, and one or two fresh items for the evening meal.

Except this morning. This morning, I'd gotten up to an empty apartment and, worse, an empty fridge. Not even a pot of coffee on the stove. It didn't matter to me that coffee these days tasted like sewage water filtered through ground bugs, the point was there was none ready and waiting for me.

I'm aware that makes me sound like either a spoiled brat or an abusive husband. The former might be close to the truth, the latter couldn't be farther from it. The fact was, Nicola also happened to be my sister. And that was a secret we'd kept from the police, who we both worked for, those same clever people who were trained and equipped to find out your worst secrets. This was definitely ours, because it hid another, and much more nefarious, truth: I'd taken my brother's name twenty-two years ago after he died on the battlefield in my arms. The police had been trying to pin a murder case on me back then, and in that moment the only exit I saw was through becoming him. Nicola had been happy enough that I survived the ghastly war, and her choices were either to turn me in and lose both brothers forever, or help me shore up the lie. She chose the second, obviously.

I was making my way to speak to Chief Proulx when she stormed into the open office area where she worked as a secretary.

"Henri, may we speak, please?" Her voice was calm but I could see a glint of panic or desperation in her eyes. Her head indicated my office would be the spot for our discussion, so I followed her in there and closed the door.

"I need your help," she said.

"I can see that."

"It's Daniel. He's been arrested."

My heart sank at the same time alarm bells started ringing in my head, blocking out what Nicola was saying next. If my colleague and her boyfriend Daniel Moulin had been arrested, I might be next—he'd started to play a tangential role in what people were beginning to call the Resistance. And the Germans were beating, arresting, and shooting people they suspected of being Resistance members.

Torturing them, too, to find out who else was working against the occupiers. I'd played a minor role in freeing someone recently, which had connected me with Daniel's brother, a major player, and I'd had no choice but to help them with an operation of their own.

"Henri, are you listening?" She was thumping my arms to get my attention because, frankly, I'd been suddenly worried about my own skin and had tuned her out.

"Wait, what did you just say?"

She lowered her voice. "Not arrested by the Germans. By us."

"You mean, the Paris police?"

"Yes, exactly."

"What for? Surely not . . ." I couldn't bring myself to say the word. There were too many people within my own Préfecture willing to sell out anyone involved with the Resistance movement.

"No, that's what I'm trying to tell you. He was drunk."

"Drunk?" I didn't understand. "Is that a crime, too, now?"

"It is if you're disorderly along with it."

"*Merde.* Where is he?"

"Pigalle substation."

"Do they know he's a *flic*? Tell me he wasn't drunk in uniform."

"No, he wasn't. But one of the men there sent a runner to let me know. Daniel was in the police academy with him, so he's being kind. And discreet."

"Thank heavens for small mercies."

"But we have to get him out of there before the shift changes."

"When is that these days?"

"Noon."

I looked at my watch. "I have a case to solve."

"A murder case?"

"Yes. Poor bastard was killed right outside our building. Did you hear anything? Where were you when I got up?"

"Depends when you got up, but no, I didn't hear anything at all. But that's not important right now. We have to get Daniel out of jail before he's found out."

"I get no coffee or breakfast, and now this is *my* emergency?"

"Henri." Her eyes pleaded with me. "He'll lose his job, his career. And who the hell knows what will happen to him then? What if he's sent to one of those work camps in Germany? Some coal mine somewhere?"

That would make him a victim, make her miserable, and make me the bad guy. I couldn't let any of that happen to disrupt what was already a pretty wretched existence.

"Pigalle, you say? I'll see if I can find a car, make it part of the investigation somehow."

Nicola heaved a sigh of relief and gave me a peck on the cheek. "*Merci*, Henri."

I nodded. "We better open that door before people start talking."

"I think we're past that. Will you go now?"

"Of course. My murder investigation can play second fiddle to your drunken boyfriend."

Nicola threw me a dirty look and let herself out of my office, leaving the door open. I still had my hat and coat on, so I started for the stairs. I was stopped by the man who'd become my nemesis, Georges Guyat. He was a useless detective and worse human being, who we all called GiGi because he had both the long face and, in my opinion, the intellect, of a horse. Right now, he was holding a box of what looked like food. Real food, too, not wartime scraps and powdered or diluted slop.

"What do you have there, GiGi?" I asked lightly.

"Contraband."

I peered into the box, which he failed to cover with an arm. "Looks like cans of good food and . . . is that cheese? And wine?"

"I told you, contraband."

"From whom?"

"A black marketeer."

I looked around. "And where is he?"

"He got away."

"Of course he did. Still, you managed to keep up with and capture a box, very well done, Detective."

"Piss off, Lefort. It's more than you've done lately." He slid the box into a locker, one of the temporary spaces we used for evidence before it got put into the more secure evidence room. "Although, I hear someone got murdered outside the apartment of the great Detective Henri Lefort, and he doesn't even hear it." He turned back to me and smirked, or maybe that's just what it looked like. "Embarrassing, *non*?"

"Not especially. I live on the top floor and am a heavy sleeper."

"Sleeping, eh? Not what I heard. More like drunk."

"Well, I'm glad to see you remain consistent, Detective."

"What's that supposed to mean?"

"You valuing gossip and rumor over facts. Not the greatest attribute for a policeman but, like I say, consistent."

GiGi puffed himself up with outrage. "I am as good a detective as you. Maybe I should come with you and show you."

"Thank you, but not necessary." That was the last thing I needed, for multiple reasons, so I jerked my thumb in the direction I'd just come from. "There's a pool of secretaries just waiting to hear your latest gossip, and maybe compare stockings with you."

The outrage was still there but his words appeared to have dried up, so I gave him my blandest smile and trotted past him, down the stairs, and into the street.

•   •   •

I'd found a car by using bluster, pulling rank, and bullying a junior officer into giving me his, which would land the lad in trouble because, or so I gathered from his babbling, he was supposed to be picking up a senior detective and driving him somewhere or other. I tried not to listen to the whining, which I found to be the best way to avoid feeling guilty.

I wound my way up to the Eighteenth Arrondissement, the streets narrowing as I got closer to what used to be the old village of Montmartre, high on a hill overlooking the city of Paris. On the way, I marveled at the lack of traffic, the dearth of cars and horses. Even bicycles seemed few and far between. I marveled, too, at how fast Paris had changed from a bustling, thriving city to a skeleton of herself, her bones still in place but her beauty and spirit rapidly waning.

Parking on rue des Abbesses, I walked the remaining way to the small police station that served this part of the city. I let myself in and walked up to the front desk. An elderly man, not in uniform, sat beside it reading a newspaper that was faded and smudged. I leaned in to look and saw it was from today, but a year ago. The man looked over the top of it and his eyes widened.

"You're Henri Lefort," he said.

"*Merde*, do I owe you money?"

"Newspapers. You were in all of them a few months back."

"Oh, so you read the new ones, too."

"No, sir. Not anymore. Stopped right about the time you saved that empress lady."

He was referring to Princess Marie Bonaparte, who I may or may not have saved from an intruder in her house. We'd become friends after that, and when the Germans requisitioned her palatial home, she moved into the empty apartment below mine and Nicola's.

"Princess, but who's keeping score?"

"Right." He clearly wasn't. "Much better for the soul to read last year's news than this, for obvious fucking reasons. I can enjoy the good news all over again, and the bad news, well, it's not really news, is it? So it's not as disturbing because I already know about it."

That was about as close to genius as I'd heard in weeks, frankly. If these pearls of wisdom had been delivered by a sober man, I would have written them down.

"You know my name, what's yours?"

"I am Christophe Duggan." He was definitely slurring. "Pleased to make your acquaintance."

"Likewise, I'm sure." I asked, waving away his rancidly sweet breath. "Are you drunk?"

"Not yet. Give me a couple of hours."

"And where's your uniform?"

"That's the funny thing. I was on duty yesterday but don't recall clocking out." He spread his hands wide. "So who knows what happened to it?"

"Well, did you walk home naked?"

He considered that seriously. "I doubt it. Someone would

have called the police, surely. And I woke up in my own bed, so I know that didn't happen."

"Do you not have a supervisor here?"

"Used to. Now I'm like a judge, I can do what I like."

"And wear what you like, apparently."

"Oh, don't worry about my uniform." He waved a dismissive hand. "It'll turn up, I'm sure. It always does."

"So this has happened bef—" I cut myself off. "Never mind, I'm here to see a prisoner."

"We have no prisoners."

"What?" I looked past him.

"We have two cells, both empty."

"But you had someone here. A Daniel Moulin."

"Ah, yes. Overnight."

I waited for an explanation but eventually realized I wasn't going to get one without pulling teeth. "Tell me, Duggan, why is Monsieur Moulin no longer locked up?"

"Ah, yes," he said again. "That would be because I let him go."

"When?"

"About an hour ago."

"And why did you do that?"

"Because he was sober. Or soberer, anyway."

"Well, someone here needs to be," I said, exasperated. "You just let the man out?"

He shrugged. *"Le camembert qui dit au bleu tu pues."*

"I don't . . . what?"

He repeated himself. "Me keeping him here, well, it's like the camembert telling the blue cheese it stinks." He shrugged again. "Life is hard enough right now, every day we are at war with our occupiers, whether we dare say it or not. Some of us are also at war with the bottle, me and your friend. That makes him my ally on two fronts, so yes, I let him go."

Again, his wine-addled logic actually made sense to me. "I don't suppose he said where he was going?"

"*Non.* Probably to look for more cheap booze. Or a bed. Maybe both."

"Perhaps he'll find your uniform in the process."

"We live in hope, Detective Lefort."

"New Year's Eve, used to be it was a good time for that."

"But we still must. In this moment, what else do we have?"

CHAPTER FOUR

The emergency nullified, I took advantage of the wheels beneath me to wind my way back out of Montmartre and over to Daniel Moulin's place to check on him. And to get his account of events so I knew how hard to slap him. It bothered me more than it probably should have, but Moulin had never been anything except a perfect gentleman and completely professional policeman. To get drunk and cause a scene was out of character for him, and I wanted to know what lay behind it.

He lived in an apartment overlooking boulevard Raspail, on the third floor. I trudged up the stairs and banged on the door, hoping it would exacerbate the mandatory hangover headache. I was surprised, though, when the door opened and a large man, half-dressed in what was going to be a German uniform, appeared. I didn't know if the *mec* had a hangover, but from the frown on his large face he certainly hadn't appreciated my loud knocking.

More surprises from Daniel? I wondered. *This should be a doozy.*

He spoke in half-decent French. "If you're looking for the previous occupant, he no longer lives here."

"Why not?"

He puffed himself up to his full height, which was about a foot taller than me. "Because I do now. Goodbye."

He started to close the door but I stopped it with a foot. "Wait. Where does he live now?"

"I don't know and I don't care."

I managed to extract my foot in time to save it from the door that slammed in my face.

On the way back downstairs I pondered what I'd just seen. Daniel wouldn't be the first person turned out of their home by the Krauts. It seemed odd to me, though, because there were so many empty apartments in Paris; there was no need to make people homeless. In my own building, which had two apartments per floor, half were empty. It was especially puzzling that this sausage-eater had picked a police officer to evict. We were just about the last group of humans that our invaders were still being vaguely polite to. Then again, there was no need to ban croissants, either, and the fuckers had done that with a vengeance. Other than needless cruelty there was a lot I couldn't explain about those bastards.

Well, the mystery of Daniel will have to wait, I thought. *I have a case to solve.*

I climbed back into the car and headed to my own building. Turning onto rue Jacob felt different—it was strange to be there on the clock, to approach my home with the eyes of an investiga-

tor. I felt a little violated, if I was being honest with myself. This was where Nicola and I had always been safe, where we lived our adult lives and held on to our particular secrets. Now here I was, parked halfway down the street and approaching my front door with my suspicions on full alert and about to question people I knew, and loved, about a murder. A year ago, Proulx would have sent anyone *but* me, but the force was stretched as thin as the shoe leather we wore these days.

I stepped into the building and got my second surprise of the day. This one was a little better, though. A young woman in khaki trousers and a white shirt was sweeping the tile floor. She looked to be twenty years old and the foreign look to her exceptionally pretty face reminded me of someone.

"Bonjour," I said, looking around. "Are you sure you're in the right place?"

"Very sure." She stopped sweeping, gave me a giant smile. and stuck out her hand. "Natalia Tsokos. *Enchanté.*"

"Henri Lefort." I shook her hand. "My pleasure. Did you move into the building?"

"Oui. I am the new concierge."

"Tsokos, is that Greek?"

"Yes, my uncle is Lucas Nomikos."

"Lucas! I knew you looked familiar." She had the slightly darkened skin tone and similar eyes to Lucas, who used to live in one of the apartments on the ground floor. He was our de facto concierge, fixing things when they broke, keeping the hallway clean and tidy, and sometimes manning the door, but only when he felt like it. Like so many, he'd left Paris as the Germans were marching down the Champs-Élysées, and we'd not heard a word since. "What is he doing? Is he well?"

"Very well, as far as I know. He works at the Prado in Spain. They gave him a room there, so he's sort of a concierge and security guard."

"I'm glad to hear it." Lucas was not the sharpest tool in the shed, but he was kind, reliable, and loyal to those who treated him well. I'd helped him out of a legal scrape a time or two, and his gratitude was unending. I had a very soft spot for him, and was genuinely pleased to hear he'd landed somewhere safe and was, apparently, appreciated. "What brings you here?"

Her pretty eyes shifted away from me, and I knew I was about to get only a slice of the truth, if any at all. "Let's just say that there were some men in uniform unhappy with a brick that flew through someone's window."

"A criminal in my building?" I laughed. "I should have warned you, I'm a policeman."

"You should have!" She laughed, too. "And here I am confessing my sins."

"Where was this unfortunate encounter?"

"Barcelona."

"Ah, then, well beyond my jurisdiction, you're safe."

She cocked her head and let the broom handle fall against her chest as she held out her wrists. "No handcuffs for me then?"

"Not today." I felt my face redden, because it sure felt like she was flirting with me, and I wasn't used to that. "So, did you move into Lucas's old apartment?"

"Yes, I got in yesterday and have been sweeping and dusting ever since." She grabbed the broom again. "Figured I might as well keep going out here."

"Well, thank you for that. And welcome to Paris."

"*Merci*. Which apartment is yours?"

"The only occupied one on the top floor." I pulled out my notebook. "While I have you here, I need to ask if you heard anything this morning related to the ruckus outside."

"No, what happened?"

"Some fellow got himself shot."

"Shot?" A look of alarm passed over her face. "By the . . ." She trailed off but I knew what she was going to say.

"I don't think so. These days the Germans seem happy to take credit when they shoot one of us. This comes over more surreptitious."

"A real murder." Her voice was a whisper and her eyes wide. "And right outside?"

"Within spitting distance."

"I'm a heavy sleeper, especially after a day's traveling and lugging bags around."

"No need for this then." I tucked my notebook away.

"So, you're not just a policeman, you're a detective?" *Definitely smarter than her uncle*, I thought.

"And solving crimes on my own doorstep now. At least, trying to."

"Please do," Natalia said. "Scary to think there's a murderer out there somewhere. Maybe close by."

"Sadly, we live amongst several thousand of them, all marching around in jackboots and wearing whichever uniform justifies their actions."

"I thought they were respectful of Parisians, that's what I heard. And one of the reasons I came here."

"For a while, I suppose you could say they were. The shine wore off after a month or two. Well, I should stop talking before you change your mind and head back to Spain."

"Handcuffs, remember?"

"Ah, yes. If you get into any trouble here in Paris, you know where I live."

She huffed in mock outrage. "So, I have to be in trouble to stop by your place?"

There she was, flirting again. Perhaps. "No, of course not." I looked at my watch, completely unconcerned with what time it was. "Stop by anytime. Now, I have to get back to work."

"Me, too," she said with that sparkling smile. "See you around."

I nodded and took the stairs, using the time it took to get to Mimi's front door to gather myself, to make the change from awkward civilian to authoritative detective. Of course, that demeanor vanished the moment Mimi opened her door and gave me a motherly kiss on each cheek. She wore a pink beret, which reminded me what day of the week it was; she'd taken to wearing it every Tuesday whenever she opened her door or went outside. She'd sewn the words "Go Home" in white thread inside, and reasoned that every time she encountered a German he would inevitably look at her bright beret. And she would know, even if he didn't, what message it conveyed. I'd persuaded her to limit the wearing of it to one day a week—there were so many small insults being thrown at the occupiers these days that I worried hers would be uncovered. And her famous name and wealth might not be the protection it used to be in the face of the kind of overreactions we'd been seeing of late.

"Come in, come in." She held the door open until I went through, then she led me into her living room. I'd spent many hours in here, telling Princess Marie Bonaparte my deepest darkest secrets. A friend and acolyte of Sigmund Freud, she'd styled herself as my psychoanalyst and turned out to be damned good at it. The free Château Pétrus she served during sessions hadn't hurt, but the woman had a knack for getting me to talk. And for seeing through the many half-truths and misdirections I'd attempted. She'd also put a name to the dragon that lived inside me, the one that roared fire every time some innocent in my presence made a sound I didn't like. No, not just *didn't like*—Mimi had compared it to an allergy, one that made my blood pressure soar and tilted a normally calm man into a raging idiot. Misophonia, we'd agreed to call it, *the hatred of sounds*. Oh, so accurate.

More than just diagnosing my misophonia, she and Nicola had been the only ones in the world to know the secret of my identity, until I told Daniel Moulin. Another reason to find that man and make sure he was on the straight and narrow. I didn't worry about him spilling my story intentionally, but booze has a way of loosening tongues just as effectively as a pretty girl with soft lips, or an ugly man sporting brass knuckles.

"What can I do for you?" Mimi asked. "Odd time for a social visit; did you get fired?"

"Funny. Truth is, they don't have the manpower to fire people."

"Even you?"

"Especially me. I'm actually good at my job."

"I suppose. But my question stands."

"Not a social visit. I'm here about the poor fellow who wound up with a bullet in his chest this morning."

"Terrible business."

"So you know about it."

"Well, Henri, believe it or not when a man is killed outside one's building, tongues wag."

"I'm sure. But did you see or hear anything?"

"No, I was blissfully sound asleep."

A common and frustrating theme right there, but it applied to me, too, so I couldn't really complain. A sound to my left made me swivel in my chair.

"Did you hear that?" My hand moved closer to my gun. "Do you have someone here?"

"As a matter of fact, I do."

"And who might that be?"

I heard a door open and close and then footsteps as someone walked toward us. A sheepish Daniel Moulin appeared in the doorway.

"My day is just full of surprises," I said.

"Good morning, sir."

"I suppose being released from jail counts as a good morning." I turned to Mimi. "I trust you know about that, too?"

"Of course." She smiled. "You know nothing gets past me."

"Very little, for sure." I turned back to Moulin, who had settled himself into a comfortable chair. "You look better than I thought you would."

"Thank you. I feel . . ." He shrugged.

"Taking the day off, are we?"

Mimi laughed. "Was it the civilian clothes? What a fine detective you are, Henri."

I ignored her. "So, what happened last night, Daniel? And since this is very much *not* a work-related discussion, please drop the 'sir' nonsense."

"I had a few too many up in Pigalle, lost my temper, and a couple of our colleagues decided that everyone, including me, would be safer in a cell for the night."

"I've never seen you drunk, let alone act out like that."

"You've never seen me after I've been turned out of my home."

"Ah, yes, I met the gentleman who moved in. Charming fellow."

"No notice, can you believe that? Three of them standing over me as I packed two suitcases. They didn't give a damn that I was a *flic*, the smirking bastards. My home now his, my belongings now his. Why me?"

"You don't expect reason and logic to apply to what they do, surely?" I asked.

"I think what made me so mad was that I tried to explain, we have a list at the Préfecture of abandoned apartments, they could have taken any one of them."

"I didn't realize we were collaborating like that."

"One of those decisions the high-ups made. It helps the Germans, yes, but it also prevents people being thrown out in the street." He snorted with derision. "Or is supposed to."

"Are you moving into one of those now?"

"That's the irony," Moulin said. "I'm not allowed to. They're reserved for the Krauts only."

"Of course they are. Well, I'm sorry, what're you going to do?"

"He'll be staying here, for the foreseeable future," Mimi interjected.

"Here?" One more surprise to add to the day's pile.

"Although, I suppose since he and Nicola are an item, he could move in with you two."

"Not one single chance in hell," I said, horrified at the idea. "Being here will be too close."

"Henri Lefort at his most charming," Mimi said.

I stood. "As I said before, this is not a social visit, and I'm only charming on my own time."

"You're here on police business?" Moulin asked.

"The shooting out front. Because I slept through it as well, Proulx saw fit to have me solve it. No point asking if you heard anything from your jail cell in Pigalle, I suppose."

"Hardly. Mimi told me about it when I got here, about an hour ago."

"Speaking of new arrivals," I said, "have you met our new concierge?"

"She's delightful," Mimi said. "And very pretty, don't you think, Henri?"

"She's about eighteen years old."

"No, she's in her late twenties, which puts her well in range." Mimi looked smugly at me.

"For Daniel maybe," I said.

"He's spoken for, and you are not."

"By the way, who vetted her?" I asked.

"I did. She showed me a letter from Lucas introducing her and giving his permission to live in his apartment."

"Good. Well, if you two will excuse me, I have more people to interview only to find they were asleep and saw nothing."

"You want some help?" Moulin asked.

"Maybe tomorrow, when you're back at work. Enjoy your day off." I patted his shoulder. "Maybe get yourself a pretty pink beret so you can match your new roommate."

I showed myself out.

CHAPTER FIVE

I started knocking on doors, determined to find one person who'd seen or at least heard the murder of Guy Remillon. On the third floor, I hammered on the door of apartment 6, which I knew was the home of Claire Raphael. She was in her late thirties, and I suspected she was a widow because her husband had been in the army, and I'd not seen hide nor hair of him in six months. I suppose I should have said something, asked after her, but people seemed to be minding their own business more these days. Me included, I suppose.

When no one answered, I banged louder and shouted, "Police, open up!"

A moment later, Claire cracked the door and peeked out. "*Oui?* Can I help?"

"Claire, hello. It's me, Henri from upstairs. Sorry to be shouting and banging, but—" I interrupted myself when I saw the state of her. "Are you all right?"

She nodded, but the smeared lipstick and tearstained eyes told a different story.

"Is someone with you?" I asked.

"No, no. No one."

I didn't need to be a detective to spot the lie.

"May I come in, please? Official police business, I promise."

"I don't think . . ." But she backed up a little and I pushed open the door. I walked past her and into the living room, where a shirtless man stood with his back to the wall in just his underwear, as if trying to keep out of sight. He was an ordinary-looking man, utterly nondescript apart from a head of thin, very blond hair, but something about him made the hairs on the back of my neck stand up.

"Who are you?" I demanded.

"My name is Maximillian Zoeller."

The name didn't ring a bell, but when I looked around the room, I saw it. I walked over to his uniform and picked up the jacket.

"You folded your clothes, of course you did. High-ranking, from the decoration."

"Yes. Obergruppenführer."

"Oh my goodness. A Waffen SS general, no less."

"You might want to remember that," he said coolly. "Who are you?"

"Detective Henri Lefort."

"Why are you here, Detective Lefort?"

"Am I mistaken, or is Germans cavorting with Frenchwomen illegal now?" His eyes narrowed and his body stiffened just a fraction. "But I'm not interested in who sleeps with who." I turned to

Claire. "There was a man killed outside our building this morning. Did you see or hear anything?"

"I heard a shot, yes." She nodded, clearly relieved that I was going to leave her situation well alone. "And when I went to the window, I saw a man running away."

"Can you describe him?"

"Not really. I saw him from behind so didn't see his face. He wore a hat, though."

"His build?"

"I would say normal. He was running quite fast, so I suppose he must not have been old."

"Did you see a gun?"

"Yes, it was . . . in his right hand as he ran."

"Which way did he go?"

"Toward rue Bonaparte."

"Can you remember anything else about him, or anything you saw?"

"*Non*, I'm sorry, that's all."

"*Merci*, Claire. You have been more helpful than anyone so far."

I put the general's jacket back, making sure not to wrinkle it.

"Are you going to report this?" he asked.

I could. And he could get in a whole lot of hot water for it. An SS general was supposed to lead by example, and when others on his team broke the rules he'd be the first to discipline them. Even if he denied it, his reputation would be tarnished, his career derailed.

"Are you paying her?" I asked.

"I am not a whore!" Claire snapped.

"I don't pay her, I don't use whores. I give her gifts because I like her."

Their shared outrage was almost adorable, but in my opinion using whores was the way to go for people like him. No entanglements and as much anonymity as you wanted. And he should want a lot, given his rank and everything he stood to lose.

"Who am I to stand in the way of love? And it's your rule, Max, not ours. So your secret is safe with me."

"Thank you."

"Just make sure those gifts include useful things, like food and wine."

A hint of a smile played on his lips. "But of course. These are hard times. Thank you again."

"Have a nice morning." I tipped my hat and left them to whatever comfort they provided each other. Hard times, for certain.

I tried two more apartments, which were either abandoned or temporarily empty. I saved for last the one belonging to Gerald Darroze. He was the building's busybody. He was in his fifties, had somehow retired from a job no one knew about, and spent his life inserting himself into the business of other people, doing his utmost to turn things miserable. If the sun shone, he'd complain it was too hot. If the clouds cooled things off, he'd complain about the shadows they threw. If complaining was an Olympic sport, he'd represent France and win gold.

I took a deep breath outside his door, and knocked. He came shuffling to it, ready to make a fuss about being disturbed, I would guess. But I silenced him with my police credentials. People like Darroze, they respected authority—the man's sole positive attribute, if you ask me.

"Monsieur Lefort." His look of annoyance turned to what might have been nervousness.

"Detective Lefort today. May I come in?"

"Err, yes, of course." He stood aside and I walked in. The place smelled musty and smoky, like someone had recently struck a match. But he wasn't smoking, and the fireplace looked cold. I wrinkled my nose, fairly sure there was rotting food in an open trash can somewhere nearby. Hopefully in the trash can. He was breathing heavily, which I found odd considering the floor seemed fairly flat to me, and led me into the living room, which was sparsely furnished with two heavy wooden armchairs and a battered leather sofa. I chose an armchair and he sank onto the sofa. I swapped out my credentials for the notebook and pencil.

"Why are you panting?" I asked.

"The stairs. Just took some rubbish out to the trash cans. Assuming they still get picked up."

"They do. For now."

"Are you here about the letter?" he asked.

"What letter?"

"I thought . . . Never mind." He pointed upward. "You are here about the noises upstairs."

"What noises?"

"Strange ones. At all hours."

"I live upstairs, Monsieur Darroze. I haven't heard anything."

"Maybe you're making them," he said grumpily.

"What kind of noises do you mean?"

"All kinds. And people going up and down the stairs."

"That's . . . what stairs are for." And this was a typical Gerald Darroze conversation. Unhelpful. "What specific noises are you hearing? And from where exactly?"

"I don't know. Two floors up, maybe three. I can never catch them in the act." *Because there's nothing to catch, maybe?* I thought, but didn't say.

"You're not giving me any helpful information, monsieur. Strange noises from somewhere doesn't really tell me anything."

"The new girl downstairs. Where did she come from?"

"She's the niece of Lucas Nomikos."

"Who?"

"Lucas, who used to live on the ground floor. He cleaned the place and fixed things."

"I didn't care for him."

"How surprising."

"Why is she here?"

"The same reason we're all here, monsieur. She lives here now."

"She's pretty, I suppose." He looked at me with watery eyes. "Then why are you here?"

"There was a shooting outside the building this morning. Very early."

"There was?"

"Did you hear anything?"

"I thought it was a window being broken, or a car backfiring."

"So you did hear it, you think?"

"I suppose I did. But by the time I got to the window, there was no one outside. Not that I could see, anyway."

"You didn't notice someone lying in the street?"

"My eyes aren't what they used to be, and I'm sure I went right to the window before grabbing my glasses. And since they turned all the streetlamps off, it's dark as pitch out there at night. Can't see what's in front of your face, let alone through a window and down into the street."

"True enough." I stood. "Thank you for your time."

"Welcome, I suppose."

He shuffled after me, presumably to make sure I would actually leave. When we got to the doorway, he asked, "So what are you going to do about the ruckus above?"

"Not a damn thing."

"Why the hell not?" His face darkened. "You're a goddamn policeman, do your job."

"I'm a murder detective," I said mildly. "Not the noise police."

"Oh, so you're too good to deal with things that disturb normal people. That it?"

"Pretty much." I stepped into the open doorway but turned back to him. "Had any cheese lately?"

"Cheese?" The ugly little man sneered. "I'm not your fancy friend who buys things on the black market." He wagged a finger. "She might want to watch her back with that, too."

"Meaning?"

"Never you mind. I suppose black marketeering isn't your job, either?"

"I'd sure love to stop all those hungry people from eating but I'm just too busy."

"Why did you ask me about cheese?"

"Because there's a fucking war going on, Darroze. Pay attention, man, people in our city are starving in their own homes. Right here, in Paris. Old people stand in lines for hours hoping to get a morsel of bread. But the real problem, that's some people finding a morsel of cheese to enjoy, and others clomping up and down stairs and making a little noise past nine o'clock."

"Later than that," he snapped.

"Oh boy, really? We should call the Waffen SS in, maybe they can just exterminate everyone who irritates you."

"At least they uphold law and order around here!"

"Are you trying to be funny?" I loomed over him. "Do you mean to tell me you actually support those fuckers roaming our streets and shooting anyone that gets in their way?"

"They don't do that," he said, but his voice was weak and he wouldn't look me in the eye.

"They damn well do, you fool. But even if they didn't, sounds to me like you'd support a few random executions of your fellow countrymen."

"Don't be ridiculous."

"Trust me, Darroze. I'm not the one being ridiculous. Not by a long shot."

With that, I put one hand on his door, stepped onto the landing, and slammed it shut, enjoying the sight of him hopping spryly out of its way and hoping the loud bang hurt his delicate eardrums.

In the lobby, Natalia was finishing up her sweeping. She gestured me to come over, but gone was the flirty demeanor.

"I heard that. With Darroze."

"Nasty little man. If he harasses you in any way at all, you just let me know. Come to think of it, you can let Mimi or Nicola know."

"Thanks, but I can take care of myself. I may be small, but I pack quite the punch." She lifted the broom. "And I'm armed, too."

"Impressive weaponry, but the offer stands."

"Thank you. I wanted to let you know, he was asking me questions."

"What kind of questions?"

"He kept asking what time I got here, if it was early or around the time of the shooting."

"He's like an old fishwife, a nosy busybody. Looking for gossip about what happened."

"Maybe. It didn't feel like that, though."

"Explain."

"It felt like . . ." She tilted her head as she looked for the right words. "Like he was worried. Afraid even."

"That he might be a victim?"

"No, that I'd seen something. Someone."

"You didn't mention this to me before."

"I know. I'd never met the man, so was giving him the benefit of the doubt. But then right before you knocked on his door, he was down here."

"Yes, he told me he was taking out some garbage."

"He did go to the bins, but he wasn't carrying a trash bag."

"He didn't throw anything out?"

"Whatever it was it wasn't very big, and was wrapped in a red cloth, maybe a towel. And it made a loud clunk when he dropped it in, so it was heavy."

"You haven't looked?"

"I'm sure I'm wrong." She shook her head. "But in case I'm not . . ."

"Better that a policeman find whatever it is, eh? Good thinking. Well, I better take a look."

I walked to the back of the building, to the storage area where the bins were kept. There was one per floor, each with a number painted on it. We were supposed to just use our own, but no one much cared if they served a communal use when one or more filled up. Even so, I started with the one for his floor. Luckily for me, they'd recently been emptied, which is why Natalia had heard the clunk, presumably. Nothing in his bin, so I started with those belonging to the ground-floor apartments, and made my way along until the last bin. Inside was a red towel, just like Natalia had said, with something nestled inside.

"Well, well. What do we have here?" I muttered to the inside of the bin. I reached in, and the moment I put my fingers on the towel I knew what it concealed. The hard muscle of a metal revolver, its curves and heft so familiar to a man who'd been a policeman for two decades and was a soldier before that. I pulled it out carefully, then with less trepidation once it was facing away from me. I unwrapped it like the Christmas present it was.

"So I was right, it was a gun." Natalia was in the doorway behind me, and she moved aside to let me escape the garbage room.

"How did you know?"

"Oh, I didn't know for sure. I've been around guns a fair bit, and people carry them a certain way."

"Carefully?"

She nodded. "And add in the surreptitious looks and, you know, the actual shooting this morning, a gun seemed like a good guess at the very least."

"And who knows what else our grumpy Monsieur Darroze has? I will be able to get a warrant to have a look around for myself, thanks to this."

Natalia's eye shifted to the front doors, a look of concern on her face that turned to surprise when a man started yelling at me.

"Lefort, what the hell are you playing at?" GiGi was red in the face. Partly, I suspected, from the walk here from the Préfecture, but for the most part it was the redness of rage.

"I was playing detective. Well, not really playing, more like being one. You should try it."

"Oh, you're so funny, aren't you?" The deepening shade of crimson in his face told me he didn't really believe that. He pointed to the street. "That car. It's mine."

"I think it belongs to the department, GiGi. And by extension, the good people of Paris who pay our meager salaries." I scratched my head, enjoying tormenting him way more than I should. "Which means, if you think about it, that some small part of it is yours. A door handle, a lug nut, perhaps? You pick."

"You *connard*." GiGi took several strides toward me and shook his fist. "I had reserved the car for the whole day. Who do you think you are just hijacking it from my driver?"

"Driver? Why do you need a driver? We're too short-staffed for that."

"That's not the point here," he snapped.

"You can't . . . Oh my goodness, you can't drive, can you?" I smiled broadly. "Well, since we're all here, would you like me to teach you?"

"No. I most certainly would not!"

"Probably for the best, I have work to do." I looked at the gun in my hand. "And you can help."

"What? I'm not helping you." He seemed to finally notice what I was holding. "What's that?"

"Evidence of a crime. And, just as importantly, my basis for a search warrant."

"What are you talking about?"

"Gerald Darroze on the third floor. Young Natalia Tsokos here as good as saw him depositing this gun into someone else's trash. I don't know if he shot Remillon or not, nor whether there's any more evidence in Darroze's apartment. But since we have no motive for the killing, it seems possible, and I aim to find out."

"Why don't you just arrest him?" GiGi asked.

"For throwing away a gun?"

"For murder. And disposing of evidence."

"I prefer my horse in front of my cart, GiGi, not the other way around."

"What does that mean?" The anger had subsided, or turned itself into annoyance.

"It means you going up to his apartment to secure the place and make sure he doesn't flush, burn, or otherwise destroy anything that might be evidence."

"No. Your case, you do it." He folded his arms and I wanted to slap his smug face.

"Time is of the essence, Detective. One of us needs to get that warrant quickly, and the other stay and secure the premises. But only one of us can drive—are you wanting to run back to the Préfecture right now?"

"Well, no. I am most certainly not."

"Then go up to Darroze's flat and make yourself comfortable until I get back."

I headed for the front doors, not giving him a chance to refuse. I did give Natalia a wink on the way past, and she smiled either at that or the rude names GiGi was calling me all the way to the sidewalk.

CHAPTER SIX

It took thirty minutes to find a magistrate and make sure he'd be there for another thirty minutes while I wrote up my application for a search warrant. I was almost done when Nicola knocked on my office door and let herself in.

"Coffee?" she asked.

"Tease. Unless we actually have some . . . ?"

"No, sorry. Didn't mean to get your hopes up."

"As someone said to me recently, hope is about all we have."

"And shitty coffee."

"Ah, yes. Indeed."

"I heard the slow, laborious typing. Sounded like you were beating the poor machine to death." She jerked her thumb over her shoulder. "You know we have secretaries who are quite good at it. And fast."

"Warrant application. Typing myself, putting it down on paper, sometimes helps me think. When I'm dictating there's too much pressure to keep talking, and not say the wrong thing."

"It's for the murder at our building?"

"It is. Gerald Darroze's place."

"That *mec*. The only man I've ever met who's capable of moaning about something I've done, while at the very same time ogling me."

"Quite the talent."

"In fact, I think he ogled me just now, while in handcuffs."

I sat straight up. "Wait, what did you say?"

"I was downstairs when he was being brought in, he gave me a look. Maybe just because he knows me." She wagged a chiding finger. "You might have started this discussion by letting me know someone in our building had been arrested."

"First of all, you started this conversation with a fake offer of coffee. Second of all, he's not supposed to be under arrest. Not yet, anyway." I felt my own temperature rising. "Who brought him in in handcuffs? It was GiGi, wasn't it?"

"Yes. I assumed you two had kissed and made up, and you'd given him orders to arrest Darroze."

"I ordered him *not* to!"

"Ah, I see." She nodded slowly. "That makes more sense."

"What does?"

"You two ignoring each other's orders and, in fact, doing the exact opposite."

"This is your fault, you know."

"What?" Her eyes widened in surprise. "How can this possibly be my fault?"

"Because I commandeered the car he'd reserved this morning. It was the only way to quickly get to Montmartre and save your boyfriend."

"Yes, well, thank you for that. But I don't see—"

"That idiot GiGi is all hot under the collar because he had to use his hooves instead of a car today. He found me at our building and was furious, and now he's arrested Darroze to get the credit and to annoy me."

"Good lord, Henri." She leaned against the doorjamb and rolled her eyes. "Please don't take this the wrong way, and by that I mean please make sure you understand I mean this in the most insulting way possible: you two are like petulant children."

"I told you, this is all your fault."

"This wouldn't have happened if you'd just apologized to him for taking his car."

"It's not his car."

"Fine, the one he properly reserved using the correct procedures for procuring a vehicle from the Préfecture fleet."

"Apologize?"

"Yes. It's when you do something you shouldn't, like you did, and then say sorry afterward."

"And as part of the apology, should I tell him *why* I took it?"

She smiled sweetly. "Not if you would like to avoid cyanide in your soup."

"With all the rationing, I'd be surprised if you could manage either soup or cyanide."

"Want to try me?"

"You are resourceful, so maybe just the soup." I laughed, wanting to end this silly argument with my sister. "Where is Darroze now?"

"GiGi told someone to find him an interview room."

"That idiot can't do anything for himself, except arrest other people's murderers." I stood. "That aside, I better talk to the man before GiGi either tries to beat a confession out of him or succeeds in talking him to death."

I walked Nicola to her desk and then found the interview room, spotting GiGi as he was about to go in.

"Detective," I called out. "A quick word?"

He hesitated, long enough for me to get to where he was. And admire the brand-new shiner he was sporting.

"Good heavens, what happened to your eye? Old man Darroze here get the better of you?"

"Don't start with me, Lefort."

"No plans to," I said genially. Instead, I gave him a shove backward and stepped into the interview room, swiftly closing the door and locking it behind me. Seconds later GiGi banged on it, and Gerald Darroze looked up, confused as to why one detective was yelling profanities at another.

"What the—" he started.

"It's all fine." I waved a dismissive hand. "He's like an overgrown, stupid baby, so he'll calm himself in a minute or so."

He did, but it took two minutes of cursing and door rattling, during which time I made myself comfortable opposite a miserable-looking (more than usual) Darroze. When GiGi finally gave up, or maybe went to get an ax, I spoke up.

"Spending time with you twice in one day, Gerald, that's a rarity."

"Why am I here?"

"Something about a murder, wouldn't you say?"

"I already told you! I didn't see it."

"You've not been arrested for seeing it, monsieur, but for doing it."

"What? That's ridiculous!"

"Well, as of right now I agree." I pointed to the door. "After all, it wasn't me who arrested you, was it?"

"That man, he came bursting through my door. I had no idea who he was, so I hit him. Of course I did."

"Ah, he's not going to appreciate that. Another charge, no doubt: assaulting a police officer." I shook my head. "You're not supposed to do that, even to the shitty ones."

"I told you, I didn't know who he was."

"Frankly, if you did know him you'd probably have hit him harder. Look, let's get down to business, shall we?"

"I didn't do anything wrong!"

"That idiot detective arrested you while I was here getting a search warrant for your place."

"A what?"

"The gun, monsieur. Care to explain ditching the gun?"

"I have no idea what you're talking about." He crossed his arms and looked even more grumpy than usual.

"Next time you dump evidence, try the river. It's dark and wet in there, and a little too deep for me to just stick my arm in and pull it out." He just stared at me. "The gun in the trash bin. Someone saw you."

"Whoever it is, they are lying. I want to go home." The hand-cuffs securing him to the table that sat between us had a different idea, and I had reason not to mind the current turn of events—I wanted him out of the way while I looked around his apartment.

"I'll tell you what," I said. "Give me permission to look around your place, and if I find nothing related to the murder, I'll come back and cut you loose."

"I don't believe you."

"I give you my word. You'll have to answer for hitting GiGi, but that's for another day."

"Will he let me go, too?"

"It's not up to him. Our boss despises him only a little less than I do, so if there's a disagreement I always win."

He thought about it for a good ten seconds. "Your word?"

"I find nothing, you're out. My word."

"Fine. You have my permission."

"Merci." I was surprised he agreed so easily. It suggested either he was innocent, or had done a good job of destroying or disposing of any remaining incriminating evidence. Still, I had him scribble on a piece of paper torn from my notebook that I had his permission to rummage through his place. "Sit tight, don't say a word to horseface, and I'll be back in a couple of hours."

"So, the person who was shot." He looked up at me as I stood to leave. "Was it the man or the woman?"

"I'm sorry, what do you mean?"

"Who was shot."

"A man. A man was shot."

"Ah. Sad. But I suppose better than if it'd been the woman."

"Monsieur Darroze, what are you talking about?"

"I couldn't sleep. That's why I heard the shot. I was sitting up reading by a candle. A few minutes before the bang, I looked out and saw two people talking. One of them had a flashlight they'd flick on every little while."

"Bullshit. You told me that you didn't see anything."

"That's after. You only asked me about *after* the bang."

I resisted the temptation to strangle the man. No one in our building would have minded, and I could make a decent case for myself in court for justifiable homicide. Instead, I took a deep breath. Of course, maybe he was lying, coming up with a new story now that he was in trouble, but I needed to hear him out.

"What did you see before the bang, monsieur?"

"It looked like two people talking. One was very tall, so I assumed it was a man."

That sounded like poor Remillon. "Did you see his face?"

"No, when the flashlight came on it was pointed at the ground. But I could tell he was tall."

"Does the name Guy Remillon mean anything to you?"

"Never heard it before, no."

"And the other person, what did they look like?"

"Quite sturdy, I'd say."

"So, another man, you think?"

"Oh, no." He actually laughed a little. "I definitely think this was a woman."

"And what makes you so sure?"

"They had on a hat."

"A hat?"

"I couldn't see what type, don't know the types of women's hats even if I could have. But I can tell you it was a woman's hat, for sure."

A sinking feeling swept through me. "Tell me why, please."

"It was pink. And not very big, I don't think. But definitely pink."

CHAPTER SEVEN

It was late in the afternoon, and by the time I got back to my building, on foot this time, I figured Darroze had earned himself a night in our jail, regardless of what I found. I was too tired to traipse back there and get him out, even assuming I found nothing. I mean, I'd given my word about that but didn't remember being specific about a timeline. And he'd thumped GiGi, God bless him, so when I went back I could argue that a cold night on a concrete bed was punishment enough. More than.

There were two things I needed to sort out, though, before the end of the day. The first was a search of Darroze's place. The second was to grill Mimi and find out why she'd lied to me.

Natalia was mopping the swept tiles when I walked in, barely recognizing my own floor, the way it sparkled.

"You don't waste time, do you?" I said, doffing my hat.

"I like to keep busy." She looked at the half dozen manila envelopes in my hand. "What're those?"

"In case I find evidence."

"Evidence of . . . ?"

I just smiled. "As effective concierge, you have a key to all the apartments, right?"

"I do."

"I need the one for Gerald Darroze."

"Henri Lefort." She wagged a finger. "Just because you're a policeman and a resident, doesn't mean I can just—"

"Good for you," I said, and meant it. A woman of ethics, I liked that. I pulled out a piece of paper from my pocket and handed it to her.

"What's this?" She read it. "That's really Darroze's signature?"

"It is."

"Oh. Then follow me."

We trudged up the stairs again, and I couldn't prevent my eyes from grazing across Natalia's slender figure. Delightful, but that kind of distraction I didn't need right now, so I looked at the back of her head. Which was also pretty. Thankfully oblivious to my attentions, she unlocked the door to Darroze's apartment, and I went in.

"Just shout when you're done," Natalia said. "I'll come back and lock up."

"Just to confirm, no one else has been in here today?"

"I mean, you and that other cop. Other than that, no."

"Thanks." I went in and closed the door behind me. I started in the living room, unsure what I was even looking for. Which may be why I didn't spot anything that looked relevant. I moved through the bedrooms but came up empty again. Unsurprisingly, the kitchen and bathroom turned up paltry kitchen and bathroom items, but nothing related to the murder. It did make me wonder, though, whether he was less interested in eating or being clean. Given how spare both spaces were, it was definitely a close race.

Back in the living room I took a final look around. I spotted some photographs on the mantelpiece that I'd not paid attention to before. One of them featured a tall man so I walked over for a closer look. I peered at the grainy picture, but it was quickly apparent it wasn't Guy Remillon, this *mec* was much older. But standing there, the faintest smell of smoke tickled my nostrils, and I looked down to see a partially burned paper in the fireplace. I knelt and carefully pulled it out with my fingertips. The paper was blue and appeared to have burned from the bottom upward. The hearth was otherwise clean and devoid of wood or ash, so it looked to me like someone had deliberately lit the paper and dropped it in here to burn. It had, but I could see in the top left corner what looked like an official blue stamp, with the German word *Untersuchung* and the first letters of another word, also German: *gen.*

I thought for a moment. *Untersuchung* meant "investigation." I had no idea what the *gen* part could mean so I turned the scrap of paper over and my eyebrows almost left my head.

"Well, well, Monsieur Darroze." A familiar name was written in neat handwriting on what remained of the paper. "Never heard of Guy Remillon, you say. Well, it looks like maybe you lied to me about that, monsieur."

I scribbled a brief description of the paper on the front of one of my envelopes, carefully slipped the burned scrap of paper inside, and sealed it shut.

Downstairs, I knocked on Natalia's door.

"Henri." She stood in the doorway, smiling. "Or is it Detective right now?"

"I mean, I'm on the clock so maybe . . . well, no, come to think of it, Henri is always fine." I was stammering like a teenager, and annoyed at myself for it. So I kept making it worse. "Unless I'm putting handcuffs on you for some reason."

She gave me a wink. "Wouldn't that depend on the reason?"

"Ah, yes." I looked down, hoping to see a deep hole that I could fall into. "Sorry, I didn't mean to . . . I just stopped by to let you know, I'm finished with Darroze's apartment."

"How old are you, Henri?"

"Much older than you."

"Well, then, how old do you think I am?" When I shrugged, she continued. "I'm twenty-nine. Which means you are older than me, but not by much I'd guess."

"I see." I was surprised; I'd already put her in her early twenties. Maybe. "You don't look it."

"Thanks." She laughed. "Mediterranean discount, I call it. Key?"

"What?"

"Monsieur Darroze's key. You're here to return it."

"Yes, of course." I handed it to her. "I locked it, but feel free to check."

"No need. If you can't trust a policeman, Henri, who can you trust?"

"Pretty much no one these days."

"That's cynical. Are you done working for the day?"

"Not quite." I didn't tell Natalia because she didn't need to know, but I still needed to confront Mimi about her lies.

"Shame. I have a bottle of wine open and I don't care to drink by myself."

"It can get to be a bad habit, I agree."

"I can't tempt you, not even on New Year's Eve?"

You have no idea how tempted I am, I thought. *And New Year's Eve has absolutely nothing to do with it.*

"Maybe later."

"I hope so, Detective Henri."

I nodded and managed to look her in the eye before blushing again and backing away toward the stairs, and safety. I marveled at the confidence of youth and beauty, and smiled all the way up to Mimi's apartment. There, I let the smile drop and banged hard on the door.

Mimi opened it and cocked her head sideways when she saw the look on my face.

"Henri, you look like someone put horse manure in your hat. What's wrong?"

"Someone put horse manure in my hat. Or, if we're being accurate, it was a heaping of bullshit that was served up."

"Do you want to come in and explain?" She opened the door wider and gestured for me to come in. We went through to the living room and I sat in the leather armchair that my backside had gotten to know so well in previous months. "Drink?"

"Yes, please."

"Good. That means this is a social call, not a work-related one." She poured a glass of red wine and handed it to me. "Not Château Pétrus, I'm afraid. Supplies are getting harder and harder to obtain."

"No matter. And just for the record, this is an end-of-the-workday visit. So police business still."

"Oh, I shall refrain then." She put her wineglass down on the table beside her chair and sat slowly. "How can I help?"

"Is Daniel here?"

"No, he's out. Didn't say where."

"Why did you lie to me?"

"What? Lie? I did no such thing. About what?"

"The man who was murdered outside."

"Well, really, that's ridiculous! What on earth makes you think I lied to you?" The faux outrage was a nice touch, but I wasn't even close to being fooled.

"The biggest problem for you in this situation is your brutal honesty," I said gently. "You're almost incapable of anything else. I could be going to Nicola's funeral and you'd tell me if I had the wrong tie on."

"I have no idea what you—"

"Which means you are horribly out of practice when it comes to lying. Especially to an experienced *flic* like me."

"Henri, I'm offended, how can—"

"Stop it," I said, more harshly than I intended. "The more you lie to me, the more I'm going to think you're involved. And I really don't want to think you're involved in a murder, Mimi."

"You can't think I killed that man. You know I don't have a gun!"

"I do know that. So I'm wondering why you'd lie." I shook my head. "No, no. You're sitting there wondering how I know, what I know. And you want me to tell you so that you can serve up a slightly altered heap of bullshit that fits the new narrative, but that almost certainly isn't the whole truth."

She looked down at her hands, folded in her lap, and thought for a moment. Finally she looked up and spoke.

"Henri, I did not kill that man. And I'm sorry I lied to you. I did speak to him right before he was shot. And yes, I heard the shot."

"Tell me. Tell me everything."

"I was just trying to stay out of it. You see what it's like now, the Germans don't need proof of anything; if they even suspect you of a crime you can wind up in a camp in the middle of nowhere being worked to death. Or they just skip that part and put a bullet in you."

"The Germans aren't investigating this. I am."

"But still. Everything is dangerous these days."

"What did you see, Mimi?" I pressed. "Why were you outside talking to Remillon?"

"Fine." She sighed heavily. "I was out early to meet someone."

"Remillon?"

"No, no. Someone who provides things to me. Things we all enjoy."

"A black marketeer."

"I prefer to think of him as a supplier, thank you very much."

I almost laughed out loud at her response. "Fine, supplier then. But you were breaking curfew, why would you risk that?"

"I have never let anyone know where I live. I'd rather risk being caught and yelled at than give my address to those people."

"The price of breaking curfew isn't a telling off, Mimi. It's way, way worse."

"Ah, for you maybe. But not if you're the Princess Marie Bonaparte, and you know that the general in charge of this area is more of a history buff than he is a Nazi."

"So you've been caught out before."

"Three times. He thinks I'm doing it on purpose to see him."

"Jesus, Mimi, are you flirting with a Nazi?"

"God no. But he thinks so, which is useful. You may even have seen him in the building."

"Why would he . . ." A vision of an SS officer with no trousers on sprang into my head. "You're talking about Maximillian Zoeller, aren't you?"

"Yes, and that's something you definitely do not need to be sticking your nose into." Her brow crinkled. "Wait, how do you know his name?"

"Let's just say we ran into each other briefly. But don't worry, I'm not concerned with why he's here."

"Good. He's an odious man, but there's a decent chance he can help keep us safe."

"Just out of curiosity, did you set him up with Claire Raphael?"

"Introduced them, perhaps. Nothing more than that."

I turned away from that rabbit hole and returned to the business at hand. "You were out meeting your supplier. Carry on."

"The way it works is, I pay him and then he sends a boy to deliver what I've paid for, to the place I designate."

"That's very trusting of you."

"Black marketeers don't last long if they take your money and don't provide what they say they will. I pay him well, no doubt his best customer, so he may be dishonest with other people but he has no need to be with me."

I nodded. "Go on."

"I was on my way back, almost home, when this tall, thin man . . . what's his name?"

"Guy Remillon."

"Remillon. He stopped me. Asked what I was doing, who I was. I could tell from his accent that he was French and not some Nazi out catching curfew breakers, so I told him to mind his own business."

"But he didn't?"

"He kept asking me who I was, if I lived in this building. And then . . ."

I waited but she was obviously reliving the scene in her mind. Having spent a year in the trenches, I knew what that could be like, so I gave her a moment before prodding her. "And then what happened?"

"There was another man. I hadn't seen him. He was in a doorway, I suppose, but it was so dark out there I hadn't seen him." She took a steadying breath. "He seemed like he was in charge, like maybe he knew this Remillon. He told me to go inside the building, to go home. So I did."

"You think they knew each other?"

"Remillon looked surprised, but I imagine I did, too. It could have been because he recognized him and hadn't expected to see him there, or it could have been shock at a stranger suddenly being there."

"And then?"

"I went inside and was on the stairs when I heard the shot. I kept going until I was in my apartment, I never even looked back."

"Can you describe this man?"

"He was . . . shorter than you. Quite short, I think. Deep voice and a stocky build. He wore a long dark coat and a hat that was pulled down, so I never saw his face. But from his voice and his build, it seemed he might have been in his forties or fifties, and maybe belonged more at the dockyards than in a coat and hat."

"His accent was rough?"

"Maybe that was it, but I didn't really hear him say much. I couldn't swear to that."

"Is there anything else you can tell me about him, Mimi? Anything at all?"

"No, I'm sorry. I can't think of a thing. And Henri."

"What is it?"

"I'm sorry for lying to you. I just wanted to stay out of it. I'm not used to the world you live in, with murder and death. I just wanted to get away from it and stay away from it. I'm sorry."

I stood. "That's all right. At least I know now. That's not a terrible description, to be honest."

"Oh, really?" She looked up, reminding me of a schoolgirl who'd just given the teacher the right answer.

"I've heard a lot worse, believe me."

It was true, I had heard worse descriptions from witnesses. But my most immediate problem was that one of those was of the same man Mimi had just described. A description provided by a woman who'd aligned herself with our invaders, and who'd described to me a man of normal build running from the scene. Someone she thought was a lot younger than the man Mimi was describing.

Is one of them wrong? I wondered. *Or is one of them lying to me?*

CHAPTER EIGHT

I was too tired to stay up to watch the New Year come in and, since my hopes for 1941 were entirely pessimistic, there seemed no reason to force the issue. Mimi was having a small gathering in her apartment, so Nicola resolved to see midnight come and go with our friend.

"I bet Natalia will be there," Nicola teased. We sat in the living room, Nicola in a black dress and me in my pajamas, robe, and slippers.

"Do give her my regards."

"How about you give them yourself?"

"I don't think that's how regards work. A third person has to deliver them, otherwise it's just *Hello*."

"Henri, you're not funny. I just thought you'd like to see her."

"She lives in the building. I can see her anytime I like."

"Not in a party dress and with a glass of champagne in her hand. And don't forget the mistletoe, that can prove very useful."

"Champagne, mistletoe. What's the point of it all?"

"Oh, Henri. We have to hold on to the smaller things in life right now. Celebrate when we can, laugh when we can. Love when we can."

"I don't feel very lovable right now."

"That's because you have to make the effort sometimes. Look past the job, look past the war, just for a little while and see what's out there that's good."

I smiled. "You'd be cheerful in a prison cell."

Nicola laughed. "If they had champagne, I'd certainly give it a try."

"Who else will be there?"

"Just me, Mimi, Daniel, and maybe Natalia. As far as I know." She gave me a disapproving look. "You afraid you might have to make new friends or something?"

"Fake jollity with total strangers, Jesus, I can't imagine anything worse."

"Well, there won't be any strangers, just friends and family."

"Slightly better," I grumped.

"You know where we are if you change your mind." She got up and walked to the door. "But change out of those pajamas, first, please."

I sat there feeling sorry for myself for a few minutes, then decided to eat the stew Nicola had prepared. It was still warm in the pot, and when I opened the lid and sniffed, it smelled a lot better than it looked. I didn't expect there to be meat in it, but I'd hoped to be able to identify one or more of the vegetable ingredients. I thought I spotted a carrot shaving and maybe a piece of tomato skin, but I decided not to press my luck. I slopped a couple of good spoonfuls into a bowl and grabbed a handful of cubed bread. The cubes were hard as pebbles; I could have painted dots on them and used them in a game of street dice.

I smiled at how the world was upside down. A year ago, croutons were a luxurious touch to a good salad. These bread-based morsels of concrete were now symbols of desperation, and only edible once they'd soaked in the stew for ten minutes. I mixed them in, sank back into my armchair, and slowly stirred.

Fifteen minutes later, I was just finishing up eating when there was a knock at the door. I opened it to find Daniel Moulin standing there in a suit.

"Nicola said you're not coming to the party," he said.

"It's an actual party now? With more people than you three? If that's the case, then I'm definitely not coming."

He laughed. "Well then, do you mind if I . . . ?" He gestured to the room behind me.

"Come on in. Something on your mind?" I walked through to the living room and took my usual seat. He perched on the sofa opposite me.

"Well, I really wanted to thank you for coming to bust me out of jail earlier. I'm embarrassed about that whole thing."

"That's all right. I'm sorry you lost your home, that seems like a bigger deal."

"It is. But a cop in jail isn't something that the brass would like to know about."

"Do they?"

"No. The *flic* who worked that night said he wouldn't say anything. I doubt you will, and I sure as hell won't."

"Your secret is safe with us," I said with a smile.

"*Merci*. Also, I gather a resident here was arrested for murdering that man while I was under lock and key."

"Nice alibi, that." I smiled, trying to make light of it, but Moulin looked at his feet, as if embarrassed. "And yes, Gerald Darroze was arrested, though a little prematurely in my opinion. But since you're here." I got up and went into my room, and pulled out the evidence envelope I'd sealed earlier. I used my pocketknife to slice it open and I tipped the charred piece of paper onto the coffee table in front of Moulin. He leaned forward and studied it a moment, and I asked, "What do you make of it?"

"*Untersuchung* means . . . ?"

"Investigation. And the dead man's name is handwritten on the back."

"This second word, *gen*—. Any idea what that could be?"

"No, but I'm sure someone at the factory could make a few guesses."

"So a German document with the victim's name. Where was it?"

"I pulled it out of his fireplace. It seems he did a shitty job of destroying all of the evidence."

"Did you find anything else?"

"No, nothing." I smiled. "So maybe not the shittiest job after all."

"Can he explain it?" Moulin asked. "It's not proof by itself, but it's pretty suspicious."

"I only just found it. I'm hoping he tries to explain it with some bullshit story that I can poke holes in to get to the truth."

Moulin stroked his chin in thought. "Why would Darroze kill this Remillon fellow?"

"No clue. He's a grumpy old bastard, but I wouldn't figure him for a killer."

"Strange times, though, Henri. A lot of bad stuff happening that we've never seen before, drives men to do things they wouldn't have done before."

"That's the truth. But I don't see any specific motive here."

"Yet."

"I need to see what he has to say about this scrap of paper."

"And I need to get back to the party," Moulin said. "You sure I can't talk you into coming?"

"I'm not dressed for it."

"Well, if you change your mind . . ."

"I know, I know. Don't show up in pajamas."

"Or do, I wouldn't care. I doubt Mimi would, either." He stood. "That reminds me. How long do you plan on staying with her?"

"Until I find somewhere else I can afford. And that's safe."

"Didn't the people above Darroze leave Paris? The Miller couple. You could get the key from Natalia and bunk there."

"They left Paris, all right." His tone was grim, though, and the spirit of the New Year seemed to have flown the coop.

"Meaning?"

"Two weeks ago. You weren't here, but I happened to be passing. The Germans arrested them, shipped them east, from what I could find out."

I sat straight up. "What? Why?"

"God knows, Henri. Some offense, real or imagined. Probably imagined. Do you know what a *corbeau* is?"

I was confused for a moment, because of course I knew the word for a crow. "The bird, or does it mean something else now?"

"It's what they're calling these letters people have started writing. French people, our own Parisians."

"Daniel, what are you talking about?"

"People write anonymous letters to the Germans telling on their neighbors. Some complaints are real, but many are invented. They are being called *corbeaux*."

"Why would anyone do that?"

"Petty grievances from the past. Trying to gain advantages in the future. Maybe jealousy, if someone has food and they don't." He shook his head sadly. "This war, it's bringing out the worst in people."

"So you think someone sent one of these *corbeaux* about the Millers?"

"That's the only thing I can think of. He and his wife were quiet, not involved in anything untoward that I know of."

"But he was English."

"Right." Moulin nodded. "I'm guessing someone let the Germans know that, or reminded them."

"But why would someone do that? Doom their harmless neighbor to a miserable death?"

"You'd have to ask the bastard who did it, Henri." He nodded. "And now for some champagne so I can forget that kind of behavior, just for one night."

I didn't think even champagne would do the trick for me, and I didn't want to bring down whatever high spirits my friends were looking to raise, so I watched Daniel leave and sank back in my chair to think and to smoke my last cigarette of the year.

Did Remillon's death have something to do with these corbeaux? *And what was the piece of paper that the grim-faced Nazi took from his body? Was it one of those poisonous letters?*

A trip to the Gestapo's HQ was not the way I wanted to ring in the New Year, but I had a job to do and, other than standing on Darroze's neck while I asked him more questions, I didn't see another way forward for this investigation. And Darroze's neck could wait a few hours. The more information I had when I went to see him, the better.

That decision made, I got up and rummaged through the kitchen cabinets. I wanted something to drink, but I wanted something stronger and darker than the bubbly being consumed downstairs. This war was reanimating deeply buried memories from when Germany last tried taking over my country, memories of death and mud and blood that I had done a fine job suppressing, until now.

When I came up empty-handed, I poured myself a glass of watered-down Beaujolais, went back to my chair, and lit another last cigarette. I stared at its glowing end, as if doing so would ward off the looming ghosts of my past and, more importantly, keep me safe from the malevolent specters hovering in the dark ahead of me.

CHAPTER NINE

January 1, 1941

I woke early and left the apartment as quietly as possible. I'd not heard Nicola come in so assumed that meant it was a late night, which in turn would require a late morning for her. The administrative staff at the Préfecture had New Year's Day off, but I wasn't allowing myself that luxury. Police investigations, especially murder, were like fish: they quickly went rotten on you, and if you fouled up a big one, the stink was hard to remove.

As I stepped out of the building onto rue Jacob, I was curious to see bundles of newspapers tied together sitting on the doorsteps of shops and other apartment buildings. I'd basically stopped reading the damn things, since the Germans had banned them from containing any actual news. In Paris, truth and information had been two of the earliest casualties of the war, and they'd been replaced by their nemeses, lies and obfuscation. I didn't know of anyone who read a newspaper in Paris anymore; the only ones that had survived the invasion were the rags printing only what the Germans wanted to see.

But these looked different, and by that I mean dangerous. I wandered over and looked down, nudging the stack with my foot as if the paper itself might do me harm. The top sheet blared out the name of the publication: *Égalité et Fraternité.* The title was missing its beginning, *Liberté,* which I assumed was the point.

Clever, I thought. *A catchy title and a call to action, I like it.* Against common sense, I liked it enough to stoop down and pluck out the top copy. It was a broadsheet folded in half, with typed copy on all four pages. No photographs or anything sophisticated, so I started reading. The first story wasn't news as such; it was a declaration of purpose, explaining that the newspaper would share the truth about the war with the citizens of Paris.

The second story was actually news, and delightful news if it was to be believed: bombers of the British Royal Air Force had attacked and devastated five Nazi-held locations—Vlorë on the Greco-Italian front, Rotterdam and IJmuiden in the Nazi-occupied Netherlands, and the German cities of Emmerich am Rhein and Cologne. One could only hope this was all true; there's certainly no way the establishment newspapers would be reporting this, if so.

I was so engrossed in reading the news that I'd not heard the footsteps approaching me. Or, if I'd heard them I'd done a piss-poor job of recognizing them. Two German soldiers in uniform stood glaring at me from five feet away. I didn't much mind the glaring, I was used to that, it was more the pistols in their hands that drew my attention. They could have been twins, tall and handsome, maybe in their mid-twenties, only one was left-handed and the other right-handed. Standing there, it was like a mirror image of the same Kraut.

"What are you doing?" Lefty demanded in depressingly good French. Quick learners, these sausage-gobblers.

"Nothing. How about you?" Sometimes I was unable to help myself.

"That is an illegal publication, and you are disseminating it!"

"Oh, easy now, soldier." I stooped and put the paper down, my mind figuring the best way out of this. "I live in this building right here." I pointed. "I just stepped out to go to work and saw the newspapers on the ground. As a police officer, I felt it my duty to ascertain exactly what they were before taking action."

"You are a policeman?"

I took out my credentials, slowly so as to not get shot, and handed them over. "Like I said, I just came across these papers. Naturally, I was planning to report their existence to my superiors."

"*Natürlich*," he repeated in German, with a heavy dose of sarcasm attached. "On your way to work, you can pick up every single one of these newspapers, in this street and all along your route."

"Well, wait just a min—"

"Think of it as police work, collecting evidence of a crime." He smirked, and as he repeated his hilarious analysis and instructions to his twin I resisted the temptation to pull out my own gun and shoot them both. I tried my words, first.

"As much as I would like to oblige, I'm afraid I don't have time to play reverse paperboy this morning. You'll have to find some other sap to do your bidding or, god forbid, do it yourself."

Lefty's eyes widened with surprise, and my guess was a Frenchman hadn't spoken to him like that in a very long time. He took a step toward me, his smirk replaced by an angry snarl.

"Listen here, you French piece of dogshit. I will beat you to a pulp and *then* you will pick up every sing—"

"Let me stop you right there." I drew myself up to my full height and hoped it projected as much authority as was needed. "You seem like a pair of good Nazis, but you don't seem to realize that on the Nazi scale you rank quite low. And by that I mean there are many people in this city who would happily order you to the front lines, should they decide you deserve it."

Lefty spat on the ground between my feet and looked about to begin the pulping, so I hurried on. "One of those men is expecting me in his office in about," and here I took a dramatic look at my watch, which I now saw hadn't ticked or tocked since midnight, "thirty minutes. Now, avenue Foch is quite a distance from here by foot, so unless you're intending to beat me up and then drive me to my appointment, I suggest you take care of these newspapers however you see fit and let me be on my way."

"Avenue Foch." Righty had heard two words of my speech at least, and judging by the color of his face and the lowering of his gun, he'd not liked them at all.

But Lefty was not yet convinced. "Who is at avenue Foch?"

For a moment, my mind went blank. Then I pictured an ordinary-looking man with sparse blond hair, and no trousers.

"Obergruppenführer Zoeller," I said.

"What is your business with him?" Lefty pushed on, and I admired his persistence.

"My business with him is none of yours. Good day to you." With that, I touched the brim of my hat as a gesture, insincere of course, of respect, and started my way up rue Jacob. Not without trepidation, though; those first steps I expected at least an order to stop, possibly a bullet between the shoulder blades. But my bluff worked. It made sense, too: better to let a brash French detective go than risk the wrath of a senior SS man. The former was a mistake they could recover from, the latter could be a misjudgment that buried them.

My relief was short-lived, as it always seemed to be these days. As I got farther away from the Nazi twins I got closer to avenue Foch, and the stories I'd heard looped in dark shadows through my mind. Everything from spy operations to torture took place at 84 avenue Foch, and too many people went into that building vertical and came out horizontal for my liking. Too many Frenchmen, in particular.

When I got there, the building itself looked like most of the others in the city, with its pale Lutetian limestone façade, elegant stonework, and wrought-iron balconies. If it hadn't been for the garish black-and-red Nazi banners I might have thought I was in the wrong place. You can trust the Nazis to let you know where you are, though, so I went up to the front door and announced myself to the two guards.

"You have an appointment?" one of them said in a less-than-friendly way.

"Yes," I replied, instantly regretting the lie.

"Wait here."

He disappeared inside and to hide my nerves I lit a cigarette. I offered one to his partner, who looked very much like he wanted to accept, but he shook his head *No* and turned his eyes back to the street.

I was halfway through my coffin nail and needing to pee

when the first Kraut appeared. Right behind him, to my great surprise, was Herr Zoeller himself, wearing a gray three-piece suit and looking as nervous as I felt. He greeted me with a curt nod, and said, "I thought it might be you."

"I don't mean to disturb you, monsieur, but I was looking for some information with regard to a murder inquiry I'm conducting."

"I see. Walk with me." We set off along the sidewalk and, once out of earshot of the sentries, he asked, with considerable suspicion in his voice I thought, "What information?"

"It has to do with the murder of Guy Remillon."

"I don't know who that is."

"I wouldn't expect you to. He's a Frenchman killed in rue Jacob a couple of nights ago. Mornings, technically speaking."

"And?"

"Someone from your side attended the body before I could go through everything he was carrying. I didn't catch the man's name, but I know he removed a piece of paper from the body."

"A piece of paper doesn't sound particularly crucial to me."

"If it was important enough for your colleague to remove, it's important enough for me to want to see."

"Why do you say he's my colleague?"

I laughed gently. "Monsieur, you work in the most terrifying building in Paris. This man was about the most terrifying human I've ever seen. I feel like there's a connection there."

We walked in silence for a minute, then he glanced over at me. "I wondered if you'd come to shake me down."

"Shake you . . . Oh, good heavens, nothing like that."

"So I see. And thank you, I suppose."

"A lot of that going on right now, I imagine."

"There is. And I opened myself up to it." He sighed. "You are right about that building, number 84. It didn't start that way, or at least no one told me this was how it would be. In such a beautiful place as this, the sounds I have to endure sometimes." He grimaced and shook his head.

"Worse for those making the sounds, I imagine."

"Hmm? Yes, yes, of course. But like any man unaccustomed to such things, I seek refuge from it, comfort perhaps."

"I don't begrudge you that, Herr Zoeller."

"Many would. Especially here." He looked over at me again. "The man who took the paper, your description of him. Would you say he looks gaunt, almost as if he's . . ."

"Already dead? Yes, that's how I would describe him."

"I don't know his name, but I think I know what he took."

"You do?" To know one thing but not the other seemed odd to me, but I'd take all the help I could get.

"He works with your people, actually."

"My people?"

"The police. Even has an office at the Préfecture, I'm told. Which is fine by me, I feel about him much the way you do."

"What is his job?"

"He's in charge of assigning investigations based on citizen complaints."

"Does he do investigations himself?"

"No, I think there are too many. He has a small army of loyal Parisians who do that for him."

"Loyal to whom?" I asked bitterly.

"Fair point. To the men who have conquered their city and who pay them."

"Funny, from where I stand that sounds more like treason than loyalty."

He stopped and looked at the sky, heavy with unmoving gray clouds. "Yes, it does all depend on where you stand, I suppose."

"The paper."

"Ah, yes. I can only think that the paper was a grant of action."

"Which means?"

"A grant of action is a letter granting authority to one of his minions to investigate a particular claim. It contains language to that effect, so the investigator can show it to a suspect, a witness, maybe a concierge to get access to a building."

"Like a warrant."

"Yes, I suppose so. But to ask questions and look around, not to arrest."

"You like to keep that privilege for yourselves?"

He let my sarcasm go. "There's a sense that Frenchmen investigating each other is less than ideal, such that arresting each other would not be tolerable. Or tolerated."

"I can imagine not."

"The grant of action contains not just permission to investigate, but a summary of the allegation and, of course, who the target is."

"The name of the complainant?"

"I don't think so; for that person's safety they are allowed to remain anonymous."

"How thoughtful of you."

"I am trying to help, Detective."

"Of course, and I am grateful for that. Just not for the system you have working here."

"Nor would I be, in your shoes." He stopped and turned toward me with his hand extended. "That's all I can tell you, I'm afraid. I shall try not to bump into you again, Monsieur Lefort."

"*Merci*. But no shame if you do." I shook his hand and watched him walk away, before slowly making my way back along avenue Foch toward the Préfecture. As I moved away from number 84 the air seemed lighter, the gray clouds a little whiter, but what I'd just learned was disturbing.

The Nazi had taken the paper for one or more of several reasons. To hide the fact that Remillon was his agent, to keep secret the target of, and reason for, Remillon's investigation, and to allow that investigation to be resumed by another of his traitorous stooges.

And that, in turn, meant a very good chance there'd be more Nazis and their lackeys snooping around my building, which was of no comfort whatsoever.

CHAPTER TEN

It was time to stand on the neck of Gerald Darroze. Not literally, of course; I was headed to the Préfecture, not the fourth floor of number 84 avenue Foch. And despite the strong temptation, to which many of my colleagues succumbed, I was never quite sure that brute force was as effective as the *mecs* who invented the rack and thumbscrews believed. Now, if you wanted a cad to agree with your position on some matter, a set of brass knuckles was an elegant tool, bringing satisfaction merely upon being produced. But if you wanted knowledge, if you wanted to possess information you didn't already have, the problem with taking the painful approach was you couldn't be sure if the man suffering under your hands was telling you the truth, or just talking so you'd stop hurting him. And there's little more infuriating than spending hours, or even days, chasing down a lead from a worked-over witness only to find that your physical exertions had served up the latter. And, of course, once you started down Knuckle Road, you could hardly double back and be your man's best friend.

Put differently, you can start out at "nice cop" and dial it up to "asshole cop," but you can't do things the other way around.

Which is why, when Darroze was brought into the interrogation room and dumped unceremoniously onto a metal chair across from me, I slid over a cup of hot coffee and a lit cigarette.

"*Merci,*" Darroze said, reaching for both.

"*De rien.*" I watched in amazement as he sipped and savored the coffee. "Good lord, man, the stuff they serve in your cell must be awful for that to taste good."

"You have no idea. I think the guards just piss in a cup and call it coffee."

"Maybe, but I'd still expect that to taste better than the wastewater we brew up nowadays."

That made him smile, and it struck me I'd never seen him do that before.

"When am I getting out of here?"

"Not up to me. But if you answer my questions, I can try and find out."

"I did already. And you promised, damn it, you gave me your word."

"Quite true, but that was only if I didn't find anything—which I did."

"What? What did you find?"

"I'll get to that, but first I have more questions."

"Then ask them."

"You burned a piece of paper in your fireplace the day you were arrested. What was it?"

"I did no such thing," he said indignantly.

"My apologies, I should restate my position on helping you out. Not only must you answer all my questions, but you need to do so without lying. That is to say, I want the truth, Darroze, and not one single lie, fabrication, misdirection, or half-truth. Am I clear on that?"

"I'm not lying."

"So the charred scrap of paper I found in your apartment spontaneously combusted."

"I don't even know what paper you are talking about. But I didn't burn anything."

As a beat cop, collaring thieves and robbers and drug dealers on the streets, you hear some of the most ridiculous excuses. My favorite, and one I heard a dozen times, was when I made a collar and found something illegal, either per se or by the manner of its being obtained, in the suspect's pockets. Maybe it was recently purloined money or a watch, perhaps a weapon, and on one occasion it was a pair of very expensive lace panties. In each case, the accosted criminal adopted a look of total and utter surprise, before promptly informing me that, "Well, you know, monsieur, I had no idea that was in my pocket because these aren't even my trousers."

Darroze was giving me the same line, with the same outraged attitude, which told me that we would not be walking down the path of truth and light together. Not yet, anyway, so I changed tack.

"Have you ever written a poison-pen letter to the authorities?"

"Poison-pen letter? I have no idea what you're talking about."

But the way he harrumphed and shifted in his chair told me otherwise, and I remembered something he'd said when I spoke to him at his apartment. I gave the tabletop a good hard slap just to let him know that the flat of my hand was working, and his jump let me know he understood.

"At your place, you asked if I was there about the letter. Who did you complain about?" I pointed my finger at him. "Do not lie to me again."

"That's not fair, though. People breaking the law in the building, right in front of our noses, and no one does anything. Meanwhile, the rest of us starve and suffer on whatever meager rations we can find."

"You little weasel."

"It's not fair," he repeated, as if by saying it again I'd suddenly be on board. "Why should she have all the food and wine she likes, while I'm eating stale bread and drinking vinegar?"

"You complained about Mi—about Princess Bonaparte, didn't you?"

"If you know, why are you asking?"

"I didn't know until just now, you idiot." I sat back and ran a hand across my brow, thinking. "When did you write the letter?"

"About a week ago," he said, pouting.

"And did you hear anything back from anyone?"

"No, but it norm—"

He'd stopped himself too late.

"You've done it before."

"I didn't say that."

"You just said exactly that, you miserable little turd. Who and when?"

"I didn't—"

"Tell me." I leaned forward and grabbed the back of his head, enjoying the look of surprise on his face before I slammed it into the table. I was kind enough to give it a little twist so his nose wouldn't drive deep into his micro brain. I needed him conscious and able to talk. For now. He pushed himself upright, sputtering more indignation as he rubbed at what I hoped would become a large bruise on the side of his head.

"You can't do that! How dare you?"

I was encouraged to have been right, to see the left side of his face blooming a nice red, and a trickle of blood coming from one nostril.

"It'll be the other side of your duplicitous face, Darroze, next time you lie to me. Who did you report and when?"

He sniffed and straightened himself up. "They were spies, it was my duty."

"Spies?"

"Exactly."

"Who were spies?"

"The Millers."

Of course it had been Darroze.

I expected to feel a rush of anger, and not a person in the world, other than Darroze himself, would have minded if I'd reduced this sorry sack of human parts to an immobile lump of blood and bones. But all I felt was a deep, dark sadness washing over me.

"Do you know what you've done?" I asked.

My gentle tone seemed to throw him off. "What do you mean?"

"The Millers weren't spies, Darroze. Monsieur Miller was an Englishman who bought and sold wine for the Truman Brewing Company across the channel. His wife was a nice, quiet lady who made excellent *millefeuilles*. And now they are either prisoners in a work camp, where they will likely die, or they are already dead."

"Well, wait just—"

"One thing you can be fairly sure of, Darroze, is that they were tortured."

He seemed genuinely surprised by that. "Tortured?"

"Yes. If you'd accused them of something else, pretty much anything else, maybe not. If you'd called them thieves or adulterers, or even Jews, they'd have been carted off but they might have escaped having their fingernails torn out on avenue Foch."

"My God," he said, his voice a whisper. "You're not serious."

"I hear that with the women, so Madame Miller in this instance, they like to strip them naked and whip them all over, then pass them to the men in the room until they're all satisfied. I'd imagine a lot of men show up in those rooms looking to be satisfied, wouldn't you think, Darroze?"

He put his head in his hands. "I feel sick."

"Oh, I do, too, but that's not the best part. The best part is that because they weren't spies, they had no information to give up, so do you know what that means?"

"What?" he said weakly, and I could tell he was dreading the answer.

"It means they were tortured a lot. Even more than if they'd really been spies and been able to spill their guts. They were probably tortured until they turned on each other because they didn't know what else to do. And if they were still alive after that, well, you better believe they'll never see each other again, not in this lifetime. So what you've done, Darroze, is subject two innocent people to the closest thing to hell that this world can serve up."

We both stared at the table for a moment, then the curiosity got the better of me.

"What did they do?"

"What do you mean?"

"What did they do to you, to deserve their fate?"

He shrugged and mumbled something unintelligible, so I slammed the table harder. "What did they do?" I shouted.

"I thought they were spies. Thought he was, anyway. Coming and going at all hours, thumping around above me and carrying expensive wines."

"It was his job, you moron."

"I didn't know that. I thought they were for bribes or . . . something."

"And the princess, is she a spy, too?"

"No, no."

"What did you say in your *corbeau* this time?"

"*Corbeau?*"

"Yes, there's a word for the poisonous, treacherous notes people like you are writing. What did you say?"

He seemed to rally, as if he had a good reason to snitch on Mimi.

"Well, you have to know I was right about this one. She is deeply involved in the black market, mostly buying. But very much exceeding her rations with food I couldn't get in a year. And," here he wagged his finger, "I'm almost certain she's providing it to other people in the building, though I'm not sure for what purpose."

"To feed them, I would imagine." It struck me in that moment that Darroze really was a curmudgeonly hermit if he didn't know that Mimi, Nicola, and I were good friends, and that Nicola and I were the main beneficiaries of her less-than-legal largesse. But I sure as hell wasn't going to tell him.

"It's not safe for the rest of us. What if she gets so bold the black marketeers start coming to the building? If the Germans got wind of that, we'd all be . . ." His voice trailed off, so I finished his thought for him.

"Tortured and shipped off like the Millers?"

"Well, I don't know if—"

"I damn well do. So you told them she was engaged in the black market. What happens next?"

"I've only done it once before," he protested.

"To great effect, you bastard. What happened?"

"Someone came to talk to me about it."

"A German?"

"No, a French policeman." He frowned as he remembered. "Maybe not a policeman, he didn't seem . . . right. But he had official papers on him, and he was definitely French, not German."

"And soon after that, the Millers were arrested?"

"I didn't see it happen," he said, somewhat churlishly.

"I didn't ask if you saw it. I'm asking about the timeline of events."

"Yes, I suppose so, soon after that."

I sat back and lit another cigarette and watched Darroze eye the packet. "Can I . . . ?"

"No. If you're lucky you'll get a final one from the captain."

"Captain?"

"Or whichever rank is in charge of your firing squad. Probably a mere corporal in your case."

"Firing squad?" His eyes widened. "They shoot people for resisting arrest?"

"Resisting . . ." I smiled. "You still think you're here for resisting arrest?"

"Well, yes, isn't that what you said?"

"You really are dumb, aren't you? If you are nicked for resisting arrest, it's in the phrase, is it not, that you are already being arrested for something?"

"I hadn't really thought about it."

"Clearly. I'm pretty sure I clearly explained that you're here on two charges, Darroze."

"What's the other one?"

"Murder. To be specific, the murder of Guy Remillon outside our building."

"No! You said that before but I thought you were bluffing." He sat bolt upright, terror written all over his face. "How can that be?"

"Well, look at us on the same page at last."

"What do you mean?"

"We're both asking the same question, finally. So, let's talk about why you killed poor Monsieur Remillon, shall we?"

We were interrupted by a knock on the door, and it swung open before I could even stand up. A smug-looking GiGi stood there, his hands on his hips.

"What do you want?" I snapped.

"Chief wants to see you."

"I'll be done soon."

"He said now." He nodded malevolently at Darroze. "Happy to take over questioning of this one."

"You don't want to question him, GiGi, you want to pound him."

"Can you blame me?"

"Well, unfortunately for you, since he pounded you first you can't work on his case."

"It's not his case I want to work on," he growled.

"Amusing, but leave him alone."

"Or what?"

I walked to the doorway, but before leaving I turned and pointed to the miserable toad that was Darroze. "If that pathetic *mec* can tune you up, just think of the damage I can do if you cross me or otherwise fuck up this investigation."

And without waiting for an answer, I grabbed GiGi by his collar, dragged him out of the interrogation room, and slammed the door shut on a cowering, cowardly Gerald Darroze.

CHAPTER ELEVEN

I dropped into a chair opposite Chief Louis Proulx, who beckoned me into his office with a wave. His glasses were perched on the end of his nose and all his attention was on a printed paper on the desk in front of him.

"That old fool your murderer?" he asked, without looking up.

"Maybe. He's certainly a nasty piece of work."

"How so?"

"He's one of those bastards writing to the Germans, snitching on the neighbors he doesn't like."

"Jackass."

"Worse. Thanks to him, a couple in our building was arrested and deported. Probably tortured to death."

"Oh, right, he lives in your building. That's where all this happened, I'd forgotten."

"Not the important detail, Chief."

"No, I suppose not. Deported, you say. What did he accuse them of?"

"Spying."

That got him to look at me. "Jesus. He couldn't go with something a little less incendiary?"

"The husband was English, I guess Darroze couldn't see past that."

"I doubt the Germans did, either." He sat back and took his glasses off. "But you're not convinced he's the killer."

"I'm not."

"Explain."

"Two things, really. First, what's his motive? I think the victim, Guy Remillon, was investigating a complaint Darroze had made."

"Against who?"

"I'm not sure yet," I lied. I didn't see any benefit of involving Mimi if I didn't have to. "Point is, if he was there because of Darroze, why would Darroze want to kill him?"

"No idea. Point two?"

"Point two is the man himself. Darroze is a coward and a sneak. I don't think he's got the guts to shoot someone himself. He's the kind of *mec* who gets others to do his dirty work."

Proulx nodded his understanding. "What's the evidence against him?"

"The concierge saw him dump a gun in a trash can at the building, and I found a burned piece of paper in his apartment that connects him to the decedent. Indirectly."

"Not exactly putting him in the lap of Madame Guillotine with that, are you?"

"I do need an explanation for him dumping the gun, though."

"What does he say about that?"

I laughed. "Funny thing, I didn't get to ask him. GiGi interrupted on your behalf."

Proulx frowned. "I told him to wait until you'd finished."

"He didn't mention that."

"He wouldn't, would he? But since you're here, I do need your help."

"With what?"

"A new task force."

"Task force?" I groaned loudly. "We don't have the manpower for whatever new bullshit the Nazis can't manage themselves."

"Feel free to tell them that."

"That's your job."

"My job is the opposite, sadly. I tell them yes and then try not to do whatever it is they want done."

"I can get on board with that aspect, I suppose. What is it this time? Gypsies? Midgets? Fat people?"

Proulx sighed wistfully. "I remember being fat. Fat and happy."

"Ah, yes." I patted my own shrunken belly. "The good old days indeed."

"Anyway, it's newspapers."

"What do you mean *it's newspapers*, exactly?" My mind pictured the single-sheeted leaflets on rue Jacob that had so disturbed two German officers that morning, so I had some idea where this was going.

"People are afraid to take direct action against the Germans," Proulx was saying. "The consequences for even minor resistance are so extreme it's not worth it."

"Precisely as the Germans intend."

"Right. So it looks like people are finding more anonymous ways to poke our friendly invaders in the eye."

"With words."

"Right again," he said. "Printing presses are being set up all over the city, seems like. People leaving stacks of newspapers, glorified leaflets really, on the streets, in shops and restaurants."

"With what aim?"

"Some are reporting on the war, the bits the Germans don't like." *Like the one I saw this morning.* "Some are more opinion-based, like the Communist ones. Some are a mix."

"What're we supposed to do, collect all these newspapers, line them up against the wall, and shoot them?"

"Yes, but first we have to arrest whoever is printing them."

"I don't want to." It was Proulx's turn to laugh, but I went on. "I'm serious. I want to arrest actual criminals. People who hurt people. Thieves, murderers, you remember them?"

"No one's stopping you, Henri."

"If you have me chasing wordsmiths all over the city, you will most certainly be stopping me. Look, I understand that the sensitive babies who run the city these days take offense at the truth being spoken to them; every conqueror always does. But they claim to be all about law and order, cracking down on criminals. Shooting writers and paperboys doesn't sit well with that."

"I didn't say you should shoot anyone."

"Oh, believe me, I don't plan on it. But what happens when I hand them over to the Nazis, do you suppose? A damn good talking-to? A polite request for a retraction?" I wagged my finger. "No, I don't think so. It'll be a train heading east, or up against a brick wall around the corner for a final cigarette."

"I have no idea—"

"And meanwhile French citizens, who we are sworn to pro-tect, are getting murdered and their murderers are wandering free around the city because we're too busy to go looking for them."

"You've already locked yours up, so I don't know that you get to—"

"That's my point, though," I interrupted. "I don't know if he's my killer or not, and if I'm now the word police how the hell am I going to find out?"

"Good lord, Henri, a detective with more than one case? Whatever next?"

"I'll thank you to leave the sarcasm to me."

"You know the murder rate has dropped significantly this past year. It's not like you're overworked right now."

"Sure, it's dropped because the Germans stopped calling it murder when they kill us, which is what, half of the deaths in the city?"

"I don't know."

"Nowadays it's only called murder when we kill one of them, or each other. And since the vast majority of the male population, who usually does the killing, is dead, in prison, or at a German work camp, are we surprised the rate has dropped?"

"I feel like you and I just had this discussion."

"I know I've had it with someone, so maybe."

"Look, you're not wrong, Henri. But whatever the reason, there are fewer homicides for you to investigate, which means you have time to do other things."

"Like crochet, or maybe knitti—"

"Work things, Henri." He was getting annoyed with me now, and I hoped he'd kick me out of his office before giving me an actual assignment. "Look, we just have to make them think we're making progress on this."

"That's how it starts, sure. We can fool them for a while, maybe a week or two. But when the papers are still being printed and no one is being arrested, what then? I don't mind making a showy, token arrest of some low-level drug pusher or prostitute—that's a risk those people know comes with their business—but for publishing a one-page newspaper?"

Proulx picked up the one in front of him and fluttered it at me. "If you fold it right, it's actually four pages."

"I don't give a damn if it's a hundred pages. Seems to me, if they're using their time to write and print newspapers then they're not getting into any other kind of mischief. The Germans should be happy it's *just* words being thrown at them."

"And yet, it seems they're not."

I snapped my fingers as a thought popped into my head. "I've got it! If you want to make it look like you're doing something, when you're actually doing nothing, I know exactly how to achieve that."

"Pray tell."

"Yes, it's perfect. You'd get zero work product, no real wasted manpower, and no results whatsoever."

"Sounds promising, go on."

"You're going to kick yourself for not thinking of it."

"If it's a good enough idea, I'm happy to."

"You give the assignment to GiGi. Not only will he not arrest anyone, he probably won't even look for them." The more I thought about the idea, the more I liked it. "He'll spend all his time sitting in cafés, sipping coffee and reading the damned newspapers, which he'll call investigating."

"My concern with him is, if he does find one of those poor saps—"

"Highly unlikely."

"But if he does, I don't know he'd exercise the discretion that you would."

"Then make it a condition of the assignment that he report any perpetrators to you before taking action."

"And what am I supposed to do with that information, exactly?"

"No idea at all." I stood and walked to the door before turning around. "After all, it's your task force, not mine." I gave him a smile and a quick bow before slipping out of his office, closing the door between us, and pretending I couldn't hear him calling after me.

● ● ●

I went straight back to the interview room, intent on asking Darroze about the gun in the garbage bin. But when I got there, the door was open and the room empty. Around the corner, a very young *flic* was typing up a report, one finger at a time.

"You see where my prisoner went?" I asked.

"The one with the busted jaw?"

Merde. I knew the answer but I asked the question anyway. "Literally or figuratively?"

"Most definitely literally."

"Who did that to him?" I knew the answer to that, too, but wanted to confirm.

"I don't know his name, sorry. I'm new here."

"I can tell. We're recruiting at elementary schools now?"

"No, sir." He blushed. "I'm twenty-two."

"Why are you not shipped off working for the Germans?"

"Honestly, sir, I'd rather not say."

"You look able-bodied, so let me guess. You have connections."

He shrugged, but wouldn't look me in the eye.

"Oh, I'm not criticizing or complaining, son. If you have connections and we become friends, then I have connections. I'm not sure what else will get me through this goddamn war, so believe me when I say I don't mind if that's true."

"I suppose it's possible my father made a contribution to someone. Somewhere."

"Bribery, not connections; that's a little different. Who is your father? You know what, come to think of it, the less I know the better." I pointed toward the interrogation room. "The detective who tuned up my witness. What did he look like?"

"Average height, balding. If I had to describe him, I'd say his face was a little . . ."

"Horse-like?"

"I was trying to find a nicer way to say that."

"Don't bother. He's known as GiGi around here for precisely that reason. And, just between us, his talents as a detective are on the equine level."

"Sir?"

"He's a terrible communicator, a horrible interviewer, a coward in a fight, would trip over a clue that was in front of him before seeing it, and is liable to kick out and damage someone for no apparent reason."

"Damage someone like your witness."

"Precisely. You know how to interview a man with a broken jaw?"

"No, sir."

"Shame, because I don't either. Other than by pencil and paper, I suppose, and who has time for that?"

"If I can help, sir . . ." He looked so earnest I wanted to pat his head.

"What's your name, son?"

"Pierre Tremblay, sir."

"And your assignment?"

"Patrol in the Latin Quarter, day shift."

"Nice gig, that one, your father really did make a contribution to someone. You patrol that area by yourself?"

Tremblay smiled. "It certainly feels like it, sir."

"Say, you ever hear of a division that investigates citizen complaints? Brand-new, the brainchild of our new lords and masters."

The smile disappeared and he either blushed again or . . .

"Yes, sir. I definitely have." It was anger in his voice.

"Tell me."

"They tried to assign me there. I refused."

"Refused? Who the hell does that these days?"

"Well, if I'm honest." He looked down at his hands. "I may have had someone back me up a little."

"Papa again?"

He nodded. "No way did I join the police to investigate my fellow citizens based on some bullsh— Oh, sorry, sir."

"No, carry on, precisely the right word."

"Based on some bullshit *mouche*."

"Agree, and calling those people flies does actual flies a disservice. Who tried to put you there?"

"The chief of the unit, Monsieur Petit."

"Noel Petit?" He nodded again. "That fits, he's a sniveling

sycophant who would investigate innocents if it moved him up the ladder."

"I don't know him, really."

"Lucky you. On several counts."

"Sir?"

"He's a vindictive bastard, and you turned him down. Instead of investigating *corbeaux*, you get a plum assignment in the Latin Quarter thanks to your father." I winked. "At some point, I may reverse my position and ask who the hell he is, but not today."

He gave me an enigmatic smile but didn't answer. I really was tempted to ask who the old boy was, but refrained. It might make me see, and treat, this kid differently, and I didn't want to do that. I liked his principles when it came to the *corbeaux*, but adults who rely on Papa too much sometimes overdo it and become entitled pricks.

"I meant it about helping, sir. I know you're murder squad, so if you need help with anything I'm game."

"I'll keep that in mind." I looked at my watch, which was still dead. "What time is it?"

Tremblay glanced at his. "One minute before five, sir."

"Excellent. I'll check back on Monsieur Darroze's jaw tomorrow. Or maybe the next day."

"Or maybe next week," he suggested.

"That bad, huh?"

"I think that detective, GiGi, hurt his hand on the man's face, maybe even broke a bone."

"And no doubt will charge the poor bastard's face with assault." I grimaced. "Either way, let's end the day's work on that bit of cheery news."

CHAPTER TWELVE

A rumor had swirled through the Préfecture that some of the high-end restaurants had been getting shipments of meat and vegetables, and were opening tonight with menus replete with the kind of fare they were serving without thought just twelve months ago.

I tried coaxing Nicola out with me, but she was feeling unwell and wanted to lie on a couch at Mimi's so she could be cared for properly. I tried not to take umbrage at the thinly veiled insult and, when I couldn't find Daniel Moulin to accompany me, I decided that a book and a good meal alone would be a fine way for a policeman to both welcome and ignore the coming of a new year.

I looked at my bookshelf, trying to decide what to take. I'd bought a dozen books in the past year I'd not had time to read, so I was absurdly excited to pick one and lose myself for an hour or two. Jean-Paul Sartre's *The Wall* was the one I'd heard most about, but a grim story about three political prisoners awaiting their own executions seemed a little on the nose. My second choice was *The Big Sleep* by Raymond Chandler. It'd gotten rave reviews in the press, but I was annoyed at the Americans for not joining the war, so the hard spine of the novel in my bookcase looked too much like the cold shoulder of the American people and politicians leaving us to face an uncertain future alone.

Ah, but not alone. The English, for all their faults, were with us. Those stuck-up, superior, arrogant English who wouldn't know good cooking if it ran up their trouser leg and nibbled on their shriveled royal peckers. But they were with us in this mess, no question of that, so I picked up my unread copy of *Mort sur le Nil*, by Agatha Christie. I was not just being supportive of the English arts, meager as they were, but maybe I could take a mental journey to a place a little more exotic than war-ravaged Paris. Sure, there'd be a murder or two, but something more genteel than I'd been seeing of late; that I was willing to bet on. And, even more reassuring, I could enjoy the story without having to catch the killer. I'd leave that to Monsieur Hercule Poirot.

I set off at 6:30 P.M., not wanting to take my chances with the 9:00 P.M. curfew. I could probably skate past trouble by showing my badge, but I'd been hearing more and more stories of trigger-happy Germans shooting first and having no reason to ask questions later, their interviewee being riddled with bullets and forever mute. But I dressed in my finest gray suit and wore a silk tie of rich claret, and stepped out onto rue Jacob with my book as if it were Agatha Christie in person and we were on a romantic date together.

The problem with optimism, hope, and a good mood were that someone was always lurking around to spoil them. In my case, it took until I started crossing rue Bonaparte before I noticed them. Two men with hats pulled low and the collars of their overcoats raised high. The only question was whether they were French or German, and the answer to that question didn't seem to matter much in the moment. Either way, they were definitely following me.

I confirmed that suspicion by taking a roundabout way, turning left onto rue Guillaume Apollinaire and then right on place Saint-Germain-des-Prés. They were still with me as I turned right again onto boulevard Saint-Germain, so I knew if they went into Les Deux Magots with me, it was no coincidence.

They didn't. Instead, they slowed as I went in, lighting cigarettes as they pondered their next move. A seedy bar sat across from the plush Deux Magots, and I was able to watch them through its large windows as they dashed across the street and ducked inside, like they were dodging a sniper's bullets.

I now had a choice to make, one made infinitely more difficult when I saw the long face of GiGi sitting at a table with two other men, who I didn't recognize. He saw me, too, and smirked. That made my mind up. I wasn't going to let two shitbirds trailing me disrupt my evening with Madam Christie, nor was I going to let the equine presence of my colleague send me back into the night hungry. I walked over to his table, mostly so I could see which part of the restaurant I'd need to sit in to have his visage hidden from me.

"Lefort," he said. "Dining alone?"

"Not exactly." I flashed the book at them. "Who are your dates?"

His smirk disappeared. "They're not dates, they are . . . colleagues, of a sort."

"Not police, though." They were too old to be rookies, and I'd have known them if they were senior or seasoned *flics*.

"Not police, no. You're welcome to join us and find out."

I'd rather eat in the kitchen, and off of the floor. "Very kind, but as indicated I have a date of my own. Of a sort."

"I don't see anyone," he said, peering behind me.

"How's the hand?" I nodded at his right paw, wrapped tight in a bandage, and his face darkened.

"It's fine. Hurt him more than me."

I said nothing in reply, just flashed a smile at him and headed for the far corner, out of view of all three of them.

A white-coated waiter appeared and asked if I'd like an aperitif. I thought for a moment. "Campari on ice?"

"We do have ice, monsieur, but no Campari."

"A glass of sherry, then. Medium."

"We have only sweet as of this evening."

"Dubonnet and gin?"

He shook his head with regret. "Neither, monsieur."

"Perhaps you could suggest something that you do have."

"Perhaps a glass of Aperol?"

"Perfect, thank you."

"Ice?"

"No, Aperol I take neat."

"Oui, monsieur." He gave a small bow and slid a menu onto the white tablecloth in front of me. I say *menu*, which implies a variety of foods from which to choose. It was more a beautifully handwritten statement of what I'd be eating that evening, the black cursive pressed into the thick card letting me know that neither waiter nor chef would brook dissent. And I didn't mind, even a little. It felt good to lean back into the welcoming

red velvet banquette, take a sip of water, and look at the people around me. They were doing what I was, of course, which was pretending everything was normal, just how it used to be. All of us pretending that the war stayed outside the gold-and-red world of Les Deux Magots, hoping too that the fare served would transport us back in time to when a visit here was a luxury and not, perhaps, the last time we ever entered the place.

So pretend I did. The place was half empty or, as I chose to see it that night, half full. The tables closest were unoccupied, but not far away a foursome of young women were giggling and clinking glasses, right beside an older couple, perhaps in their seventies, who kept looking at the young women and smiling. *Those two remember the good times*, I thought, *and have the kindness and decency not to begrudge it to others.*

Most of those in the restaurant were older, and I ignored the reason why, admiring the fine suits of the men and pretty dresses of their women. My waiter, who I'd noticed walking with a limp, brought my Aperol and set it down next to my book like it was the last drop of the stuff on the planet, which maybe it was.

"*Merci*," I said. "Your leg, it hurts still?"

"Not for twenty years."

"Ah, the war."

"*Oui, monsieur. Vous aussi?*"

"Yes, me, too. I managed to escape with all my limbs intact, though."

"Better a limp than a wounded mind, there are plenty of those even two decades later."

"Too many. And here we are creating more."

He stood up straight and smiled, which surprised me. "*Ah, non, monsieur.* Out there maybe." He nodded toward the large picture windows. "But not in here. In here, we have Aperol and Pomerol, plenty of Burgundy and, if you order quickly, a cut of beef like you have not tasted in months. Maybe years."

"Is that so?"

"The war has had a strange effect on businesses. Before the Germans arrived we were mainly a café, with a few *petit* snacks to serve. Then they arrived," he nodded disdainfully toward the window, "and so many restaurants went out of business. But because of our reputation we were able to expand our services a little, serve meals in a way we didn't before."

"I'd not thought of that," I said. "But you're right, until now I'd only come here for coffee or an aperitif." I looked out into the darkness. "But I still refuse to be grateful for any damn thing they've done."

"Understandable, and I agree."

We both fell silent as two men walked into the café. They wore expensive suits with crisp silk ties, and their shoes were recently polished. The edges of my mouth dipped, as they did for my waiter friend, and I imagine he was thinking *Gestapo*, too. Both of us, however, were smart enough not to say anything out loud. They were like snakes, these Gestapo types. Blended in with their civilian clothes, or at least trying to, they were all cool and calm until you stepped too close or spoke too loud. Then they were deadly, their bite as fatal as that of a viper and their blood as cold. These two looked innocuous enough: one was tall with aquiline features and darker skin than Nazis usually liked to sport. The other looked like an accountant, with soft features and thin blond hair. *At least a snake looks like a snake*, I thought.

"Only a few cuts of that beef left," my waiter murmured, and I didn't need warning twice.

I smiled and picked up the card. "Then I shall order one of them, my good man. If you don't mind, I shall have the foie gras to start matters."

The bow was deeper this time. *"Bien sûr, monsieur."* He limped off on his mission, and I took a sip of Aperol, letting it roll around my mouth and linger on my tongue until it disappeared of its own accord. It was a complex citrus drink, with hints of orange and vanilla, bitter but less so than Campari, a kinder and gentler member of the same family. And in the moment, it was perfect.

As I waited for my meal, I savored the smells of other's people food, the full and rich aroma of grilled meat coming through the swinging doors that led to the kitchen, the delicate and fleeting smell of a baked fish wheeled past me on a squeaking wooden trolley.

I noticed, too, a man walking slowly past the window to the restaurant. He was one of the two who'd been following me, I was sure. He'd swapped hats with his colleague, a simple but sometimes effective bit of misdirection, at least when the subject had no clue they were being followed. He was pretending to read a newspaper as he walked, but it was cold out there and he was more interested in wrapping his coat around himself to stay warm. I smiled, feeling oddly safe and secure, and most certainly warm, inside Les Deux Magots.

Patrol all you want, friend, I thought. *If you don't disappear of your own accord, I'll just leave out the back. And I'll be leaving nice and warm, with a full stomach.*

Interestingly, the two Gestapo men noticed him, too, which made me wonder if they knew the guys on my tail or were just good at spotting their own countrymen. But my limping waiter soon drew their attention, pouring lukewarm water and taking their drink orders as slowly as possible. I turned to my book for company, glancing up in hope every time the swinging doors swung, more than ready to eat.

The foie gras was extraordinary. I didn't even bother smearing it on the stale bread they served with it, so rare was this creamy, fatty pleasure. I had a glass of Bordeaux with it, and ordered another when my flank steak arrived, surrounded like the last man on a battlefield by a ragtag squadron of vegetables: a few skinny carrots, a potato that had been quartered and roasted in salt, and thick slices of what was either a turnip or parsnip. I didn't ask which, because I didn't care.

When I'd finished, the waiter swept the plate away and stooped to speak in a low voice. "We do have two desserts, but my honest recommendation is to savor what you've eaten for as long as possible. They are both edible, although the apple tart is more tart than apple, but neither is good enough to warrant confounding the deliciousness of the meal you've just enjoyed."

"I appreciate the tip. Then just the bill, if you would be so kind."

"Very good, monsieur. And please excuse me but there is half a glass left in the bottle you've been drinking. I can't serve it to anyone else, so if you will forgive me . . ."

He poured and, naturally, I forgave him, and then sat there for a few minutes longer, until the bottle was all the way gone.

I don't know whether it was the food or the wine, probably both, but I was most of the way to the front door before I remembered my lurkers outside. In a moment of poor timing, I was beside the table of the well-dressed Gestapo men when I remembered, and they gave me suspicious looks when I stopped in my tracks.

"Ah, excuse me." I gave them a genial smile. "I just wanted to recommend the apple tart for dessert. Quite special."

They nodded their thanks, which were also suspicious, and I turned and walked back toward the swinging doors to the kitchen. When the waiter came through I swiveled him quickly back the way he came with an arm around his shoulders.

"Monsieur, is everything—"

"Everything will be fine, my good man. I would just prefer to leave from a back door, if you would kindly show me the way."

"You are in trouble with the Germans?"

"We're all in trouble with the Germans, it's just a matter of when it catches up to you."

He grunted and led me through the kitchen, past the curious gazes of the chef and his two underlings, and into a tiled back hall where empty crates lay across each other as if someone had once stacked them, but since then they'd been kicked into new places for being in the way. I caught whiffs of rotten vegetables and raw meat that should have been cooked days, even weeks ago, and should probably now be thrown out. Or served to the Germans.

He pointed to the back door, past the staff bathrooms, and I waved my thanks and headed toward it. I pushed it open and stuck my head into the cold air. The alleyway to my left was empty save for a few piles of rubbish, so I pushed the door wider and stepped outside, the fresh air making me pull my coat closer around me. A quick check to my right revealed a pathway to boulevard Saint-Germain, and my way home.

And then a match flared in the darkness, and two men stepped out of a doorway in front of me. I thought about turning and running, maybe ducking back into the restaurant, but one of the men flicked on a flashlight, illuminating not me or them, but a gun in his partner's hand. A gun that was pointed at my gut from a distance of no more than six feet.

"Monsieur Lefort. Come with us, please."

"It's Detective Lefort." I thought a spot of bluster would be a good way to begin, but they didn't.

"Your title doesn't impress us, Lefort. This way."

"And what if I refuse?"

He was quick, I'll give him that. The one with the flashlight was on me in a second, and he drove the metal of his light into my stomach, knocking the wind out of me, and almost my fine meal. He followed up with a firm right cross to my jaw and, as the lights dimmed in my head and my book fell from my hands, I heard him say either "Not an option" or "Stupid *cochon*."

"You're the pig, not me," I tried to say, but my face was in the gutter before I could utter even one of these words.

CHAPTER THIRTEEN

They must have had a car waiting, one they'd had much practice throwing suspects into, because I was tossed like an old jacket onto the rear seat, my head still spinning and my breath barely filling my lungs. I didn't bother trying to keep track of where they drove me; the destination wasn't my worry. I already had a good idea about that, so it was what they planned to do to me when we got there that made my heart beat out of my chest.

Worst of all, I had no idea what they wanted from me—as far as I knew, I'd not run afoul of any of their new rules nor insulted any of their superiors, directly or indirectly. After less than five minutes the car slowed and turned into what was obviously a cobbled courtyard. We stopped, the door at my feet opened, and I was dragged out by my heels, hauled upright, and marched so quickly into a building I didn't have a chance to orient myself or see anything useful at all.

Inside, I was dragged up two flights of stairs and then dumped onto a wooden chair that faced its unoccupied twin. The two men left me alone and I looked around, but the only thing visible was an open door to a bathroom. I wouldn't have minded a piss, the wine was working through me quite nicely, but I figured doing anything without express permission would see me on the hard end of another flashlight, or worse, so I waited.

And waited.

Finally, a door opened and my eyes opened wide with surprise when the Nazi accountant from Les Deux Magots came in.

"My name is Klaus Altmann. And surely you didn't think it was a coincidence." He didn't look like an accountant anymore. His pale blue eyes were intense and his thin lips were set in what was more a grimace than a grin, and they reminded me of a razor blade.

"Why am I here?"

"You are a police detective, how can you not know?"

"Perhaps I'm a bad one?" Humor seemed stupid, but it was all I had in the moment.

"Not from what I hear." He raised a finger. "Ah, and you were right. The apple tart was excellent. Even better than the pâté."

I assumed he meant the foie gras, which showed that he had the tastes of a philistine. Suddenly my future dimmed even further, but I told myself that if he'd hated the apple tart maybe I'd be in more trouble.

"Good, I'm glad you enjoyed it."

"And I didn't want to disturb your meal, Detective Lefort.

Plus, it doesn't look good arresting police officers while they dine, especially in an establishment like that."

"I suppose not."

"No reason why we couldn't both enjoy a nice meal, don't you think?" He didn't wait for an answer. "So, back to why you're here." He cocked his head to one side. "You really have no idea?"

"None."

"You are the sole policeman living in your building on rue Jacob, are you not?"

Sort of, I thought, picturing Daniel Moulin. "Correct."

"Which suggests that if there is illicit behavior taking place in the building, either you are a terrible police detective." He wagged his finger. "Which we ruled out by speaking to your colleagues."

"How nice of them," I muttered.

"Or . . ."

"Or what?" I asked, although I clearly wasn't in the mood for guessing games.

"Well, I think that leaves us with one possible conclusion, does it not?"

"And that is?"

"And that, Detective, is that you are fully aware of aforementioned illicit behavior. Which raises an even more interesting question. Are you merely ignoring and thereby sanctioning it, or are you actively involved in it?"

"I promise you, I don't know what you're referring to."

"How disappointing." He frowned. "I do hate to press you on this, I always get the truth in the end. So I will ask one more time, are you looking the other way or actively taking part?"

The annoying thing in the moment was that I truly did not know what he was talking about. I could think of a couple of minor, to me at least, things happening around me, but without knowing what he was talking about I wasn't going to start throwing crumbs, and maybe the lives of my friends, his way.

Unfortunately, the fact that I didn't know what he was on about was even more annoying to him than to me. With a deep sigh, he said, "Stand up." I did so. "Undress completely."

I didn't immediately, as the only man I willingly undress in front of is my doctor, and even then I'm not thrilled about it. My hesitation resulted in him putting two fingers to his mouth and blasting a screeching whistle my way. Within seconds two men, I assumed the ones who'd deposited me here, stormed into the room wielding thick rubber truncheons.

"I won't ask politely again."

I began to undress, slowly, to give my mind time to come up with a way to talk myself out of whatever this was. *Should I give up his colleague who visits my neighbor for interesting rendezvous? Perhaps I could just wield his name? Should I assume this is Darroze's doing and . . .*

"Look, if this is somehow related to something that idiot Gerald Darroze has come up with, I can assure you—"

"Darroze?" Altmann looked at his thugs and then back at me. "Never heard of him."

"He's the only bad apple in the building that I'm aware of." I stopped unbuttoning my shirt, sensing a glimmer of interest from Altmann, and thereby a glimmer of hope for me.

The German leaned forward. "And what has this Darroze been up to?"

"Nothing illegal as far as I know, but he's been writing poison-pen letters to the authorities to get various people in trouble. For example—"

"I didn't say stop," Altmann snapped. "You have twenty seconds to be naked, or my men will do it for you. And as you know, they are not gentle."

I didn't see an option, so did as I was told. As humiliating as this was, my main sentiment was anger. When you've lived among men in the trenches, the normal boundaries surrounding the human body disappear. You eat, sleep, piss, shit, wash when you have to and when you can, no matter who's around. Much like prison, I imagine, but with more mud. So I didn't care that much about being naked, what I cared about was this bully *making* me get naked. As a cop, or despite being one, I never much cared for authority, and I positively hated it when a colleague abused his power. One of the many reasons I despised GiGi: he was your classic bully with a badge.

Once naked I stood in front of Altmann with my hands on my hips, looking as defiant as I could in that situation. Which probably wasn't very.

"No longer a policeman," he said. "We're all pretty much the same when stripped down past our outer trappings."

"I suspect there are some differences," I said, unable to help myself.

"Ah, the question of manhood." He was disappointingly unbothered by the implied threat. "Even that fails to remain unchanging."

"Look, Altmann, can we skip the . . . whatever this is and get down to business. You've got me naked and presumably have other things in mind, but as you pointed out I am a policeman with a job to do. And plenty of other things in mind."

"Business? What business do we have with each other?"

"Since you're the one who dragged me here, I'll let you tell me."

"I have two items to discuss. The first relates to newspapers.

Not even newspapers, ridiculous scandal sheets. Pamphlets, maybe, being printed by troublemakers and scattered around the city."

"If you're about to ask who's doing the printing, I will have to disappoint, because I don't know."

"I read a report with your name in it, Detective. The suggestion was that early one morning you were spreading these scandal sheets out in your own neighborhood."

"I told those idiots I just came across them, same as they did."

"Those idiots, as you call them, didn't seem to believe you."

"Well, since they're idiots, that shouldn't count for much."

"I think you know who put them there, and where they are being produced."

"I do not."

Altmann looked over to the two thugs behind me. *"Wanne."*

I had no idea what he was talking about, didn't recognize that word, but didn't get a chance to ask for clarification. The men approached me and the larger of the two buried his fist in my stomach, and while I was wheezing and gasping to get air back into my body they hauled me into the bathroom next door. I saw a bathtub full of water, and in a moment the men had pushed me down ass-first into it, so my legs were hanging over the edge. In a flash, they looped a rope noose around my ankles and cinched it tight.

And I didn't resist, because I couldn't. I was utterly paralyzed by the freezing water that gripped me like the fist of death itself. I could hear my own weak gasping sounds as I fought for air, and it seemed like every muscle in my body was contracting to squeeze the oxygen out of me. Before I could recover at all, they pulled the rope to the end of the tub, submersing me entirely.

Out of instinct I reached for the edge of the tub to pull myself up, but they were pros, they'd done this a time or two before, and one of them slid a metal grate over the top of the bathtub, pinning me inside.

The pain from my stomach was nothing compared to the cold of that water, which seemed to turn my very bones into ice and set my body shaking and quivering from the inside out.

I don't know how long they let me suffer in there, but it felt like an eternity before strong hands reached in and dragged me over the lip of the tub and dumped me on the floor, still gasping and shivering like a half-drowned mongrel yanked from a frozen pond. Eventually, I noticed a figure in the doorway. Altmann.

"Now then, does that help your memory when it comes to newspaper production?"

"I . . . I . . ." I worked my jaw until it felt loose enough to let me speak properly. "I . . . can't remember something I don't know. I would tell you."

"Would you, though? I mean, I know you're a policeman and all, but if it was one of your friends, I'm guessing you'd keep that to yourself."

"None of my friends are doing that. I would know." I gingerly pushed myself into a sitting position, still shivering.

"It's amazing how much people remember in the tub." He nodded to his henchmen. "Back in, two minutes."

My protests barely escaped my lips before they were drowned and frozen out, so swift were his men in dumping me back into that frozen hell. Even if I'd wanted to confess, I couldn't, because one of them pulled hard on the rope around my ankles, dragging my head under the water. I pressed my face against the grille, sputtering and gasping for air, my eyes pleading as my lips froze on my face and turned purple with the cold. The men just laughed at me, and one leaned over and spat on me. Humiliatingly I didn't mind, was even grateful for a split second of warmth on my face, until they tugged on the rope and dragged me under again.

The two minutes lasted two lifetimes, and they left me on the floor, shaking like a leaf, no doubt confident that I was in no state to stand up, let alone run away. They were right to be so confident—the only thing that seemed to work on my body was my heart, but even that couldn't decide whether to race from the suffering or slow from the freeze, so it fluttered and paused, and then thundered against my icicled ribs, and I thought it would surely sputter out entirely. As I lay there alone, slowly, painfully slowly, the furry edges of warmth and feeling nudged away the chill, life creeping back into my body until I was able to some-what control the shaking of my limbs and lips.

After what seemed like an age, the two heavies ambled in and grabbed me by the armpits. They carried me like a sack of pota-toes to one of the wooden chairs and plonked me down. Altmann sat down opposite me, a small smile on his face as he spoke.

"My friends here want to remove your fingernails with hot tongs."

"I don't know anything," I stammered. "I promise you."

"They really do heat the tongs, but I've never seen the point of that. Isn't removing the fingernails enough?" He glanced over his shoulder at the men as if it was a real question, then turned back to me. "I mean, if having your fingernails torn from the ends of your fingers, one bloody yank at a time, doesn't do the trick, it seems unlikely a little scalding of the torn flesh would make a difference."

I grimaced at the images he was thrusting into my head, but he kept talking.

"Then again, I'm not the expert in such matters. I'm certainly learning, but these gentlemen are, well, at the top of their game, you might say."

"I don't know anything," I said again.

"And it'd be a shame to ruin those fine typing fingers for nothing, wouldn't it, Detective?"

I nodded in genuine agreement.

"Some other sap would have to type up all your reports for you, wouldn't they? For a while anyway, say—" He looked back again. "For three months?"

"At least. And if they don't get infected," one of them said with a snarl. "Red-hot tongs help with that. More pain on the front end, but potentially less permanent damage."

"Well, now." Altmann slapped his leg merrily. "I told you I was learning, and that makes perfect sense. Hot tongs it is from now on."

All this banter was clearly a hoot for them, and part of the act, but I was getting tired of it and, along with feeling, I was regaining some of my nerve.

"Look, Altmann, if you pull out every fingernail, toenail, and tooth I still won't have any information to give you. I truly don't know who's behind the pamphlets." Probably not smart to be giving him ideas vis-à-vis my teeth, but my deck was short of cards to play, sincerity not just being the best in my view, but pretty much the last.

He stared at me with those ice-cold eyes for a moment. "You'll be losing only the ones on your left hand today, Lefort. And I'll let the boys use their hot tongs to save you from later infection." His grin was about as malevolent a smile as I'd ever seen. "And in exchange for my thoughtfulness and generosity, I want something in return."

"What's that?"

"You will find out who's making those damned papers and turn them in to me."

"You know, my boss already asked me to do that, and when I declined he assigned another detective."

"Well, now, that's very interesting. Why would you decline, if you're not involved?"

"Because I'm a homicide detective, not a newspaper detective." There went my mouth again.

"You're whatever kind of detective I say you are," he snapped.

"Look, think about this. If I was putting out those papers, I'd have jumped at the chance to head up the case, wouldn't I?"

"And why is that?"

"Because I'd know exactly which directions not to look in. It'd be one of the best ways to keep myself safe, don't you see that?" I could hear the desperation in my own voice, but it was warranted—one of the thugs had left the room, I could only assume to begin heating his tongs.

Altmann stared at me in silence again.

"That actually does make sense," he said finally. "But if it's not you, it's someone. Who is the man who accepted the assignment?"

"Not someone who would print anti-German newspapers."

"And how can you know that?"

"The man is not just an idiot, but he's also spineless and has no leadership skills whatsoever. I've yet to work out how he was accepted into the police force, let alone how he made the homicide unit as a detective. And quite apart from his cowardice and incompetence, I'm fairly sure that if your lot actually win this war he'd happily start saluting your fearless leader."

Altmann's eyes narrowed, as if he was trying to figure out if I was being sarcastic.

"What I'm telling you," I went on, "is that GiGi is loyal to one person, one cause: himself."

"GiGi?"

"He looks like a horse. Smells like one, too. He was at the Deux Magots, when I was." I suddenly wondered if that was a coincidence.

Surely, it had to have been? Even he wouldn't go along with this, would he?

"Write his name down." He handed me a pencil and small pad of paper, so I did. It did feel a little like snitching, but in giving up someone's name I'd also made it as clear as I could he wasn't the mastermind these Germans were after.

"He's not your man," I repeated. "And given his policing skills, I find it highly unlikely he'll find your man, either."

"Oh, I don't need him to do that."

"You don't? I thought—"

"Not at all. I have you for that." He slowly rose and stretched. "Now, put your clothes on and be on your way. One of my men will be checking on your progress later this week, and I expect good news."

CHAPTER FOURTEEN

January 2, 1941

I woke up the next morning after a night of tossing and turning, my ears catching and exaggerating every sound in the dark. I'd jumped out of bed three times when I couldn't recognize those sounds, but each was innocuous. The fear didn't subside much, and I realized this was how I felt when around people—if my misophonia wasn't being actively triggered, it sat like a cloak of anxiety around my neck, waiting for a sound to suddenly tighten and choke me into a rage. It was my own form of shell shock, a sudden wave of terror caused by something that was over, finished, but that lurked in my head ready to remind me, to torture me all over again.

My body ached, too. I didn't remember being beaten or even unduly roughed up. Hell, maybe I was just getting old. Either way,

I didn't want to leave the comfort and safety of my bed, and I most certainly didn't want to go to work, or even set foot in the street outside my building.

Fucking Nazis.

Maybe I could start my day investigating the case right here, on rue Jacob. Baby steps. I did have one issue to resolve, certainly. Mimi and Claire Raphael had both seen the man who killed Guy Remillon, and both had been able to describe him to me, at least a little. The problem I had was, those descriptions were not just different, they were incompatible. Contradictory. Mimi had seen a shorter, stocky man and Claire a taller, younger, thinner man. I'd been inclined to go with Mimi's version since it was closer to how Gerald Darroze looked, but then a thought struck me.

Merde, were there two killers? I wondered.

I'd put the discrepancy down to the generally awful ability of people to either remember or describe people and things that they've seen. Especially in the dark and in moments of high stress, which this would have been. Time to revisit them both.

I hauled myself out of bed, but when I stood my knees buckled for a second. They'd really done a number on me, those sadistic bastards. But eventually I managed to get dressed, although I noticed that when I was knotting my tie, my hands trembled. Flashes of that room, that tub, that indescribably cold water kept leaping around in the back of my head and it was all I could do to push them away. I skipped washing my face.

I started with Mimi, since she was the closest.

"You look terrible, Henri." She stood in her doorway, a worried look on her face.

"Bad night's sleep, is all."

"You sure?"

"I'd know, wouldn't I?"

"With you, one wonders." She glanced past me, as if worried someone else was watching, then moved aside to let me in.

"What was that about?" I stepped inside and followed her into the living room. "A nervous little look there, are you expect—" I stopped, and my mouth gaped. "Mimi, what the hell is that?"

"The reason for the paranoia. Now hurry, close the door."

I did, staring at the stack of newsletters under the coffee table. "Mimi, you can't have those here. You can't have them anywhere."

"I am well aware, Henri. I only just put them there, not five minutes before you came knocking."

"Explain, damn it."

"I was outside for my morning stroll, and someone had left these up and down the street. I knew if the Germans saw them, they'd come knocking on doors, knocking them down most likely."

"Quite possibly."

"And these days, if you ask me, they don't much listen to whatever answers you give them, they just decide what's what. And I have no desire to go to one of their work camps, thank you very much."

"So you picked them up and stuck them under a table."

"Yes. Not the best hiding place, but then I'm hardly a professional criminal. I was planning to burn them, but then you interrupted. Sit."

I did. "Hey, get to it, don't let me stop you. We can talk while you burn."

"Talk about what?"

"The man who shot Guy Remillon."

"I already told you." She stooped to gather the pamphlets. "I didn't see his face."

"Could it have been Darroze?"

"Oh, I don't know." She walked to the fireplace and knelt. "Wouldn't I have recognized him? Even from the back?"

"It was early, the light was low. And how well do you know Darroze?"

"Not well." She dumped the propaganda into the grate and reached for a box of matches.

"Crumple them up, they'll burn faster and more completely. More surface area per page."

"Thank you, Professor," she muttered, but started to do so. "You could always help."

"I'm busy conducting an interview."

"Right, of course, apologies, Detective." She glanced over her shoulder. "Although I suspect the interview is over, since I don't know any more than I've told you. Which means you could help."

"No, ma'am. That could be considered tampering with evidence, a serious crime in this jurisdiction." I stood.

"Henri?" She paused and looked at me again.

"Princess?"

"If you're not going to help, would you kindly fuck off and close the door behind you?"

"There's really nothing else you can tell me?"

"Nothing."

"Well then, I would hate to distract you further."

I let myself out and headed for Claire Raphael's apartment, catching her as she was letting herself out. I didn't stop, instead using my momentum to sweep her back inside.

"Monsieur Lefort, what are you do—"

"I'll be brief, I need to ask—" For the second time that morning I saw something that not only did I not expect to see, but that I most assuredly did not wish to see. Seated on the couch was General Maximillian Zoeller, with a startled look on his face. It wasn't his expression that caught most of my attention, it was the man kneeling on the floor with his head pressed into the general's naked lap. The scene was so bizarre I had to confirm my eyes were really seeing it, which I did by noting his nicely folded trousers draped over the arm of the sofa.

I pointed to the man's head, which continued to bob up and down.

"Why is he not stopping?" I asked, horrified. "Stop it, man, for the love of all that's holy."

"He's deaf," Claire said weakly.

"Make him stop," I implored Zoeller.

"Yes, yes, of course." Zoeller put two large hands either side of the man's head and plucked it from his lap. I turned away, or started to, so I wouldn't see the effects of the man's ministrations. But as I did so, I caught a glimpse of his face.

"How old are you?" I asked.

"He's deaf," Claire reminded me.

"How old is he?" I asked her instead.

She shrugged, and behind me Zoeller spoke up. "How old do you want him to be?"

"Well, given the law, general decency, and your own age I would hope he'd be around forty. Which he clearly fucking isn't."

"He's not a child." Zoeller was tucking himself away, and displaying a remarkable amount of hutzpah for a man who'd just been caught with, quite literally, his pants down.

"That's good to know, because I'm fairly certain that your

people disapprove of men being serviced by boys, even more than they disapprove of men being serviced by men. Which, I do believe, one could classify as a fatal amount."

"Are you threatening me?" Zoeller sounded almost curious, but I could see a trace of fear in his eyes. As an SS general, he wasn't used to being challenged, let alone threatened. Then again, I would guess not many men had ever had this much leverage over him. *A dangerous amount of it*, I thought. *For both of us, perhaps.*

"Look, Zoeller, I don't care how many men you have between your legs, or anywhere else for that matter. I do care if they are boys, however."

"He's not."

I pulled a notebook from my pocket and scribbled out a question, which I showed to the young man as I handed him my pencil.

Quel âge?

He looked at me, this thin little person who must not have been more than fourteen. He took the pencil and wrote, *Mon choix.*

"I didn't ask if it was your choice, friend," I muttered. I pointed to my question, but he just shook his head and glanced at Zoeller, who stood and started pulling on his trousers. "What's his name?" I asked the German.

"Antoine," Zoeller replied, and I was oddly relieved that he at least knew that.

For his part, Zoeller put a hand on the boy's shoulder and steered him toward the door. On the way, he scooped a parcel wrapped in string out from under his folded jacket.

"If you're done with him?" Zoeller asked, and I refrained from the obvious response, which was, *Are you?*

"Please." I gestured him to let the lad out, and as he did he thrust the package into the boy's grateful hands.

"Food," Zoeller said, nodding toward the door where the lad had just exited. "More useful than money."

"And whose fault is that?"

Zoeller ignored that, instead asking me, "What happens now?"

"The way I see this, you slowly gather your things, which gives Antoine a head start to wherever he's going. Then you also depart to wherever you need to go, and I get to ask the questions of Madame Raphael that brought me here in the first place."

"Nothing else?" Zoeller asked.

"Nothing at all."

"That's probably best. For us all."

He shrugged on his jacket before sidling past me to the door. He paused for a moment, as if to say something more, but decided against it and let himself out.

"He's right, you know," Claire said quietly.

"About Antoine not being a child? Because—"

"No," she interrupted. "About food being more valuable than money these days."

"And he keeps you supplied?"

She smiled, which caught me off guard. "Do you know what I did before I married my husband?"

"No, I do not."

"I was homeless. I'd left school, my parents were both addicted to opium, and I didn't want to watch them kill themselves in front of me. Slowly, of course, but it was happening all the same. So I moved around the city making money where and how I could. Yes, even doing that. But I never touched drugs, not even alcohol."

"That sounds rough."

"I'm not asking for your sympathy, monsieur. That's not my point. I'm telling you that, like most people I've ever known, I will do what I have to in order to survive." She pointed to the couch. "And what you just saw . . ." Her voice wavered for a second.

"You facilitate that to survive. I get it and I'm not judging you. I might judge him a little, but not you. I was just surprised, that's all."

She laughed gently. "Well, last time you saw him with his pants off, he was with me."

"True." I smiled. "A man of varied tastes."

"*Oui.*" Her own smile waned. "You have no idea."

"Nor do I wish to." I cleared my throat to signal a change of subject. "Now, then, why I'm here."

"Why you barged into my apartment, you mean."

"Hey." I held up an apologetic hand. "That lesson has been learned, believe me."

"What questions do you have?"

"The same ones as before, actually."

"I don't understand."

"The man you saw running, the one who killed Guy Remillon. Are you sure he was of medium build, and younger?"

"Did I say younger? I didn't see his face, so I don't know how—"

"Sorry, no. You presumed it from his gait, the way he ran."

She nodded, in thought. "Yes, that sounds right. If that's what I said, that's how I remember him. Which is vaguely, to be clear."

"Yes, of course." I didn't want to put an image in her head, but I didn't know how else to ask the question. "Could the man have been Gerald Darroze?"

"Darroze? The nosy *mec* who lives in this building?"

"One and the same."

"I don't think so." She squeezed her eyes shut, remembering the scene. "I don't know. The thing is, it was all so unexpected and happened so fast. I mean, if it was him and you knew it was him, I'd be surprised but I can't . . . I can't say it definitely *wasn't* him."

"I'll settle for that. Tell me, could there have been two men?"

She thought for a moment. "I didn't see two but . . . it was dark and I wasn't . . . yes, I suppose. I'd be surprised but it's possible."

"And you've not remembered anything new since we last spoke?" A man can live in hope.

"No, sorry."

"Well, thanks for your help and apologies for ruining your morning." I went to the door.

"Oh, that's all right. He'll be back."

"With Antoine?" I couldn't be sure the kid was, well, a kid, but it still wasn't sitting right with me.

"That I don't know," she said. "But Antoine can't provide some things that I can. Some things he's very fond of indeed."

"Thank you, and I rarely say this, but that's all the information I need." I opened the door and stepped halfway out before turning back. "I don't know how many people know about you and him. But some things are happening in our city that makes me worried if the wrong person finds out."

"What things? What do you mean?"

"There have always been nosy people, like Darroze. But now, it's different. Now they are telling things to the Germans and people are being hurt because of it."

"The English couple."

"Yes."

She put a hand to her mouth with the realization. "Gerald Darroze caused that?"

"I'm afraid so. And whatever he told the Germans wasn't even true. Which means . . ."

"I need to be careful."

"Yes, you do. No more strange men busting into your apartment." I said it with a smile, but I didn't get one back.

"I know what I'm doing is dangerous. Life for me would be more dangerous if I didn't do it, though. And if things change, go back to how they were, then I'll adapt and survive in a different way." She shrugged. "Or the same way, I suppose. Whatever I need to do, I'll do."

She was such a sweet-sounding, delicate thing it was hard to imagine the rigors she'd endured, the harshness of life that had somehow preserved her physical person but hardened and tinged her soul. I liked her, though; she was a rare pigeon. She flew for herself, by herself, and didn't seem to much care what those below thought of her.

I closed the door behind me and turned right into Natalia.

"Jesus, woman. You keep popping up like a . . . a . . ." I couldn't think of anything, because she was just smiling up at me. And I liked that smile, quite a lot.

"Are you stepping out on me, Henri Lefort?" She said it playfully, but I blushed a little anyway.

"I'm working," I said stiffly.

"Ooh, is she a suspect?"

"You know what, let's go downstairs." I trotted down behind her, and when we got to the ground floor I asked, "Do you know what goes on in her apartment?"

"My concern is what happens in the building, not what people do in their own homes."

"Not an answer to my question."

"Yes, it is." She crossed her arms as if to let me know it was the best answer I was going to get.

"Well then. Tell me, Mademoiselle Tsokos, what were you doing lurking outside her door?"

"I'll have you know, Detective, I was not lurking. I was looking for you and heard voices."

"By pressing your ear to the door?"

"The walls are thick, Henri, and so are the doors. How else do I achieve that?"

I laughed. "You are something. Why were you looking for me?"

"Let's go get lunch. I want to talk to you about something."

"Lunch? It's barely ten o'clock."

"Breakfast, then."

"You want us to go, right now, to one of the many open and well-stocked restaurants still operating in Paris."

"No, silly, there are hardly any of those. I want us to go to my restaurant."

CHAPTER FIFTEEN

She lied to me, it wasn't a restaurant at all, but the moment we stepped inside I stopped caring. I'd not smelled grilled chicken like that for what felt like years, despite my recent treat at Les Deux Magots. In this place I could hear it sizzling, but it was the spices that teased and taunted my senses—full and rich, tangy and light, utterly unidentifiable individually to me, but then so are the stars that make the night sky sparkle like a black silk cloth sprinkled with diamonds.

The house, which is what it was, sat several streets behind boulevard Arago, the only home in a row of small shops and, a year ago, several places to eat and drink. There was no sign over the door, and the place itself appeared to have just two rooms downstairs—a now-empty place to eat making up the front of the space and a kitchen at the back. A wide archway separated the two rooms, which is why I could hear the chef at work. The floor was covered in bright and thick rugs, with not a stick of furniture in sight.

"They either traded the furniture or burned it as fuel." Natalia was reading my mind, apparently.

"God, it smells divine."

"There's no god, silly man. Our neighbors to the east have proven that twice this century."

"Hush, you're spoiling the moment." I took another deep sniff and looked around. "So, we just pick a spot?"

"Shoes off first, please." We both removed our shoes and put them against the wall by the door. Then she pointed to the farthest corner. "Over there?"

Like most cops and former soldiers do, I rushed to get my back against the wall and preserve my open line of sight. Natalia either didn't notice or didn't care, and settled down cross-legged opposite me.

"What is this place?" I asked, still looking around. "And how the hell do you know about it, of all people?"

"Why shouldn't I know about it?"

"You just got here!"

"Well, true." She laughed. "As you may have noticed, there are a lot of closed restaurants and bistros in this area."

"Unsurprisingly."

"Right. Well, a few of the owners pooled their remaining resources. There are three chefs, they rotate, but the place is open pretty much all day and all night."

"Where do they get their supplies?"

"No, no." She wagged a stern finger. "That is most definitely a question you do not ask. Not here."

"They won't mind you bringing a cop in here?"

"The way this place works, the only people who know about it are invited by people who know about it. The circle grows, but slowly and carefully."

"Only the trusted."

"Exactly." She took a deep inhale through her nose, her eyes closed to savor the aromas. "And who in their right mind would come here, smell this, and then give it up to the authorities?"

"Not me, that I can assure you."

"Glad to hear it."

A man appeared carrying a silver tray. In his fifties, he wore a white shirt and trousers, which matched his turban.

"Welcome," he said, stooping to place the tray in front of us. "Tea."

"*Merci*, Amit," Natalia said.

"Nice to see you again, Mademoiselle Natalia." He gave us a bow and disappeared through the archway.

"You know each other's names."

"You noticed, well done. Is that intriguing to you?" Her eyes sparkled and I knew she was going to drag this out and tease me as much as possible.

"Well?" I waited for my explanation.

"Most good business owners get to know their customers, it's quite normal."

"What's not normal, though, is that he knows yours. You've not been here long enough."

"Apparently you're wrong about that." She flashed her dark eyes at me as she sipped the hot tea. "Mmm, try it. Delicious."

I did, and it was. I put my cup down and tried again.

"Are you going to tell me how you know about this place? And how they know you already?"

"Yes." She took another sip of tea and said nothing.

"But you're going to make me work for it."

"You know, they just bring out food to you. No menu, no choosing, they just bring it to you."

"What if I don't like what they bring?"

"Then I'll eat it. I may be small, but I'm all stomach."

"Yeah, seems unlikely we'll find ourselves in that situation. What did you want to talk to me about?"

"Oh, you're giving up that easily?"

"Not playing your game, Natalia," I said with a smile. "You'll tell me when you want to."

"That's true. Do you, the police—" She stopped herself as Amit appeared with another tray, this one carrying two silver plates of food. He put them down carefully in front of us, along with a clay pot containing cutlery. "Looks and smells like heaven, Amit. Thank you."

"Yes, thank you, Amit. My name is Henri, by the way."

"Pleased to make your acquaintance, Monsieur Henri." He gave the little bow again and left us to stare down at our food.

"Looks like chicken, hummus, some sort of potato-and-turnip hash. I had that last time; trust me, it tastes better than it sounds. And flatbread, of course."

"Of course." I plucked a fork from the clay pot with my right hand and picked up the plate with my left. I breathed in the rich aroma of what was certainly lamb, and the exotic smell of the curried potato hash. I dipped my fork into the latter and tasted it.

"Why don't you eat here every day?" I asked Natalia. "Every meal?"

"It's not free, you know. Plus, they have a once-a-week rule."

"Which apparently doesn't apply to you, since this is at least your second visit in a matter of days."

"You just assume that I came straight from Greece to rue Jacob, don't you?"

"You stayed here first?"

"They have three rooms upstairs for . . . newcomers."

"Newcomers. Odd word choice."

"Thanks." Natalia dipped her bread into the hummus and chewed on the end of it. "Wonderful."

"Do we the police . . . ?" I prompted, with a mouthful of hash. "You were asking me something."

"Ah, yes. Do you keep records of those who come and go from Paris?"

"The mass exodus of last year?"

"Partly. We can start with that—is there a list or other accounting of who left? More importantly, who left and didn't come back?"

"I don't think so. Why?"

"We'll get to that. What about records of people who lost their homes directly to the Germans?"

"You mean, like the Millers?"

"It sounds macabre, but yes. Like them."

"I don't think we do, but you can bet the Germans will have a list."

"Very helpful, Henri, I'll just invite them to lunch and ask for it."

"Good point. Wait." I snapped my fingers. "Daniel told me there's a list at the Préfecture of abandoned apartments."

"Why?"

"I think the idea was to steer Germans into those, instead of kicking people out of their homes."

"Makes sense, I suppose."

"Why do you want to know?"

"That's another question you might not want to ask."

"And yet, I am." I tried a mouthful of lamb and wanted the taste to last forever.

"Let's say I'm asking for other newcomers."

"I'm not sure that'd be the best idea." I gave in and swallowed. "Damn, that's just so good. Just once a week, huh?"

"*Oui*. Why is it not a good idea?"

"Because of all the *indics* we have around now."

"Is that what we're calling snitches these days?" Natalia forked hash delicately into her mouth.

"*Indics, mouches*, take your pick."

"What about them?"

"The more buildings you're using, the more likely you'll have one containing a *mouche*. If they hear or see anything new and unusual, they're likely to report it. If they even *think* they hear or see foreigners in their building, they'll report it."

"What do they get out of it?"

"I've been trying to figure that out. A sense of power and control, maybe?"

"Do you think they know that they're sentencing people to death that way?"

"I honestly don't know. Some of them must, surely. Either way, I'm not sure your plan is the safest."

"Maybe not. I don't suppose there are any entirely empty buildings."

"It's possible. You'll have to invite the Krauts to lunch and ask them."

"I feel like that might spoil the greatness of the food."

"Quite likely; they've spoiled everything else."

We ate in silence, savoring every bite. Even the noise of her fork scraping the plate didn't annoy me. She chewed quietly, though, for which I was grateful. Explaining my condition every time I ate with someone new was one of the biggest barriers to a romantic relationship. Even though I'd not taken anyone out in a year or more, I was fairly certain that punching one's paramour for smacking her lips was still frowned upon.

Eventually, Natalia looked up at me. "How do you think it'll all end?"

"The occupation of France, or the whole war?"

"I think they'll both end soon after America grows a spine and helps."

"You think they will?"

"Surely. They have to. Although their president seems, as I say, a little spineless."

"I met a journalist last month, an American. He said that Roosevelt is a much better bet than the guy he beat."

"Did your journalist say it's going to happen?"

"America join the war? No, but I got the impression he thought it would. Which means we just have to live through this pile of *merde* for another year."

"Is that how long you think it'll take the Yanks to spank the Germans?"

"It's just a guess."

"Seems like too long. They have so many soldiers, so much modern fighting machinery."

"One thing I do know, from personal experience: wars last longer than you think they will. Much longer."

"I can make it a year." Natalia wiped her plate clean with the last of her bread, and I did the same. "Maybe two."

"Dear lord, don't let it be that long."

We fell silent as Amit reappeared to clear away our plates and present us with dessert: small and flaky, but utterly delicious, triangles of baclava that, Natalia said, was Amit's specialty.

"Can I assume from these delicacies that he knew you were coming today?"

"You are a clever man, Henri. Yes, he knew."

We looked up as the door to the place opened and two men walked in and kicked their shoes off next to ours. They nodded to us and went to the far corner, where they settled themselves on the floor as we had.

After Amit had served them tea, he came to us for the dessert plates. As he collected them, I said, "I'll take care of the bill, please, Amit."

"Bill?" he asked. "There's no bill, Monsieur Henri."

"I don't understand. You can't provide customers that level of deliciousness and not charge for it."

"Oh, we charge our customers, of course."

"There you are then. I'll take care of it for us."

"*Non, monsieur.* No bill for you. Employees eat for free." With that, he gave me a wide smile and disappeared into the kitchen.

"What just happened?" I asked Natalia. "He thinks I work for . . . what's this place called?"

"No name."

"A restaurant with no name?"

"Yes. Much safer that way."

"What a strange world we inhabit." I sighed, then returned to the question of the bill. "Why did he call me an employee?"

"Because you are. You haven't done any work yet, but you're on the payroll as of today."

I let that sink in. A few weeks ago, I'd agreed to help a little with some of my friends' shenanigans against the occupying force, but at least they'd had the decency to ask before signing me up. I smiled as I realized I'd been taken.

"That's the real reason you brought me here, isn't it?"

But Natalia just batted those pretty eyes and rose from the floor, beckoning me to follow her with a crooked finger and a smile that told me all I needed to know.

CHAPTER SIXTEEN

Outside, Natalia made me wait while she dipped into the alleyway behind the restaurant "to get something." I lit a cigarette and waited, as content as I'd been in a very long time. My belly was full for the second time in days, I'd eaten that fine meal with a pretty girl, and for the moment no one around me was killing or being killed. Even the specter of that ice bath had receded.

When Natalia came back, she had a leather satchel over her shoulder and a smile on her face.

"What's that for?" I asked, my feeling of content slipping sideways into suspicion.

"It's for carrying things, Henri. Normal purpose for a bag, if you think about it."

"Funny. It's not the bag I'm worried about, it's whatever happens to be inside it."

"Just a few pieces of paper."

"Not a gun or anything illegal?"

"Just a few pieces of paper. No gun."

We started walking, but I didn't feel as reassured as she intended. "I'm sorry, I don't mean to be paranoid, but why would someone give you some pieces of paper in a satchel in an alley?" I glanced over but she said nothing. "I mean, if it's all legal and aboveboard."

"I didn't say the papers were legal."

I stopped. "Jesus, Natalia, what do you have in there?"

"Information."

"About what?"

"I honestly don't know." She looked up at me. "I don't, I promise."

"Where are you taking it?"

"We."

"What?"

"You mean, where are *we* taking it."

"Natalia—"

"It's a delivery from the restaurant to a bookshop. Pick up today, drop off tomorrow. And since it comes from your new part-time employer, who just fed you very well, I might add, then this is now a 'we' job."

"A dangerous job," I said grimly. "And apparently I get to risk my life for some unknown information."

"The food was more than worth it." She took my arm and we started walking again. I didn't mind that at all.

"Why does it take two people, no, why do we *risk* two people to deliver some papers?"

"I would have thought it was obvious."

"Not to me."

"It's safer this way."

"How so?"

We rounded the corner onto boulevard Arago and all but stopped in our tracks.

"*Merde.*" Natalia clutched the satchel to her body and my blood ran cold at the sight of German soldiers setting up a checkpoint, placing wooden barriers across the road and sidewalk. It would be just my luck to be caught doing something illegal the very first time I did it. Within minutes of my first job. And I knew what would happen, to both of us. Some of it, anyway.

"Come on, this way." I tugged her to my left and, as casual as we could be, we strolled into the Denfert-Rochereau subway station, disappearing into its gloomy stairway with a growing sense of relief.

I'd not been on the Métro for many months, preferring to walk or abuse my privilege as a policeman and drive an official car, and I was surprised how crowded it was. Natalia tucked the satchel under her arm as we wound our way through the crowds to the platform for the northern-bound train.

"Why so many people?" I wondered aloud.

"No cars or even bicycles anymore," Natalia reminded me. "It's how ninety percent of people travel these days."

A train rattled and clanked toward us, and we moved to the front to be in first class. I didn't mind mixing with the masses but I was going to do it in comfort.

The doors opened and we found two empty seats next to each other. "It feels safe down here," I said.

"Yes, it does. Maybe not if you're in the last car, though. I'm not sure those folks ever feel safe."

"Those folks? What are you talking about?"

"Oh, you don't know." She shook her head. "Not exactly an in-touch, man-of-the-people *flic*, are you?"

"What don't I know?"

"Quite a lot. But in this instance, that the last car on every Métro train is reserved for Jews."

"Reserved for them, or they're required to use it?"

"Right, saying it's reserved makes it sounds like a privilege, which it's not."

An elderly man in a tweed suit beside Natalia looked up from his newspaper. "Good riddance, if you ask me. Those people have been usurping our economy, our city for too long. About time they went to the back of the damn train."

"*Those people*, old man, are your neighbors," Natalia snapped. "They're the people who make your fancy suit and guard your hard-earned money."

"Steal it, more like." He narrowed his eyes. "You're pretty swarthy, shouldn't you be in that rear carriage with your Jewish friends?" He looked back at his newspaper, but the bear had been poked. And enraged.

"Do you know how this goes, you ignorant old fart?" Natalia flushed with anger, and pointed her finger at his chest as she berated him. "It starts with the Jews, and then they'll move on to, well, pretty much everyone who doesn't have lily-white skin. Gypsies, Arabs, Negroes, of course. And after they're all gone they'll start picking on the disabled. War heroes with one arm, people who became disfigured fighting for this country."

"I seriously doubt—"

"I'm not done, *connard*, so shut your mouth and listen. Listen good because once they're happy all the crippled people are gone, you know who they go after next?"

"Well, I . . . I—"

"You. They go after you, because like crippled people, drunks, and drug addicts, you are a drain on society."

"I'll have you know, young lady, that—"

"Oh, it's not me saying that, it's the men in black uniforms who've decided that whatever fine service you gave to your country is a matter for the past, and because you have no value to the Fatherland anymore, it's your turn to be exterminated."

She turned back to me, leaving the old man sputtering with indignation. I'm fairly sure I would've caught a dozen flies with my open mouth, if there were flies in first class, which there weren't. I went from surprise to anger when the old man regained his composure enough to twist in his seat and grip Natalia's shoulder. I leaped to my feet, grabbed him by the lapels, and hauled him upright.

"Now you listen to me, you withered prick. You can spout your hateful bullshit all you like and all I'll do is argue with you. But you put your hands on my friend here and I'll throw you off the goddamn train. Between stations. Am I clear?"

"Don't you threaten me," he mewed. "I'll call the police at the next station."

"The problem with that, you spineless maggot, is that I am the police."

I watched the confusion and doubt run circles around in his eyes, then I threw him back into his seat. I winced when his head cracked against the window, harder than I intended but maybe not as hard as he deserved. He groaned and I heard mutterings around me, ones less supportive of my interference than I would have liked, so I pulled out my badge and showed it to everyone in the carriage.

"If anyone has any doubts or concerns, I am indeed a policeman. And he can count himself lucky a headache is all he's getting from me today."

That seemed to calm everyone down, or at least shut them up, and we exited at the next station without further incident. As we walked along the platform, Natalia said, "I can protect myself, you know. Especially from a seventy-year-old."

"I know. But it's my job. I'm a cop, remember."

"Exactly."

That seemed like an odd thing to say, and when I looked at her she was smiling.

"Stop being so damn cryptic, woman."

"You asked earlier why it took two people to deliver papers."

"And you never answered . . ." I thought about what I'd just said, and what she'd just agreed with, and it dawned on me. "I'm a policeman. Less likely to get harassed and searched, certainly not by the French authorities."

"Right, but go a step further."

"I suppose I can take the satchel and put my handcuffs on you, if it came to that. No one will interfere with a cop arresting someone."

"See, look how clever you are. Your brain and handcuffs are both of great value to our cause." She nudged me playfully with her elbow as we climbed the stairs to the street. Playfully or flirtatiously, I wasn't quite sure which. "And I'll answer your other question now, if you like."

"I don't know what other question you're talking about, but I'm listening."

"My uncle Lucas knows Amit. Knew Amit, I guess, when he lived here. He connected me with him as a place I could stay, as he wasn't sure what was going on at rue Jacob. We knew the Germans were taking over entire buildings, kicking people out."

"They still are, but mostly on the Right Bank, luckily for us."

"Much less likely where Amit lives." She smiled. "Not as chic."

"The Gestapo does prefer chic."

"Those sexy leather boots and coats." She shuddered. "Jesus, sorry, I can't even joke about it, nothing those people do is funny."

"Maybe when we kick them out."

"You think we will?"

I didn't know how to answer that properly, but tried anyway. "I suppose I do. I can't imagine this is our life forever, can you?"

"I'll go back to Greece before living like this forever."

"Why did you come here, then? Why now?"

"I didn't want to. My father said the war was coming to Greece and it was going to be bad. Italy and Germany together, we wouldn't have a chance. Which means a lot of dead Greeks. He didn't want me to be one of them."

"But why not England or even America?"

"He said England would go the same way as Greece, just not as quickly. And because of the fight they put up, my father said the Germans would be more brutal. And America? I don't know anyone there. I think I would hate it, there with all those rich people doing nothing to help us over here. And being so far from the people I care about, how would I know what happens to them?"

"They have newspapers in America."

"Sure, for the big stories. But the newspapers everywhere have stopped listing the dead, you may have noticed. So how do I know what happens to my father, my sister?"

"Who picked Paris?" I asked, as we hurried across rue de

Seine. I still wasn't used to the lack of traffic, the emptiness of the road itself feeling like a temporary lull.

"He did. Maybe we both did, a compromise. We knew it was more settled and from there things didn't look too bad. The bombing never really happened, there was no fighting."

"Crazy times when an occupied city is the safe place to go."

"Like the eye of a hurricane, I suppose. And I only have to do this delivery stuff for a little while, to pay back Amit for the lodging."

"Good, because it's not safe." I felt a wave of relief, for us both. "So I'm only needed for a little while?"

She laughed. "I suppose that depends on how many meals you want from his restaurant."

"Wait, we're near home. I thought we were delivering those papers to a bookshop."

"We are. Just not today. Step by step, my friend." She gave me the sweetest of smiles, and I was annoyed at myself for giving in to her at every step of this dangerous new endeavor.

"Fine, but until I get another meal like that, you're on your— *Merde*, what's going on here?"

We'd rounded the corner into rue Jacob, and both of us slowed to an almost-stop at the sight of two German soldiers apparently guarding the door to our building. The bastards were in black uniforms, too, which meant they were the worst of the worst. The kind of soldiers for whom killing other soldiers on the front lines wasn't quite enough.

"Keep going," Natalia said under her breath but with a big smile because one of them was looking right at us.

"Don't act too happy, they'll know something's wrong," I said, annoyed. Not at her though, at them. "Or be pissed off that you're happy and change that."

We kept going, and they kept watching us. When we were close, one of them said something in German that I didn't catch. I just shrugged and spread my hands out in the universal *I'm sorry* signal.

"Speak English?" he demanded.

It was a funny thing to me, and I'd come across it several times at this point. Most of the fuckers who'd taken over our country didn't speak our language, and, whether or not we spoke theirs, most of us pretended we didn't. Many of them did speak English, however, so the little that we said to each other was in the language of the country they couldn't conquer. Yet. I'm sure I enjoyed the irony more than they did, but I was also sensible enough not to point it out. Especially when the young woman next to me was carrying papers that could get us killed.

"Yes, I speak some English," I said. Fluency, which I had, would be suspicious, so I knew to play it down.

"Do you live here?"

"Yes, my name is Henri Lefort. I'm a detective with the Paris police."

"Lefort?"

"Yes. And this is—"

"I don't care who she is." A nasty little smile crept onto his face, and my stomach dropped. "It's you we want to speak to."

CHAPTER SEVENTEEN

"Go inside," the SS man said. Then, when we started to move, to Natalia: "You live here too?"

"Oh, now you care who she is," I muttered in French, and instantly wished I hadn't.

"Was hast du gesagt?" he snapped at me.

"Sorry, I was saying that she does live here, on the ground floor."

Natalia flashed me a look that could have been amusement at my wit, admiration for my quick thinking, or annoyance at me being an idiot. I was pretty sure it was the third. The Nazi narrowed his eyes and watched as we went past him into the lobby, then followed us in.

"Wait," he said, then shouted something in German I didn't

catch up the open stairwell to someone I couldn't see. Then I heard footsteps clattering down toward us.

"Can I go?" Natalia said to the SS man, in her sweetest baby-girl voice. "I have to go pee-pee."

"Yes." He waved her away as if she were a bad smell. "We don't need you."

"Thank you." Natalia glanced at me and, along with her precious cargo, turned and walked away to her apartment. When I turned to see who was coming down the stairs to greet me, my stomach decided to clamp a little tighter. The man who stood before me, flanked by two more of his minions in black uniforms, was the dead man from the cells, the half-human, half-corpse-like Nazi I'd so freely insulted to his lifeless face. The very same man who'd taken what I assumed was a letter giving Remillon written permission to investigate . . . something.

And now here this *mec* was, standing in front of me, investigating . . . something.

Looking at his gaunt face and beady eyes I was not exactly feeling warm and fuzzy, but maybe this was a chance to find out what that piece of paper said exactly, find out what Remillon was investigating that might have got him killed.

"We meet again," I said, as cheerily as I could muster.

"You are Henri Lefort."

"I am."

"Not what I expected." His French was better than he'd let on at the Préfecture. Sneaky bastard.

"I'm not sure how to take that."

"I was told you are a clever man, a good policeman."

"Well, that's very nice to hear. Sorry if I disappoint."

"You most certainly do."

"Again, apologies."

"Clever, they said. So have you solved the murder of that Frenchman?"

"Still working on that. And, as it happens, I have a question for you, the answer to which might help me."

"Unsolved still, eh?" He pointed straight up toward the top floor, which was a relief, because for a split second I thought he was throwing a spontaneous salute to his Führer, which I most certainly would not have returned. "And here I am, in the very building that houses this supposedly clever detective, investigating crimes he apparently has absolutely no knowledge of." He smirked toward his underling. "Can you imagine being so clueless and unaware?"

I was on high alert by now. He was wrong in thinking I was unaware of criminal activity in my building, but absolutely right that I was clueless as to which one he was there for. And I sure as hell wasn't going to offer up a smorgasbord for him to choose from. I tried to steady my breathing, control the panic rising in me, because this conversation seemed headed in a very familiar direction. That ice bath suddenly loomed large again.

"Yes, I'm sorry. What are you talking about?"

"You are aware we have imposed certain restrictions out of necessity, are you not?"

"Quite a few, I'd say."

"You are insolent."

"Respectfully, Herr . . . sorry, what is your name?"

"I am Standartenführer Ernst Hahn."

"Well, Standartenführer Ernst Hahn, respectfully I'm also very busy. As you pointed out I have a murder case to investigate and—"

"One that happened on your doorstep."

"Indeed, I'm aware, so—"

"Quite the hotbed of criminality, no?" A thin eyebrow rose quizzically over a dead eye.

"Still to be determined, I'd say. If you care to clarify?"

"You are familiar with all the owners and tenants?"

"I believe so. Although we've had some vacancies and some additions lately, so it's possible with everything that's going on someone new has joined us I don't know about or haven't met." Which was me, like any smart man unsure where the conversation was headed, giving myself some wiggle room.

"There are two apartments to each floor, correct?"

"Correct." Safe ground, I liked it so far.

"And one staircase to access each floor."

"One main staircase, yes."

"As I thought." He opened his mouth to speak but it just hung there, as if he really was dead finally. Except that his eyes widened, just a little, at whatever he was seeing behind me. Rather, *who* he was seeing behind me. I turned.

Maximillian Zoeller.

This time Hahn did snap out an impressively crisp salute, one that Zoeller returned less enthusiastically. Which, being Hahn's boss, he was entitled to do.

"Sir, what are you doing here?" Hahn asked.

"I'm investigating a matter."

"What matter?"

"None of your concern. What are *you* doing here?"

"We had a report of fraternization with someone in this building. One of our people with a woman, and maybe . . . more than just a woman."

I looked hard at Zoeller, but whatever he felt inside he kept hidden.

"Aren't you supposed to be looking for whoever printed that newspaper?" Zoeller snapped.

"*Jawohl.* But some were found near here, so I thought because I have this case, too, I would kill two birds."

"Sex is not your priority, Standartenführer. Subversive propaganda is."

Yeah, you would say that, you Nazi pervert, I thought, and briefly wondered what would happen if I gave Hahn the information he wanted. Very briefly wondered, because there was no way in hell I was inserting my lance into this joust.

"It's just that an . . . agent of ours was killed in the street here. It's possible he was killed by whoever has been—"

"I said propaganda, Standartenführer." Zoeller was almost shouting. "Not sex. Do I make myself clear?"

"Yes, Herr Obergruppenführer. Perfectly clear."

"Good." Zoeller looked over at me, no recognition in his eyes. "Who is this man and what did he tell you?"

"He is a detective who lives in the building. I was going to ask him—"

"My question," Zoeller interrupted with exaggerated patience, "was not what you were going to ask, but what has he told you."

"He's told me nothing, Herr Obergruppenführer."

"My name is Henri Lefort, and he's right, I haven't told him anything." I knew a lifeboat when I saw one, for both me and Zoeller. "Mostly because I have no idea what he's talking about. Fraternization? Never seen anything like that in this building."

"He is not a very good detective," Hahn said, a little sulkily I thought, and I wondered if Zoeller would mind if I punched the fucker for singing that tune again.

"Do you have a suspect?" Zoeller asked, ignoring my comment and Hahn's. "I suppose you would need two for fraternization. Well?"

"Just the Frenchwoman on the third floor."

"You interrogated her?"

"A little. She hasn't given me a name yet, but she will."

"I'm sure." Zoeller looked pensive for a moment, and I knew he was working all the angles. He absolutely couldn't have Hahn interrogate Claire Raphael, that much we both knew. Finally, he said, "Bring her downstairs. Put a pillowcase over her head."

Hahn started to move, then paused. "A pillowcase, sir?"

"Make it two." When Hahn didn't move, Zoeller sighed, as if having to explain something to a child. "It will disorient her. Make her more afraid and more compliant. By the time you get her to avenue Kléber half the work will have been done."

"*Jawohl*, Obergruppenführer." Hahn snapped his heels and directed two men to follow him upstairs. A different kind of sickness swept over me, the fear for myself dissipating but a terror for Claire Raphael rushing in to take its place. I didn't see a way this could end well, and it was physically painful to me that I couldn't figure a way out of this for her. We listened as the SS men banged on her door, as she opened it, as the soldiers yelled at her and grabbed the pillowcases, at her wailing as they covered her head and dragged her down the stairs to where we stood.

"Stand still and be quiet, woman," Hahn commanded, as poor Claire stood trembling and sniffling before us. "Did you want to question her, *mein Herr*? I am willing to do it, either here or at headquarters."

Zoeller put a hand half on his chin, half covering his mouth, and said, "Headquarters." The change in his voice, the slight mumble, was imperceptible to his men I was sure, but I noticed it. With that, the hand over his mouth, and the two pillowcases, he was gambling that Claire wouldn't recognize him and plead for his help. And, of course, in doing so give away the secret that would likely land him in front of a firing squad. So far, it was a bet he was winning.

"*Jawohl*, Obergruppenführer, avenue Kléber it is," Hahn said, snapping out another salute. But his arm was still on the way up when I saw Claire's head lift a fraction, and the beginnings of a muffled question come from her.

"Oberg—"

Zoeller punched her hard in the face. Hard enough that her head snapped back and she hit the wall with a *thunk*. She slid down it, groaning with pain and confusion. Zoeller acted cool as a cucumber, and my glance at Hahn suggested he'd not fully understood what just happened.

Still winning that bet, I thought.

"This situation is ridiculous," Zoeller said, harrumphing for effect. "Hahn, do you suspect anyone in this building is producing that damned pamphlet?"

"Here?" Hahn looked confused. "No, sir, not yet anyway."

I didn't like the *not yet* part, but kept my trap shut.

"Then this is what we will do. You and your men continue your investigation into that. I will interrogate this woman myself."

"How will you get her to headquarters? I will leave a man to help you."

"No, no need. I want our resources on that propaganda."

Zoeller pointed to me. "I will use the French detective, he will help me." His tone grew more serious. "You're not suggesting I'm incapable of controlling this sorry French slut, are you?"

"No sir, not at all. Never!"

I almost smiled at Zoeller's ability to bring the dead to life. Hahn was like a newly animated zombie, except he was the scared one.

"Very good, then get on with it." He ushered Hahn and his men out onto the street, and we watched as the heavy door closed behind them. Then he turned to me.

"Well, now, Detective," he said grimly. "Quite a situation we have here. Any suggestions?"

"I do. We take the sack off her head and get her to a doctor."

"I was thinking more long term."

"Well, avenue Kléber sounds like a bad idea, no matter who takes her."

"Agreed. I suppose I could just shoot you both and say you tried to help her escape." He frowned in thought. "Which would also relieve me of another problem."

The icy grip of fear tightened in my guts again. "Me seeing you with that . . . young gentleman. About which, and I am more than happy to give you my word on this, I never saw nor heard a damn thing."

"Which is more effective at keeping a secret a secret, though? A promise, or a bullet?"

"If I'd wanted to spill the beans, I had my chance."

"Not the same as being asked questions while hanging upside down with bricks tied to your balls."

"I've had the cold bath treatment, that was more than enough."

"What?" That clearly surprised him.

"One of your colleagues seemed to think I had information about the pamphlets."

"Which colleague?"

"He introduced himself." The man's pale face drifted into my mind. "But it's what he did rather than his name I seem to remember."

"How very rude," Zoeller said. "I always make a point of making people remember me."

"Build rapport before extracting fingernails?"

"Seems like the least I can do."

"The least you can do is not pull fingernails."

He laughed softly. "If my new friends answer my questions satisfactorily, then I don't. It's in their . . . hands, quite literally." He laughed again, amused at his own pun.

I looked over at Claire Raphael, who was stirring and moaning gently. "Yes, well, back to the matter—"

"At hand?" He was grinning now, and it crossed my mind that a happy Zoeller was one less likely to put a bullet in my back.

"Precisely."

"Lay her on the floor. On her front."

"On her front, why?"

"Yes, facedown, I don't want her seeing me if the pillowcases come off."

"Ah, right." A shot of relief warmed my stomach. He wouldn't care if she saw his face if he planned to kill her. And me.

I knelt beside Claire but she jerked back as I put my hands on her shoulders.

"Claire, it's Henri Lefort. It's all right."

"Henri?" Her voice was weak and afraid.

"Yes, it's me. I'm going to lay you down on the floor, we're still in the building. You need to just lie there for a moment, nice and still. Got it?"

"The floor? Yes, yes."

"I'm going to help you. Here we go." I swiveled her body so her head was away from the wall and, under Zoeller's amused gaze, helped her to lie facedown on the tiled floor.

"Now you." Zoeller looked at me, unblinking.

"Me? Why?"

"Good question." His eyes seemed to harden into black stones as he unholstered his pistol and held it by his side. "I suppose instead of lying down and accepting your fate, you could *actually* try to escape. That would make this much more realistic, now, wouldn't it?"

The relief drained from my body and I felt sick. And I couldn't take my eyes off his pistol, one of those ugly Lugers the Germans loved so much. *God, they really have to ruin everything* was the odd thought that ran through my mind.

Zoeller interrupted my irrelevant musings. "Think you could make it to the door, Lefort?"

"I'm not as fast or agile as I used to be. Plus, you're in the way."

"Yes, quite the hurdle, aren't I?"

"Maybe if you just put the gun away?"

"Ah, that would make it more fair." He spread his hands wide. "But then how would I shoot you?"

Over his shoulder I saw the door to the building open, inch by inch, but because he blocked my view I couldn't see who was coming in. I opened my mouth to say something—I didn't want Zoeller to be startled and shoot either me or the incomer—but before I could speak, a slight figure ghosted through the opening and in a moment Natalia Tsokos was beside and slightly behind Zoeller.

With a revolver pressed lightly against his spine.

"You're not shooting anyone, Nazi," she said through gritted teeth. "In fact, what if you're the one dying today?"

CHAPTER EIGHTEEN

The smile that had been on Zoeller's face melted in an instant, but he had the good sense not to move. Natalia was small and light, but the gun in her hand was more than adequate to cut his spine in half and paint his guts all over, well, me unless I moved. That calculation made, I stepped to my right, just in case.

"That is a very bad idea, young lady," Zoeller said, but there was a measure of fear in his eyes, which I enjoyed immensely.

"Henri, take his gun," she said. When I'd done so, she went on: "I'm the new concierge for this building, monsieur. I don't let my residents get shot for no reason."

"And your guests?"

"The invited ones, same rule."

"Am I not such a guest?" he said.

"You're an unwelcome one. And anyway, I have plenty of reasons to shoot you."

"Plenty more not to," he countered. "Lefort, explain it to her."

My mind was working overtime. "He has a point. If you kill Zoeller, they will round us up like sheep and do nasty things to us until we tell them what happened."

"Very nasty things," the German added.

"Shut up, Zoeller," I barked. I was annoyed at his tone, but also at the dawning realization that shooting him probably was, in fact, a terrible idea.

"We could take him and dump his body somewhere else," she said.

"We could, indeed. But that Hahn character knows he was here. So here is where they'd start looking, and Natalia, I've been asked questions the Nazi way. I don't want that again, not for me, you, or anyone here." An image of Nicola being dragged into that house on avenue Kléber convinced me I needed to think my way out of this before any triggers got pulled. And in a way that allowed Zoeller not just to live, but to leave us alone.

"Then what?" Natalia asked.

"I give Zoeller his gun back and you put yours away. He goes on about his day and we go on about ours. We all agree this never happened and no one bears anyone else ill will. How does that sound, Herr Zoeller?"

He seemed to think for a moment before nodding. "I can live with that."

"It's the only way you live," Natalia growled, clearly unhappy with this resolution.

"Then that's what we'll do. We have your word?"

"You have my word." Zoeller put out his hand and I handed

him back his pistol. I looked at Natalia and said, "And you have ours."

She held my eye for a moment, then withdrew her gun and I saw Zoeller's shoulders relax with relief. He looked to his left and we both watched as Natalia reluctantly uncocked her revolver and tucked it into the back of her trousers.

"Time to resume our respective days," Zoeller said, and walked to the front door. When he got there, he turned and we watched as he made to holster his Luger. At the last second, his arm flashed up and Natalia and I froze in place. I wondered if we'd been fools to trust him, to put our gun away before he put his away.

"Don't worry, Lefort," he said grimly. "I'm not going to shoot you. I am a man of my word, and the three of us have an accord."

"Glad to hear it," I said.

"But she does not." His gun arm dropped a fraction and I saw he was pointing it at Claire Raphael. Before I could say another word, he closed one eye to confirm his aim, and, with a bang that momentarily deafened us in that closed space, put a bullet into the back of her head.

Natalia dropped to her knees beside Claire and I looked to where Zoeller had just been standing, a space that was now empty. I would gain nothing by chasing him so I knelt beside Claire as well, hoping against hope he'd missed or just grazed her. But I knew before my knees hit the tile that it was hopeless. The pillowcases covering the front of her face were soaked with blood, which meant the bullet had gone through the back of her head and out of the front. And I'd seen enough exit wounds to know how much worse than entry wounds they were. Natalia clearly hadn't and was trying to work the pillowcases off.

"Natalia, no." I grabbed her wrists.

"Why? She might be—"

"She's gone. The bullet went through her head. Her brain is scrambled, her face destroyed. She's dead." Not the softest landing I'd given someone, but better she hear what happened than see it. Slowly, she sank back on her heels and stared down at Claire's lifeless body.

"That monster. That monster."

"I know. I'm sorry."

"He murdered her. In cold blood."

"A lot of that happening these days." Angry eyes flashed at me. "I'm sorry, you're right. She did nothing to deserve that."

"If you'd let me shoot him, she'd still be alive."

"Maybe, but not for long." I gripped Natalia's shoulders. "You have to understand how these people work. I wasn't making it up when I said that if we kill him his buddies would be back here to exterminate probably everyone in this building. And the ones on either side of us, too, most likely."

"So, we don't ever fight back?"

"We do, we jus—"

"We just let them shoot us in cold blood and walk away?"

"Yes!" I didn't like it any more than she did, but she had the hotheadedness of youth working against her. "But we do fight back, just not in a way that gets us and a whole load of other people killed."

"Then how?"

"Still working on that." I looked down at Claire's body. She epitomized this damn war. A harmless, kind woman who did everything she could, everything she had to, to survive. And yet she still wound up with a set of pillowcases over her head and a bullet in her brain. In the last war at least it was mostly soldiers that got killed, men who had guns in their hands and knives in their belts. This time around, anyone at any time could find themselves pushing up daisies.

Which brought me back to the problem in front of me, a problem Natalia was also processing.

"What . . . what do we do with her?" she asked.

"Normally we'd call the police." Stating the obvious was always a strong suit for me.

"We could do that, say we found her like this."

"No. They'd interview us, and if we got one detail wrong they'd know we were lying. And believe me, unless they send GiGi, they'll know we're lying."

"Why?"

"Because it's almost impossible to lie in detail. It's even harder for two people to lie in detail and have their stories match."

"Then what do we do?"

"For now, get her out of sight. Your apartment is easiest."

Natalia grimaced but didn't argue, and she helped me drag poor Claire Raphael into her tiny apartment, leaving her on an old rug that immediately stained red from the blood-drenched pillowcases.

"Now what?" Natalia asked.

"I'll get a car from the Préfecture. I hate to say it, but the only safe thing is the river."

"Do you know who killed that man outside the building?"

I gave her a look, because that question seemed like an odd response to me suggesting we dump a neighbor's body in the Seine.

"No, why?"

"Do you even know why he was killed?"

"I have an idea."

"And?"

"And I'll share it with a non-civilian colleague when I'm good and ready."

"What if there's a murderer on the loose, what if we're in danger living here?"

"Jesus, Natalia." I laughed at the ridiculousness of her objection. "Look at what's lying at your feet."

"Who, not what," she said softly.

"Not anymore, I'm afraid. Look, of course we're in danger living here. Every goddamn day, every goddamn minute."

"That's not what—"

"If you're worried there's some lunatic prowling the streets, or this street, then don't be. That's not what's going on."

"And I just take your word for that." She crossed her arms like a grumpy old woman.

"Yes, you do. Look, are you able to help me tonight or not?"

"What if we get caught?"

"Then we get a bullet in the brain, too." I sighed. "We'll go after dark but before curfew. It won't take long, it's not like we can have a ceremony."

"Henri, Jesus."

"Sorry. I just . . ." I didn't know what. Was exhausted? Was becoming immune to death? A little of both maybe. "Can you help or not?"

"Yes, of course."

"Thank you." I wiped my brow, suddenly feeling not so great. "I need to get to work, find a car."

"Fine. I'll . . . wait somewhere else."

"And best not to tell anyone about this. Everyone who knows is in potential danger, understood?"

"Understood."

I walked to the Préfecture, glad to feel my limbs moving and grateful to feel the cold air on my face. Once there, I perched on Nicola's desk and, because she was who she was, she could tell something was wrong.

"Henri, what is it?"

"Claire."

"Claire Raphael?"

"*Oui.*"

"*Merde*, what has she done now? She's going to find herself in deep water if she keeps doing what she's been doing."

I grimaced. "Unfortunately, that prophecy is truer than you know."

"Henri, stop playing games. What happened?"

I lowered my voice. "Her boyfriend shot her. In the head. In our building."

Nicola's hand flew to her mouth. "Oh no."

"He was covering his tracks, and I'm pretty sure he was seriously considering shooting us, too."

"Us?"

"Natalia was there."

"That poor girl, she's too innocent to see that."

"A little late for that."

"So, Claire. Where . . . what are you . . . ?" Unsurprisingly she didn't know the right question to ask. Who did anymore?

"She's at Natalia's apartment. We have to be . . . discreet."

"Oh my god. The river?"

"We can't have authorities, either theirs or ours, asking questions. So yes."

"You'll need—"

"A car. That's where you come in."

"I can't, Henri."

"What do you mean, you can't? That's your job. Or one of them, anyway."

"It used to be. The whole office is down to just three, now. If you want one you'll have to get permission from Chief Proulx."

"More red tape, that's what this place has always needed." I slid off her desk and headed toward my boss's office, breezing through the door without knocking. Proulx jumped at my entrance and I wondered if he'd been napping.

"Sorry to wake you, Chief," I said. "I need a car for this evening."

"Oh, certainly, which one would you like?"

"Well, it doesn't matter really. As long as it has petrol in it I'm fine with—" I stopped myself. "Ah, that was sarcasm, wasn't it?"

"Well spotted."

"Thank you, sir, but I do need a car."

"No chance."

"In these ever-changing times I'd say there's always a chance, wouldn't you?"

"I would not. Not when it comes to you having a car tonight."

"Why not?"

"Because we now have just two, and both are spoken for."

"Hang on." I pointed out toward the bullpen. "Nicola said we have three."

"My back, along with my worn-out shoes and my seniority, have permanently requisitioned one of them. So two."

"Well, I only need one."

"Out of the question."

"Why?"

"Both are being used tonight."

"For what?"

"A raid."

That caught me by surprise. "A raid? What raid?"

"One you don't know about."

"And why is that?"

"Because, Henri, you are a detective. Your job is to solve murders, something you're surprisingly good at. My job, on the other hand, is to supervise lots of policemen, including, but not limited to, detectives. For example, policemen carrying out raids."

"What kind of raid?"

"None of your business."

"Jesus, Louis, don't tell me you're helping the fucking Germans by grabbing people from their homes. What is it, Jews? Blacks? Gypsies?"

"None of those," Proulx snapped. I could tell I'd hit a nerve, and I was glad to have done so. "We don't take part in those."

"Yes, we do."

"Not when I'm giving the orders."

"Not yet."

"Lefort." His face had turned red and he waved an angry finger at me. "You think my job is easy? Every day I do shit that could get me killed, that saves lives, that . . . that fucks with the Germans. So don't you dare come in here and act like I'm part of the problem." He calmed himself, which entailed dialing down from angry to irritated. "Did you solve that murder yet?"

"Not yet. I mean, I know roughly the reason he was killed. I think."

"You think."

"I'll be sure when I catch the killer and he confesses."

"So, it's a he?"

"Good question. When he or she confesses."

"And why do you think Reb . . . what was his name?"

"Remillon. Guy Remillon."

"Why do you think he was killed?"

"He was working for the Germans, investigating these goddamn *corbeaux* for them. I think he showed up to our building to either look into one of those letters, or maybe meet the *mouche* who sent it."

"I'm confused. We have a man in custody for his murder. Either he did it or didn't. Why are you still investigating if you made the collar? Go get your confession and wrap it up."

"Two reasons, since you ask. First, I can't get a confession because that lunk GiGi broke my suspect's jaw. Second, I want to gather enough evidence so that, once my suspect Darroze is able to gab again, there'll be no point in him lying."

"But you're sure enough it's him to keep him locked up." Proulx was a soft-hearted man, despite his efforts to make everyone think otherwise. "Seems like bad practice to lock random suspects up while we search for evidence of their guilt. Makes it look like we decide before we find evidence."

"Oh, he's not behind bars for murdering Remillon. Yet."

"No?"

"No. He assaulted a *flic* while being arrested."

"While being arrested for . . . ?"

"Being a *mouche*."

"That's not a crime."

"It must be, otherwise he wouldn't have been arrested for it."

"Henri," he began, but gave up. We both knew my logic, while frequently fallible, was utterly exhausting at all times. "Go find your evidence."

"I need a car tonight."

"Ah, right. We finished that conversation already. You asked, I said no, and now you leave."

"Boss, please."

Proulx heard something in my voice, and cocked his head. "What do you need it for, Henri?"

"Better I don't say. I promise it's police business, though." Not entirely a lie. A car might prevent this policeman from being shot, and a dead Henri Lefort would mean a vacancy at the Préfecture that Proulx would have to fill, a bunch of cases he'd have to reassign.

"My hands are tied, Henri. Both cars are needed tonight. Unless . . ."

"Unless what? I'm game."

"You lead the raid. I give you a car, you . . . do whatever it is you need to do, then grab the team and lead the raid."

I did not like that suggestion one bit. But I needed the car, badly.

"What's the raid?"

"Illicit newspaper production. We think we've found where they are producing that pamphlet everyone's been finding."

I groaned loudly. "Not that again."

"Afraid so. And it's called *Égalité et Fraternité*?"

"That's the one. The Germans have asked us to shut it down, they feel like it looks better if we do it rather than them."

"They still give a damn how they look?"

"Some of them do. Fewer and fewer."

"What happens to whoever we find?"

"Depends."

"On what?"

"First of all, whether they start shooting at you. If they do, you shoot back. If not, you arrest them."

"Yeah, I get that. My question pertains to what happens after we arrest them."

"I imagine they will remain in jail until there's some sort of trial at which they get to present a defense to an impartial judge or jury."

"Yes, that does seem likely. Especially in this enlightened age."

"Or they get a bullet in a dark alley. Look, Henri, no one's asking you to execute anyone."

"My point exactly."

"Meaning?"

"Arresting someone is equivalent to putting a bullet in their brain. There's no trial, not even a pretense of justice. The sausage-munchers want examples, not justice."

Proulx ran a hand over his face and his shoulders slumped. "I'm so fucking tired, Henri. Look, I don't have the answers, I don't have any solutions, and I can't tell you what's justice and what's murder anymore. The only thing I know, right this minute, is that the only way you get a car tonight is if you lead that raid. Am I at least crystal clear on that point?"

CHAPTER NINETEEN

The black Renault, the oldest, crappiest vehicle in what was left of our fleet, only just fit in the alleyway behind our building. The car's gears ground and grated every time I worked the clutch and lever, setting my teeth on edge. That was one of the many irrational problems with misophonia—I could unintentionally annoy the hell out of myself.

I was even more on edge when Natalia was nowhere to be found. I knocked on her door at six sharp, five minutes before the sun officially set, expecting help moving the body of poor Claire Raphael. My knuckles were still warm from the rapping when I saw the piece of paper sticking out of the jamb, at what was eye level for Natalia but not for me.

Had to go out. Emergency. Sorry. Door is unlocked, hope you manage.

I groaned out loud and let myself in to find Claire lying where we'd left her. I found a large blanket, and rolled her stiff body onto it so I could drag her to the back door. A quick glance into the shadowy alleyway told me the coast was clear so I opened the rear door and dragged my poor dead neighbor into the car, depositing her indelicately onto the floor behind the front seats.

"Sorry, my dear, no time for a soft touch." I said it to the pillowcases that still encased her head.

I covered her with the blanket and climbed into the front seat, panting a little as I settled myself in. The gathering darkness gave me some comfort, as did the fact I was driving a police car, but since the Germans had moved in both things had taken on new meaning.

As a homicide detective I'd been at the top of the food chain and I could have driven a stack of bodies around the city in broad daylight without a care in the world. But now I only commanded respect if the lowly, gun-toting grunt of a foot soldier decided he wanted to give it to me. His options ranged from saluting me and wishing me a fine evening to shooting me in the head, all with the same consequence: none.

Likewise, the dark provided cover just like she always did. But now she was an excuse for aforementioned grunt to question my business. To search my car. The trick was to take smaller roads, a winding route out toward the Boulogne-Billancourt area. There were closer dump spots to the east, but that could mean Claire's body floating through the city. And even these days, that could attract unwanted questions and provoke an investigation that ended up on my doorstep. And my doorstep had been busy enough, thank you very much.

The car rattled and groaned, its engine misfiring on the low-grade fuel it was drinking, but I made it across the river and was making steady progress toward the Bois de Boulogne when I hit a roadblock on boulevard Suchet. I saw the glowing cigarettes of the two guards before the wooden barrier, and cursed them as I slammed on the brakes. I wound my window down and, despite the cold air, I felt sweat on my forehead. I just hoped these two *mecs* wouldn't notice.

"Sprichst du Deutsch?" one of them asked.

"Nein," I lied. *"Police. Je suis police."* I showed him my credentials and he waved his friend over. They huddled for a moment.

"Get out of the car," the second one said in passable French.

"Why? Look, I'm in a hurry." Quite true, I had to dump the body and get back to the city in time to lead the fucking raid I'd agreed to. "You see I'm police, why are you stopping me?"

"Where do you go?" the second man asked.

"I'm meeting a colleague on the edge of the woods."

"Why? It's night."

"A policeman's job is never done." I said it with a friendly smile, but I wasn't sure he'd even understood.

The first soldier produced a flashlight from his belt and shone it inside the car, blinding me and then sweeping the light through the interior. I hoped to hell I'd covered Claire completely, but even if so he'd see a lump covered by a blanket.

The light paused. *"Was ist das?"*

The moment of truth. I looked at the second soldier and said, "Please don't disturb that. It's evidence. Important evidence."

"What, exactly?"

"A body. A woman was shot."

This was a new one for them. They stared at my police

credentials again, turning them upside down and inspecting them from every angle.

"Why no ambulance?" the second soldier asked.

"She's dead. There are no ambulances, and one wouldn't help anyway."

"Who killed her?" His tone amused me, more mild curiosity than in-depth interrogation. He might have been asking me about the engine capacity of the car I was driving.

"I don't know yet," I lied again. "But every minute matters in an investigation."

They handed me back my papers and whispered to each other for a moment, then one of them lifted the wooden barrier and the other stepped out of my way. With a huge sigh of relief I accelerated as hard as I could, which was not very, past them and into the safety of the darkness beyond.

I couldn't help but marvel yet again at the world we now lived in—one where I, a police detective, was dumping the body of a neighbor in the dark of night. A world where that was absolutely the best option, and one where two soldiers were more interested in smoking their cigarettes in peace than investigating why a cop was driving about town with a fresh corpse on the floorboards of his car. In that moment, as confusing as it all was, I was grateful that we all had our own missions and interests, and that a plot twist that started to lead these two soldiers down an unexpected path meant it was easier just to turn and walk away.

I kept the windows down as I drove, immune to the cold and desperate to find the spot I'd once picnicked on with Nicola. It was slow going, what with my headlights doused and the streetlamps out, but I finally found the spot. I killed the engine and sat in the chilled silence for a moment as my eyes scanned the bank. I twisted in my seat and looked behind me, making sure there was no one there.

During the day, the Bois de Boulogne was a pleasant place to take a stroll, picnic, and generally people-watch with a bottle of wine. At night, this two-faced park showed her dark side. Prostitutes and drug dealers sold their wares, usually to each other, and men with knives lurked in the shadows to take the wallets of those who lingered too long.

I saw no one, though, so I stepped out of the car and opened the back door. I put my hands under Claire's shoulders and heaved her out of the car and onto the ground, the blanket falling away as it caught on the door sill. It was a short drag to the river, a stone parapet with a three-foot drop to the water, and I got her there with a little puffing but no real trouble.

At the water's edge, I hesitated. This suddenly seemed so wrong, everything about it. Claire didn't deserve this. I knew many had died unnecessary deaths, of course, and many more would. But right there I had my hands on the body of a woman who'd just tried to survive a world she didn't create. For her to disappear forever in the black waters of the Seine seemed like the ultimate insult. *You lived, you failed to survive, and now you will just disappear from the world.* This act, dumping her body, making her a forgotten person, was the opposite of everything I stood for and believed in.

And yet, it was still my best option.

I knelt beside her and pulled the crusted, stiff pillowcases from her head, and I grimaced when they stuck to her face, or maybe it was her hair. I dropped them into the water and gave them a moment to float away, then looked at her face, destroyed by the exiting bullet just as I knew it would be.

"I'm sorry, Claire," I whispered. "I'm sorry you died and I'm just as sorry this is happening. You deserve better and I'm sorry I couldn't protect you." I waited for a second, as if for a reply, then gently rolled her onto her side and over the edge of the parapet. I saw her for just a moment after the splash, and then she was gone. I stayed on my knees, a deep sadness coursing through me, and I punched myself on the thigh to stop the tears coming.

"Monsieur." I wheeled around, staggering to my feet at a man's deep voice. He stood twenty yards away, a young woman next to him. They were both Black, and she looked scared, he watchful. They were both dressed in clothes that might once have been nice, but were now dirty and threadbare. "Who was that?" the man asked.

"None of your business." My hand twitched but I didn't want to escalate this, to make it an armed confrontation, if I didn't have to. One corpse per night felt like a good limit.

"I can make it my business." He smiled, which was unexpected. "Or not."

"I'd appreciate not."

"Ah, but perhaps something in return."

"A bribe." I could tell him I was a *flic*, but something in me resisted that. Maybe I didn't want a civilian to know that the police were rolling bodies into the Seine these days. Maybe it was something else but, like my gun, that was a weapon I wanted to keep holstered. For now.

"*Non, monsieur.*" He shook his head dramatically. "I am training a new employee here. Alice. I do not expect anything for free, and I do not seek bribes."

"Then what?"

He didn't say anything, just shoved her toward me. Her head

dropped and she slowly shuffled to where I was standing. As she got closer I could see how young she was, probably not even close to being twenty.

"For a modest fee," the man was saying, "you can help me with her education."

"Is she your daughter?"

He laughed gently. "God, no, not possible. Got my balls blown off the last time the Krauts invaded France."

"Managed to keep mine."

"And now, for a small fee, you can use them."

"Not interested." Now felt like the right time to provide the gentleman with full disclosure. "I'm a cop."

"I doubt it." The man smiled again. "Do cops dispose of their cases in the Seine nowadays?"

"Do you know a Frenchman who's not a cop who still drives a car and carries a gun?" I opened my jacket to show him.

He glanced between me and the Renault, as if he'd not noticed the car before. He shrugged.

"Cops like pretty girls, too, don't they?" He was persistent, I'll give him that.

"I'm sure many do. I prefer them about my own age. You know, not children."

"Is that so?" The man took a step forward. "Alice here can be any age you want her to be."

"Like I said before, not interested. Go on about your way."

"What if that way involves telling the authorities about a French cop dropping bodies into the river?"

"Why would you do that?"

"I hear they give rewards for things like that. I'm sure a dirty cop would get me more francs than Alice would."

"I'm not a dirty cop."

"Normal procedure, was it, what I just watched you do?"

My patience, and mood, was running low and I calculated the best way to get rid of this *mec*. "How much?"

"For her mouth? Why don't you ask her."

The girl turned her large eyes up to me, and I could see she was shaking but trying not to. I was suddenly fed up, beyond fed up, with this night.

"You know what?" I looked past the girl and directly at her pimp. "I'm taking her somewhere safe. We have a whole new batch of pricks running Paris right now, I don't have the time or energy to deal with a prick like you."

"What are you talking about, she's my girl." His voice hardened and he took another step toward me, putting him about ten feet away.

"You're a former soldier, for God's sake. Is this what you fought for, to live like this? Make her live like this?"

"You think I chose to fight?" He spat on the ground. "I didn't choose that life any more than I chose this one."

"Well then, comrade, you're out of choices again. Walking away is all you have left."

"Not without her."

"Do you think I'm negotiating with you?" I put a hand on her arm and steered her toward my car.

"Stop, asshole, you're not taking her anywhere." I looked over and a silver blade had jumped into his hand. "I don't give a damn if you're a cop, you try and take my property and I'll cut you to pieces."

"She's a kid, not your property."

"Fuck you, she's mine. Get your hands off her." He pointed the knife at the girl. "Alice, come here right now. You don't, you know what you'll get."

"You hit little girls, too? Yeah, of course you do."

"Alice, right now!" he snarled.

She twisted in my grip and looked up at me. "Please, monsieur, let me go. Please."

"You want to go with him?" I asked.

Her reply was a nod, but the head drop was also a sign of defeat, of submission, an acceptance of her world as it was.

"Let her go!" the man shouted.

"So you can beat her and pimp her out? No, I don't think I will."

The man raised his knife and I pulled out my gun and aimed it at his chest.

"Oh, is that what you're going to do, cop?" he sneered. "Shoot me? Dump me in the river, too? Give me that little bitch back, you won't see us again. She'll be losing a finger because of this little performance, but what do you care?"

I hated him in that moment, this man who'd worn the same uniform as me, a man I might have fought and died alongside. A man who had failed the purity test the Germans were now applying to their conquered people, to us, a test he'd failed by being born. But I didn't feel sorry for him. Maybe I should have, but he'd chosen his path and it was to enslave this girl, and maybe others, so he didn't have to work for his money. His plan was to ruin this girl's life, add her to the stack of women in this city who started out with little and wound up with nothing, broken and empty.

As we stood and stared at each other, a gust of wind gathered pace and disturbed the branches nearest to us, and all around they clattered and chattered like voices telling me what to do. I don't know if I listened to them or to the voice in my own head, but my finger slipped onto the trigger and tightened. I didn't even aim, I just waited for him and his knife to move toward me, to get close enough so that I didn't need to, close enough for the trigger to give way. And so I did two of the three things he'd taunted me to do. I shot him dead, and I rolled his body into the River Seine. Then I watched as a young girl named Alice ran away into the darkness of the woods, if not safe then at least safe from him.

CHAPTER TWENTY

There were only three of us available to raid what Chief Proulx had called the newspaper office, but was in reality the ground floor of a shuttered bistro on rue de l'Eglise in the Fifteenth Arrondissement.

"I thought we weren't supposed to do this unless we had at least four men?" The question was a fair one, and posed by the youngest of the group, a uniformed *flic* who I assumed had joined up to avoid the rigors and torments of elementary school.

"Procedures aren't what they used to be," I told him. "What's your name?"

"Gregoire Vacher."

"Well, Vacher, it's just the three of us. You're welcome to sit this one out if you're unhappy with the balance of things."

"No, sir, of course not."

"All right then." I looked over at the third member of the team, Albert Durand. He was a fellow homicide detective and an asthmatic, and I'd never seen him exert himself beyond climbing the stairs to work. He even took breaks doing that. "You volunteer for this, Albert?"

"What do you think?"

"Me neither. So, let's get this done and done safely. To be clear, I don't care if we arrest everyone inside, or everyone escapes. I want us all to sleep comfortably in our beds tonight. That's our priority." I laid out the plan. "I'll go around back, there's an alleyway that'll take me to the rear doors. You two give me time to get there, then head inside. I'll go in the back and we'll meet in the middle of this fearsome, traitorous newspaper office." The kid looked anxious, like he had a question he didn't want to ask. "What is it, Vacher?"

"Sir, I'm not sure when I'm allowed to shoot someone. If they try and run away?"

"Let's plan on not shooting anyone at all. For anything. If they try to run away, you can tackle or even chase them if you want." Durand snorted derisively. "But let's not shoot anyone unless they're actually pointing a gun at you. Clear?"

"I'm not shooting anyone even if they do," Durand grumbled. "Just about had enough of this damn war, I'm ready to exit any way I can."

"You should probably take a day off, with that attitude," I chided him.

"This *is* my day off, for fuck's sake."

"Well then, let's get on with it and get you back home." I lit a cigarette and the three of us strolled along the sidewalk until I cut across the road to the alleyway. The smell of garbage rose all around me, and twice I had to step over the legs of men sleeping on their beds of rags and torn clothing. At least, I assumed they were sleeping; it wasn't in my purview to be checking for pulses. It wasn't just for Durand that I wanted this over; I was bone-tired and wanted a strong drink to help me forget how the evening had unfolded.

When I reached the back door to the former bistro, I put my ear to it. Nothing. I tried the handle and was pleased to find it unlocked. I'd been prepared to shoot the door open, but having told Vacher to keep his pistol holstered I was glad I could, too. The door squeaked a little as I eased it open, and I cursed myself for not bringing a flashlight, because whatever was in front of me lay in total darkness.

I flipped open my lighter and sparked up a small flame, enough to let me see five steps ahead, and probably more than enough to get me shot by a trigger-happy newsman. As I made my way down a long hallway, I could see a dim light glowing in front of me.

A sudden crash ahead and to my right, followed by Albert Durand cursing wildly, told me my comrades had also neglected to bring flashlights. I almost laughed at the absurdity—Vacher had his youth and inexperience as an excuse, but Durand and I were just chumps.

I froze as I saw a flash of something, or someone, at the end of the hallway, and I questioned my eyes. Maybe just a shift in the shadows, the darkness playing tricks. Then I saw it again, maybe someone darting toward the main dining room, where Durand and Vacher were, then doubling back.

"Police!" I called out. "We don't plan on shooting you, so please do us the courtesy of showing yourselves, and with your hands up where we can see them."

Whoever was there declined my invitation, so I pressed slowly on into the kitchen proper. It had been deserted for some time, and now had more spiderwebs than pots and pans. Dust and grime coated the surfaces I touched, so I stopped doing that. I held my light high above my head but saw no one.

"Henri, in here." It was Durand. I followed the sound of his voice and pushed through double swinging doors into the restaurant. One of the men had switched on a table lamp, and I could see most of the space. It was like the kitchen, mostly empty but what remained was dirty, broken, or upside down. Except for one part of the room, the part Durand wanted me to see.

It was away from the windows, against the back wall, where a man working there had a view of the main doors and could safely see out into the street without being seen himself. A large stack of folded papers sat on the floor and lay spread out on a large steamer trunk.

"I think we found our newspaper headquarters," Durand said.

"You sure about that?" I asked. "I just see newspapers. Shouldn't there be some kind of printing press?"

"These too, sir," Vacher said. He poked with his foot at several large rolls of blank paper that were laid out in neat rows on the floor, and I wondered how people managed to get their hands on so much of what was considered a rare resource.

"But no printing machine?" I looked around and saw an area against the wall that looked oddly empty. I turned on another lamp close to the space and inspected the floor. "Looks like there was one here. Look at the ink on the floor and walls."

"They moved it?" Durand asked. "Do you suppose they knew we were coming?"

"I believe newspaper presses are pretty damn heavy," I said.

"Meaning?" Vacher looked at me, then at Durand, then back at me.

"Meaning they didn't just see us walking up the street and make a run for it. They knew we'd be here." I shook my head and tutted, and Durand smiled when I said, "I'm telling you, no one can keep a secret these days."

"Is there an upstairs to this place?" Vacher asked.

"The brief I got from Proulx said the apartment above closed off access to the restaurant, but feel free to check it out." I pointed to a door we'd not yet opened. "I'd guess that's it."

I watched as Vacher headed that way, coming back disappointed when his pathway was nailed shut and plastered over.

"What now?" he asked.

I looked around at the empty space, and a thought struck me. "There's no door to a cellar, but these places all have one. Maybe an outside entrance?"

"I'll go look," the ever-keen Vacher said.

"I'll go with you," Durand said reluctantly. "Henri, you might want to grab a few newspapers, pamphlets, whatever they are, so we're not going back completely empty-handed. We can pretend we interrupted and prevented a print run, or some bullshit."

I liked his bad attitude—it was just how I felt about what we were doing. "Will do," I said.

As they left the room, and the building, I went to the trunk to gather up some of the sheets of newspaper. As I got close, I thought I heard a noise from behind it. *Rats?* I wondered. Just what I didn't need. I tapped the trunk with my foot, but nothing moved. Or squeaked. I kicked it a little harder to be sure, and heard something.

From inside the trunk, and of that I was positive.

I unholstered my gun, hoping I didn't have to use it again tonight, and pointed it at the trunk's lid, then reached down to where the latch had clicked into place. I pressed the button to release it, and quickly flipped the lid of the trunk open. Inside was a slender figure, a teenage boy maybe, curled into a fetal position with their hands over their head. In the dark I couldn't discern any features, nor whether the person had a weapon close at hand.

"Hey, get up, get out of there. Slowly, and show me your hands. Any twitchy movements and I'll blow your head off. Got it?"

The figure in the trunk grunted as if to acknowledge my threats, and then started to unfurl itself. Whoever it was wore blue overalls and a wool hat pulled low over their ears, and they pushed themselves to their knees, facing away from me, before slowly rising to their feet.

"Turn around," I commanded, keeping my voice loud so my colleagues might hear and come back me up. "Slowly."

Still standing in the trunk, the slight figure of a woman turned slowly toward me, one hand reaching in slow motion to the hat, which she drew off her head just as our eyes locked, and my jaw fell open.

"Oh, no," I started. "Jesus Christ, no."

"Henri—" she began, but stopped when we heard voices. Vacher and Durand.

I grabbed my suspect by the arm and dragged her out of the trunk just as the two men walked back into the room. Before they could get a look at her face in the gloom I slammed her into a nearby corner, snatching her hat and jamming it back on her head, pulling it as low as I could.

"Ow, you're hurting me," she protested.

"Good," I said, and meant it. "Fucking stand in the corner and don't you dare move until we've cleared this place."

I grimaced as Durand held up his own lighter and peered in

her direction, but he was quick about it, as if he didn't recognize our capture, or didn't care who it might be.

"There's a cellar, but nothing down there," Durand said. "Unless we're hunting enormous spiders, cobwebs, or mouse shit."

"We're not," I said, placing myself between the two men and the woman in the corner. "Vacher, I was distracted, as you can see. Grab a handful of these shitty newspapers, you're in charge of getting them to the station. We can show them to Proulx in the morning."

"Yes, sir." Vacher moved to the trunk and stooped to gather the printed pages. "You want me to take the prisoner, too, sir?"

"No, I'll take care of her myself. You get those out of here now, and call it a night. I'll stay here and ask her some questions, but nothing for you to do."

"Very good, sir. But do you need me to stay and help interrogate her?"

"Do I, an experienced homicide detective, need you, a teenage rookie, to stay behind and assist me as I interrogate a terrified suspect?" I clapped a hand on his shoulder, which had slumped midway through my sarcasm. "No, son, I do not. Not even close."

"Yes, sir. Of course." Durand and I watched as Vacher grabbed a second armful of newspapers. "This enough, sir?"

"More than."

"Very well. Good night, Detectives." Vacher hesitated. "If you're sure I can't help with the woman?"

"Oh, no." Durand was gruff. "We can handle this, don't you worry."

I couldn't tell if he'd seen her face, but either way he sounded like he was prepared to give her a rough time of it.

"Albert, you can go, too. I can manage this."

"Against protocol," he said, and we watched Vacher leave with his trove of worthless evidence.

"Also against protocol is doing a raid with three people," I pointed out. "You seemed all right with that."

"This is different." He stepped close enough that I could see his face in the dim light. His eyes suddenly crinkled and a smile spread over his face. "I want to be here when you tear this young lady to shreds." He tutted exaggeratedly. "Dear, oh dear. Nicola Prehn at the scene of the crime, whoever would have thought?"

"Not fucking me," I growled. I put a hand on Nicola's shoulder and spun her around, and her eyes flashed angrily at me.

"You don't have to treat me like a damned criminal."

"Except you are one, *non*?" Her defiant tone only angered me more. "What the hell are you doing here?"

"My bonnet blew off in the wind and drifted in here. I came to retrieve it."

I had to admire her temerity. "Your bonnet?"

"Yes."

"On this cold but windless night, the bonnet you were wearing on top of your woolen hat blew off your head, through a closed door, and into this abandoned restaurant."

"Exactly."

"And into the trunk?"

"I got scared when I heard three gruff men coming inside in the dark. You can't trust anyone these days."

"Apparently not," I said, glaring at her.

"I think I'll leave you to bring her in," Durand said. "Or try to; I assume she'll escape."

"Unfortunately," I said.

"Well, you should make it believable," Durand said.

"Meaning?"

Without warning he punched me in the face, a blow to my cheekbone that sent me tumbling over the trunk, and sent Durand into a fit of coughing. To my dismay, Nicola went straight to his side, putting an arm around him as he doubled over, hacking and wheezing away like the asthmatic he was.

"Albert, I'm so sorry, are you all right?"

"What the—" I began, as I propped myself up on my elbows. "What about me?"

"You're fine. You've been punched more times than Jean Despeaux."

"Who the hell is that?" I asked.

"Don't pretend you don't know, just because you despise boxing. There, there." She patted Durand's back as he slowly regained his breath, hands on his knees before he straightened himself up.

"I'm too old to punch people," he said, his voice weak. "Remind me of that if I ever start to chase someone. For now, I'm going home."

"Albert," I said, getting to my feet.

He stopped and half turned, with a smile. "You're welcome. And don't worry, some people can keep a secret still."

I smiled, too. "Thank you."

He looked at Nicola. "You take care, young lady, it's not a safe world. And make sure you don't forget your bonnet."

We watched him walk out, and when he was gone I turned to Nicola.

"Do you know what would have happened if it'd been some other *flic* than me who pulled you out of the trunk?"

"Or Durand," she said sulkily.

"If it hadn't been one of us. Even now I have to write a report that will make me look like an idiot for letting you escape. And maybe even raise suspicion I'm involved."

"Well, you're not."

"Aren't I? How am I not if I just let you go?"

"You're not just letting me go, I'm escaping."

I couldn't tell in that moment if she was trying to be obtuse or helpful, but again I felt that wave of exhaustion from the constant danger, from the lies and deception, and mostly because I felt like the life we'd once lived was not just gone, but gone for good. And I didn't like this new one, not one bit.

"Go home," I said. "Pour me a large glass of wine, but go home and wait."

"Henri." Her head dropped and her tone was soft. "I'm sorry you had to find me. I'm not sorry for . . . other things I'm doing, but I didn't mean to put you in this position."

I looked her in the eye, my sweet, efficient, smart, and utterly unpredictable sister. "Well, I think we just agreed to be happy it was, in fact, me in this position, and not GiGi or some other officious prick cop."

"GiGi would never have found me," she said with a gentle laugh.

"Go home, Nicola. I'll be there soon after."

"Where are you going first?"

"Isn't it obvious? I have to spend at least ten minutes looking for my escaped prisoner."

And, with that, my captive rose to her tiptoes, kissed my cheek, and disappeared into the darkness.

CHAPTER TWENTY-ONE

In the relative safety of our apartment, I could have cut the tension between us with a knife. I didn't have the energy to peel a banana, though, let alone start cutting things, so I sank into my chair in the living room, grateful eyes on the excessively large glass of wine Nicola had placed on the side table.

She puttered around the apartment until I'd taken three large gulps, then came and sat opposite me, tucking her legs under her as she got comfortable on the couch.

"Where do we even begin?" I asked, rubbing a hand over my no-doubt exhausted-looking face.

"I was there to clean up, that's all."

"Oh, so your bonnet didn't really blow its way in there?"

"The day you see me wearing a bonnet . . ."

We both smiled, grateful for the moment of lightness.

"I need to know what's going on." I took another drink, smaller this time.

"See, I was thinking it's better if you don't." She held up a hand. "Not that very much is, at all. It's just that . . . you're a detective, you have certain reporting obligations and I wouldn't want to put you in a difficult position."

"Like finding my sister hiding beneath incriminating evidence at the scene of a crime?"

"Exactly." She clapped her hands in delight. "Much better that you don't, right?"

"Yes, of course. But since someone did, better it's me than the kid Vacher who was there, right?"

"And Durand . . . you think he'll be . . . ?"

"Don't worry about him. He knows on which side of his bread the butter gets spread."

"I've always liked him."

"I've always wondered why he became a cop. He doesn't like work, exertion . . . people."

"He has a good heart, Henri. He just doesn't like to use it."

I found a half-full pack of cigarettes in my jacket pocket, which mostly served to remind me I was too tired to take off my jacket. I had the energy to light one of the coffin nails, though, and watched Nicola frown through the first puff of smoke. She was of the belief that smoking was unhealthy, and she might be on to something. But of all the things out to get me, a slender, calming smoke seemed the least dangerous. Especially when paired with one of Mimi's wines.

"So then." I took in and released another lungful. "What are you into?"

"Like I said, I was there to clean up a little. I heard your lot enter and panicked."

"Hmm. If panicking is your thing, I would suggest you stick to secretarial work and leave the clandestine shit to other people. Did you notice that the latch to the trunk which you panicked yourself into had closed?"

"What do you mean?"

"I mean that if you'd been as quiet as a church mouse and I'd not heard you, you would still be in that trunk now. And maybe tomorrow. And if no one knew to look for you, your mummified corpse would have been found in maybe a year or two. You locked yourself in without even realizing it."

"What's your point?" Her tone was defiant, but she squirmed on the sofa as if the truth of what I'd said had hit her in an uncomfortable way.

"My point is that you're not good at this secret stuff. It's not in your nature, it doesn't suit you, and you don't have the head for it."

"I'm just a secretary, I get it."

"Don't take offense." I sat forward and looked hard at my sister. "Why would you want to do something you're not good at, when that thing is liable to get you killed?"

"I hear you, Henri. I'm listening."

"Does that mean you'll stop?"

"Yes, of course."

"Merde." I sat back, took another sip of wine and yet another puff.

"What?"

"You're a terrible liar."

"I said I'd stop."

"I know what you said. It's what you mean to do I'm worried about. Who else is involved?"

"I can't tell you." She got up and poured herself a glass of wine.

"Just because you're my sister doesn't mean I won't throttle it out of you."

"Yes, it does." She sat down again, cupping her glass in her hands. "Any chance you'll just let this go?"

"What do you think?"

"I know you're worried about me. I do. And I was careless today, even though I wasn't really doing anything wrong."

"The Germans wouldn't agree with you. If they'd caught you there you'd be in jail right now, probably being measured for a firing squad."

She grimaced. "They measure you for that?"

"Sure. If you're small they stand closer." I was making it up, but didn't mind the image being planted in her head. "Look, I'm not going to throttle you, Nicola, as much as I might be tempted. But I do need to know who else is involved. Of my friends, at least."

"Henri, no one is *involved* in anything. I was asked to get rid of those papers to avoid trouble with the Germans."

"We'll start there, then. Who asked you?"

"I'm protecting you by not telling you."

"In my experience, they torture first and ask questions later, so no you're not. Was it Natalia?"

She sat up, seeming genuinely surprised. "Natalia? Why on earth would you think she's involved in anything? She's basically a child."

"A pretty resourceful one. Also, weren't you suggesting I take her out and romance her?"

"Fine, she's not a child. But she only just got here."

"And you're not taking orders from a child who just got here?" I smiled.

"I'm not taking orders from anyone."

"Nicola, look." I sighed, and cast about for the right words because I didn't think trusting me should be this hard. "I can't protect you if I don't know what you're doing."

"You said that already."

"And I'll keep saying it, because it's true. I assume Daniel is involved."

"Daniel's . . . Daniel. He's actually not doing anything at all, just his job as a cop and his job as my *copain*, which is to look out for me."

"And my job as your brother."

"Oh my." She fluttered a hand in front of her face. "All these strong, brave men looking out for me. How incredibly oppressive."

"When you stop getting yourself locked in trunks, maybe we'll back off."

"Can we change the subject for a moment?" she asked, sipping her wine.

"As long as you know we're not finished."

"That's fine. Do you know who killed that man, Guy something?"

"Guy Remillon. And no, I don't."

"Oh. Does that bother you? Are you close at least?"

"It does bother me, and yet . . ." I stubbed out my cigarette and resisted the temptation to light a new one right away. "And yet, it doesn't at the same time."

"I wondered."

"What do you mean?"

"You're normally so driven, you work eighteen, twenty hours a day until you catch your killer. On this one you seem . . . distracted?"

"Trying to keep my sister out of jail." I smiled, and she smiled, too. "I think it's because of who the victim was, and I hate that about myself."

"Meaning?"

"Meaning, in the grand scale of things, I find it hard to care that Remillon is dead. He was a sneak, a snitch, a traitor. Best I can tell, the world isn't any worse off now he's gone. It may even be a better place."

"Does he have family?"

"An elderly mother. Shit, I should go see her just in case she knows something."

"You think she might? Know something I mean."

"She can at least tell me more about my victim. If he's the ass that I think he is, she may not even care that much he's gone."

"This doesn't sound like you. Judging your victims."

"I know, and that bothers me, too. I think I'm realizing that all lives aren't worth the same. Just as we're created differently, with different gifts, abilities, and needs, so we live differently and in doing so, making the choices we make, we become worth different."

"Calm down, Plato," she said, but her smile was kind.

"It's true. The president of the United States, hell, the head of every country, has a protective detail at all times. Why? Because his life is worth more than the homeless man slowly freezing to death under a bridge half a mile away."

"You may be right, Henri. But you're in the wrong job to make those decisions. The last thing you get to do is decide whose death matters and whose doesn't."

"I know. You're right. Even if he was a shit, did he deserve to get murdered?"

Nicola smiled. "You know what, maybe he did."

"Seriously? I thought you just said—"

"Yes, I said you had to investigate no matter what. Here's my point: maybe he deserved to get shot. If that's the case, then maybe whoever shot him has a good legal defense and won't get punished. But you won't know until you finish your investigation."

"As ever, you speak wisdom. And, as ever, it's fucking exhausting."

"You're welcome."

"I do have a good idea of *why* he was killed."

"All right, then. Let's start with that."

"He was working with the Germans, investigating a complaint against someone in the building." I explained about the *corbeaux* and the snitches who operated on behalf of the Germans to snoop and see if the poison-pen letters contained any truth.

"So if the so-called *mouches* report back some degree of truth, the Germans themselves get involved?"

"I think that's how it works. Saves the bastards manpower on the front end, and staves off ill will in case of a false report."

"Makes good German sense," she said grudgingly.

"Yeah, I suppose so."

"So who was Remillon investigating?"

"Claire or Mimi probably. Maybe both. Or it may have been something to do with the newspapers found in the street, or maybe that Darroze snitched on someone else here."

"That's the other thing, hasn't Darroze been arrested for the murder? Was it not him?"

"It could have been. There's the gun he hid, the burned note in his fire grate. But why would he kill the person he basically summoned to do an investigation?"

"What if the investigation was over, and Remillon found that Darroze had lied? Maybe he'd get in trouble for making a false report, and knowing Remillon would say something to the Germans he decided to kill him?"

"Maybe. It doesn't fit the facts that well, with Mimi seeing Remillon approach the building, not leaving it."

"What does Darroze say?"

"Nothing. GiGi broke his jaw, and even if I had time for him to write out his answers, if we give him a pencil he'll likely throw it across the room. Or use it to give us a message."

"What message?"

"To take his pencil and insert it somewhere unpleasant."

"Maybe, but if he's innocent, why wouldn't he cooperate?" Nicola pressed.

"Well, he's technically under arrest for assaulting a policeman. Plus, he's angry. About the arrest, the broken jaw. And he's an angry man to begin with, that's why he told on his neighbors."

"But you're still not sure which one?"

"Honestly, I think it must have been Claire. The SS were here on some kind of suspicion, I assume from a Darroze *corbeau*. But, even though he didn't know it at the time, that meant telling on a senior SS officer, which can't be good for anyone's health."

"So, maybe . . ." The wheels were turning in Nicola's head, and I enjoyed watching the pieces slot into place. "That German, Zoeller, right?"

"Right."

"Is he capable of killing Remillon? More than anyone in this building, surely."

"Agreed." I grimaced at the memory of him executing my neighbor.

"Simple answer. Zoeller did it."

"Simple?" I almost choked. "Oh, right, I'll pop over to avenue Kléber and slap some cuffs on one of the most senior Nazis in Paris. Simple as committing suicide."

"So leave it unsolved. Who cares, Henri? People are dying every day in this damn war, what's one more body among all that carnage?"

"If I find out it was Zoeller, I might just do that. But until I do, there's a killer out there. Maybe Zoeller, maybe not. But if not, I need to know."

"I don't see why."

"A minute ago you did, you chided me for judging my victim. And you're right, this is my job. But if we're back to talking about things we don't understand, it's how you were at that restaurant risking your life for . . . leaflets."

"Henri, I went to clean up. I knew that restaurant had been used to print news leaflets and that a lot of them had been found on our street. I put that together with the murder on our doorstep and figured if someone found the place, even though it was abandoned, they'd be back asking questions."

"And if you're doing nothing wrong, why would you mind people asking questions?"

"Are you serious?" She looked at me like I was an idiot. She made a good point. "They dragged you into a torture room and did horrible things to you, with zero reason. You think I want those people coming back here with even a hint of a suspicion of wrongdoing?"

It made sense, she was absolutely right about that. But I also knew she was lying, hiding something.

"I'll let it go," I said wearily. "But if you won't trust me, if you insist on keeping your secrets, then I'm deadly serious when I say that next time I might not be able to help you."

"Oh, Henri." She walked over and stooped to kiss my head. "You still think this is about protecting me. Adorable." She paused for a moment. "Henri, what happened with Claire?"

"You sure you want to know?"

"Yes."

And so I told her, all of it. I told her the story of Claire's pointless and unnecessary demise, and also of my role in covering for Zoeller. She sat in silence but the tears streamed down her face, her sleeve soon damp from wiping them away.

"Will he come back?"

"Zoeller? I doubt it, he has no reason to risk that."

"What about the boy?"

"Hopefully long gone."

"What a monster that man is. How can you doubt he killed Guy Remillon?"

"I don't doubt he's capable, but as you said, there are a lot of people dying every day. Zoeller's not killing them all, so maybe he didn't kill Remillon."

I watched as she took herself to bed but, as tired as I was, I wasn't ready to lie down and close my eyes. Maybe I just didn't want tomorrow to come.

CHAPTER TWENTY-TWO

January 3, 1941

The next morning, I woke before dawn and made the worst cup of coffee since the first South American, or whoever the hell it was, discovered how to squeeze juice from a coffee bean. It tasted like water filtered through dirt, but I imagined it to have energy-giving powers and it was hot enough to sting my tongue and help open my eyes. That was useful since I'd decided to make a list of possible suspects, which would be as much a guide as a record because I wasn't sure where to go next in the investigation.

I ruled out Nicola. She'd lied to me and was up to something sneaky, but she wasn't a killer and she'd just told me not to give a damn what a shit Guy Remillon had been, and to do my job anyway. I couldn't imagine the real killer telling me to solve the crime, so she was out. I ruled out Daniel Moulin, too. Not only was he in jail during the killing, but Nicola would surely have known he was involved and, again, not pressed me to investigate the way she just had.

What about Mimi? She'd lied to me, and been seen with the dead man moments before he was killed. Any real detective would have kept her as a prime suspect. But I knew her. Mimi may also have been up to something—what the authorities would call smuggling, but what she saw as trying to live a normal life. Normal for her, which meant a continued supply of wine, cheese, and foie gras. As much as Mimi was willing to do for the fine things in life, I was sure that cold-blooded murder was a giant step too far.

Gerald Darroze was my best bet. He'd hidden what was almost certainly the murder weapon, was a prize asshole, and was willing to consign people like Claire Raphael and the Millers to fates worse than death. Was he capable of shooting someone himself? I'd changed my opinion on that. Previously, I'd thought him too much of a coward, more inclined to get others to do his sneaky bidding and dirty work. But when their own lives were at stake—and invertebrates always have an overinflated sense of danger when it comes to themselves—I'd known cowards to shoot people themselves. They just did it with their eyes closed.

And so now I happened to think he was, absolutely. The question was, though, did he? For now, he headed my list.

And then there was Natalia Tsokos. Sweet, friendly Natalia. But behind those pretty brown eyes did there lurk a cold-blooded killer? I wasn't big on coincidences, and Remillon had been killed the very day she showed up. Pure chance? Maybe. She certainly had a few secrets, like the work she did to earn her keep above the restaurant with no name.

I looked up when Nicola stuck her head through my doorway. "You're up and about, I see. Damn your soul for making that vile coffee."

"Let's not misrepresent my actions. I replicated to the best of my ability what used to be coffee, and you know perfectly well you drink that swill at your own risk."

"Whoever thought we'd be getting up in the morning and drinking hot toilet water?"

"The Germans," I said grumpily. "I'm pretty sure they planned all this."

She smiled. "I'm headed into work. I'll try and make something a little less poisonous, if you're headed in."

"I will be. Maybe in an hour, perhaps less."

She looked down at my desk. "List of suspects?"

"Yes."

"Am I on it?"

"Not really. I mean, I wrote your name down, but only so you wouldn't feel left out."

"You're a sweetheart."

"I just know how you like to be included in things."

She stuck her tongue out, then closed my bedroom door behind her. I listened to hear the apartment door shut, and turned my thoughts back to the building's newcomer and her possible secrets. Then again, these days we all had those, and I was more aware of that, more a living embodiment of that, than anyone. That Natalia would deliver a few papers in exchange for room and board made her less a suspect and more of a pawn. And what would her motive have been to kill Remillon? None that I could think of; she'd simply not been around long enough to have one. Unless she was sent here by some dark mysterious force to do precisely that, but there was no evidence she was a contract killer, and that theory seemed more far-fetched than Nicola being the murderer.

After Natalia, I was left with two other possibilities, one of whom was Claire Raphael. I had no evidence it was Claire, even though she may have had the best motive of all. I reminded myself, though, it was only a motive if she *knew* Darroze had complained about her and Zoeller. And the way the anonymous *corbeaux* worked, it seemed unlikely she would have had any idea. Plus, she was happy enough to talk to me, she didn't avoid our chat like a guilty person might. If what she told me was true, at most she might have seen the killer. Although what better confusion for a killer to sow than to describe a different person running from the scene? And that would account for the differences in the appearance of the man running away, why she and Mimi gave different descriptions—because Claire invented hers.

Or maybe Mimi did? My head was spinning with the possibilities, and then I remembered there was yet another one. Maximillian Zoeller. Maybe someone had tipped him off about an investigation into Claire Raphael's secret German lover. It might be a smart move for some underling to save the career and maybe life of such a senior Nazi; Zoeller would no doubt be in his debt for that. What if Zoeller knew Remillon would be coming in advance, had intercepted the Frenchman, and dispatched him before he could do any damage?

All questions, and too few answers. I looked up from the desk in my room as the early morning light filtered through the threadbare curtains that covered my windows. I liked to awake to the dawn, it felt natural to me. It got me to work early in the summer, and late in the winter, but no one seemed to mind the irregularity. Now, the sun was reaching out from the horizon, spilling over the roofs of the surrounding buildings into my bedroom, tinged red before it rose above the clouds that would filter out its intensity, its color. After yesterday, this blood red morning seemed appropriate, but I wasn't sure if it was a warning or a remembrance. I hoped to God the latter; I didn't want more bodies piling up on my watch. I did not need that today.

Action, however, was needed. I had my list but I needed to rule people out, or otherwise. I wanted to talk to the dead-looking Hahn to see what he'd taken from Remillon's body, but I also very much didn't want to talk to him. I had a strong sense that any encounter with the man wouldn't go how I intended. And because I suspected I knew why he'd taken the note, I didn't see the benefit in crossing paths with him. Not yet, anyway.

My best bet for now was Darroze. He could tell me who he sent notes about, who he was snitching on. That could narrow my focus. I hoped he might have an explanation for hiding the gun but, as I thought about it, I tested that piece of evidence in my head. Hadn't he denied doing that? And who was it who'd seen him and reported it? Natalia Tsokos.

And there I was, going in circles again.

I focused my mind on Darroze. Even if he didn't want to talk to me, there was another task I could accomplish while there. One that would either reassure me that one of my suspects was being truthful, or confirm my suspicions that they were very much being deceptive. And a spot of confirmation, be it positive or negative, would make a nice change from the way this investigation had been going lately.

A light rain and a cold wind swept across my face as I stepped out of the building, and my eyes dropped to the place on the sidewalk where Guy Remillon had been killed. I had seen a hundred crime scenes before this one, and most had been washed from my mind by time, but I wondered if I'd ever step out of my building into rue Jacob without thinking of a dead man. I damn well hoped so.

I was shivering by the time I got to the Préfecture, and when I tightened my belt because my trousers were slipping down I realized that both were caused by recent weight loss. Which was caused in turn by my terrible diet and long days. I resolved to hit Mimi up for some bone-padding cheese or pâté. Surely she would not disappoint.

My first stop was at Nicola's desk, where she handed me a mug of something she'd made. I took a sniff and grunted.

"Better than your effort," she said.

"A low bar. Also, we're the police, can't we go requisition or confiscate the real stuff?"

"Only the Germans have the real stuff, so good luck trying that."

"Oh, right." I perched on the edge of her desk and lowered my voice. "Well, I have a mission that may be as complex as finding real coffee."

"Intriguing. And judging by your tone and body language, it's a secret mission."

"I prefer to think of it as needing discretion, not secrecy."

"But it's case-related, not personal?"

"Absolutely. I need you to call this location, have the local police find a particular person, and call us back when he can be on the line."

"That doesn't sound particularly challenging. Who is it?"

I smiled and reached for a pencil and paper. I wrote the man's name and where I believed him to be and passed it to Nicola. Her eyes widened as she read it.

"Are you serious?" she asked.

"Very. Think you can manage?"

"If anyone can, I can."

"Precisely my thinking. I'll be in the building, and back here soon enough if you're quick. This is important."

"I'm guessing so." She looked back at the name. "Well, this should be interesting."

I patted her on the top of the head, mostly because I knew she hated it, and went to find Gerald Darroze. I'd thought about having him brought up to an interrogation room but decided a trip to the cells underground might be better. If nothing else, he'd be out of reach of GiGi's fists. No way that lazy bastard was taking all those steps downstairs, not even to punch a man in handcuffs.

When I got down there, I was surprised to see young Pierre Tremblay as the lone guard.

"Your family connections didn't save you from cell duty?" I asked.

"Yes and no." He smiled. "The alternative was some German-initiated raid on . . . I'm not sure. Some people who've done nothing wrong, would be my guess."

"And a good one, no doubt." I liked this kid more and more. "I'm here to see my old friend Gerald Darroze."

"Ah, the chatterbox."

"He's regained the use of his jaw?"

"No, it's . . . sarcasm, sorry."

I smiled. "Well, hand me a pencil and paper, I'll see if I can get him to write me a story."

He did so. "Best of luck. Here's a key. Suite nine."

I made my way to Darroze's cell, banging on it to let him know someone was coming in, then sliding open the eye-level slot so I could be sure he planned to behave himself. It's my experience that men with busted jaws don't tend to start fights, but in this job you can't be too careful.

Inside the cell, I closed the door behind me and looked down at Darroze, who sat on his iron bed. He looked pale and tired, and it struck me that jail food probably wasn't designed for people who couldn't chew. Stale bread and undercooked turnips were a challenge for most people, for Darroze all but impossible.

"I know you can't talk, Gerald, but I was hoping you'd still be able to help me with a few things."

He looked up at me, suspicious, and spread his hands wide, which I took as an invitation to keep going.

"Are you still saying you didn't kill Guy Remillon?" He nodded. "Do you admit you wrote to the authorities, snitching on someone in the building?" He crossed his arms and looked down, as if he didn't like how I'd phrased it. *Too bad*, I thought. I repeated the question and eventually he nodded. "How many letters?" He held up two fingers, and I put the pencil and paper on the bed. I needed him to answer the next question and not just agree with whatever I was saying. Plus, I only had one guess and wanted him to think I knew more than I did. "Write down the names of . . . the people you complained about."

He stared at the paper and pencil for a while, then picked them up and wrote, *What's in this for me?*

That made my blood boil. "You selfish prick. A man is dead because of your little notes. And look, if you're telling the truth and you didn't kill Guy Remillon, it's very much in your interest for me to find out whoever did. On the other side of that coin, if I don't finger someone else for it then there's a good chance you're swinging for his murder. Or maybe it's the guillotine, I can't recall what we're using these days." I gave him a big smile. "Hey, maybe they'll let you choose. You can draw whichever one you prefer. Do it right now if you want; in these days of red tape and heightened bureaucracy it's always a good idea to get a request in early, don't you think?"

He started scribbling and I wondered if he really was expressing a preference, but when he handed me the paper again it had just one name on it.

Claire Raphael.

That was the one I expected. I was sure her name was on the piece of paper Ernst Hahn had taken from Remillon's body. I reasoned that Hahn had taken that piece of paper because it mentioned that Claire had been seeing an unnamed German, not something Hahn and his buddies wanted the French police looking into.

"Fine, we can start with this. What did you say about her?" I asked, before remembering who I was talking to. "I mean, did you complain that she was having an illicit affair?" He nodded. "With a German?" He nodded again. "Did you write down in your complaint the German's name?"

Darroze snatched the paper from my hand and scribbled something.

Only that he was an officer. Didn't know his name.

"You said you wrote two letters. Who was the other one complaining about?"

He wrote: *Not until you get me a better cell and food I can eat.*

"How about I just slap your stupid, broken face until you tell me?"

He scribbled painstakingly slowly: *Anything you beat out of me will be a lie.*

He sat back, his arms crossed over his chest, a defiant look in his eye.

"I'll see what I can do," I said, and let myself out of his cell. I went to Tremblay and found him talking to a breathless uniformed *flic*, the one who'd manned the cells when I came down to see Remillon's body.

"Paul Renaud, monsieur," he reminded me.

"Renaud, that's right. You relieving Tremblay here?"

"No, sir. I came looking for you. Nicola Prehn sent me."

"Everything all right?"

"Yes, sir. But there's a phone call for you, one you've been expecting. She said it's important and for me to hurry and get you."

"Important." I rubbed my hands together in anticipation. "Yes, it most certainly could be. Let's go."

CHAPTER TWENTY-THREE

I started for the stairs but stopped and turned to Tremblay.

"Go to the evidence locker, the one on the first floor," I said. "There will be a box of food in there. Grab the soft stuff, pâté, cheese, that kind of thing, and let Darroze eat as much of it as he wants."

"Are you serious, monsieur?"

"Yes, and tell him you're working on getting him a nicer cell."

"Am I?"

"Hell no, but lie to him."

"The food." Tremblay looked concerned. "If it's in the evidence locker, isn't it evidence?"

"That room is not refrigerated, kid. It's also populated by flies, mice, and probably rats."

"So . . ."

"So within a day or two, if not already, whatever perishable food is in there will no longer be evidence. It will be rotten or eaten. Maybe both."

"*Oui, monsieur*, understood. Do that now?"

"The sooner the better, I would say. Thank you."

That task assigned, I all but ran back to the squad room. When I got there, I panicked for a moment because I didn't see Nicola holding a telephone; instead she was sitting on her desk.

"The call you wanted," she said, somewhat unnecessarily I thought. "The operator has the Greek police on the other end."

"Excellent. Where's the phone?"

"Henri, what is the call about? What on earth is in Greece related to the murder?"

"Not what. Who. It's always the who that matters, my dear. Now, the phone?"

"Proulx's office. Thought you might want privacy."

"Good thinking." I started in that direction and she hurried after me.

"Then who?" she asked. "And why didn't you tell me about it?"

"You like surprises."

"I like *some* surprises."

"You'll like this one. I think."

"Did you tell anyone about this? How much is this phone call costing?"

"No, no idea, and I don't care."

"But Henri—"

I ignored her protests and went through the open door into Proulx's office, where the phone sat on his desk. I tried swinging the door shut, but Nicola stopped its progress with her foot, and then stationed herself in the doorway, leaning casually against the jamb. I picked up the heavy handset.

"This is Detective Henri Lefort."

"Yes, sir. Stand by, connecting you now."

"Hello?" A deep voice came on the line, along with a lot of crackling. He gave his name, which I didn't catch, and said: "I don't speak French, only English."

"English is fine with me," I said.

It had taken him some work, the slow-speaking Greek policeman told me, but they found my man and brought him in. And without telling him what it was about, which was key. They just handed him the telephone and when he spoke, he sounded a million miles away. And very scared. At first, he said something in Greek but the cop told him to use English or French.

"Hello? Who is this?" His voice was so faint and the line so crackly I could barely hear him, so I spoke loudly myself.

"Lucas, *bonjour*, this is Henri Lefort. In Paris."

"Henri . . . in Paris?"

"Yes."

"This is even possible?"

I assumed he meant the technology, which I didn't begin to understand myself so didn't try to explain.

"I know, it's like magic." I was all but shouting, and everyone in the office had stopped what they were doing to listen. "Lucas, I have to ask you some questions."

"What questions? What's going on?"

"Lucas, do you have any family members in France?"

There was a pause, and I was afraid we'd been disconnected. But after a moment, I heard his voice again: "Yes."

"Who?"

"My niece. Natalia."

"What's her last name?"

The crackling picked up a notch, and I thought I heard him say *Tsokol*.

"Say that again. Better yet, spell it."

Another pause. "T-s-o-k-o-s."

I hated not being able to look him in the eye, I couldn't even hear him properly to gauge his tone, his reactions to my questions.

"How old is she?"

"I'm . . . not sure. Late twenties, I think. We'd see each other at family gatherings but we aren't that close."

He was giving me all the right answers, but I still wasn't convinced. I looked over at Nicola, but couldn't read her expression. Like everyone else in the room she was listening intently to my side of the conversation, as enraptured by the fact this was happening as by what was actually being said.

"She's your brother's daughter, yes?"

"Yes. Wait, no . . ." There was a click and the line went silent for three seconds, then a woman's voice came on.

"This is the operator. The other party has disconnected."

"Please reconnect with them," I said, impatient.

"I will try."

I waited, shifting from foot to foot with the phone pressed to my ear, a series of clicks, buzzes, and static coming down the line to me. Finally, the operator came back.

"You are connected. Go ahead."

"Hello?" I said.

"Hello again." It was my slow-talking Greek counterpart.

"Did you hang up?"

"I didn't, your friend did."

"I'm not done with him."

"He doesn't want to talk to you. Want me to beat him?"

"No, I do not. You can threaten to, but please don't actually hurt him."

He muttered something in Greek, I assume calling me soft or weak, then I heard him speak to Lucas Nomikos. And after thirty seconds or so, Lucas himself came on the line.

"Henri. I'm sorry."

"Lucas, please don't be. You remember Christmas of 1936?"

"Christmas, what does . . . ?" And then a chuckle of laughter. "Yes, I know what you're talking about."

That Christmas, Nicola had bought me a bicycle as a present. She'd asked our concierge Lucas to store it for her, so I wouldn't see it until Christmas Day. He'd put it in the back room where the garbage bins were, a place I rarely if ever visited. But I had gone in, I couldn't even recall why, and seen this brand-new bicycle with a Christmas ribbon on it. I'd wheeled it out into the lobby and found Lucas standing there, eyes wide and looking guilty.

"Whose bicycle is this?" I asked.

"It's mine."

"Yours."

"Yes." He'd blinked but otherwise stood still like a small, Greek statue.

"And the ribbon?"

"It's Christmastime. I like ribbons."

"Lucas, this is not your bicycle. It's a present for someone, and since you're trying very hard to lie to me, I have to assume it's a present for me."

"I . . . no, really, it's . . ."

"You want to ride it for me, prove it's yours?"

His shoulders slumped and he gave in at that point, because he could see what I'd already figured out: he was maybe five feet, four inches tall, whereas I was over six feet. There was simply no way in the world his feet would reach the pedals on this bicycle, let alone him be able to ride it.

"I'm sorry for lying," he'd said, eyes downcast.

I laughed. "Please, don't be. Let's just pretend I didn't see it, eh? That's easy enough."

He looked up and the relief on his face was evident. "Yes, I think so."

Now, I could picture that handsome face grinning with the same relief, and when he spoke his voice sounded clearer.

"Ach, I could never lie well, Henri. And to you, not at all."

"I know, Lucas. But I have more questions. You won't get in trouble with me, but make sure no one listening on your end speaks French."

"He doesn't, he already told me. What questions?"

"Wait, just a moment." I put the phone down and went into the squad room, where I turned on an old radio that no one much used. It crackled into life and I turned the tuning knob until I came across some booming band music, no doubt some patriotic shit the Germans were putting out. Then I raised my voice so everyone in the room could hear me.

"If anyone turns the volume down or otherwise touches the radio, I will shoot you. Nicola, please stand guard."

"But I want to—"

"*Everyone* wants to listen in, but no one is going to." With that, I turned the volume up to the maximum and hurried back into Chief Proulx's office. I shut the door behind me and turned my back to it.

"I'm back, Lucas. And my first question is, who the hell is she?"

"I don't know. Really."

"Not good enough. Tell me what you do know about her."

"She's not my niece, but she's on your side."

"Explain, please."

"Henri, like I just said, I don't know very much at all, I promise. But some people came and paid me some money, good money, to say she was my niece if anyone asked about her."

"Who apart from me would that be?"

"I don't know. Germans, I suppose."

"She's some kind of spy?"

"I don't know, Henri, but I assume something like that."

"When was this?"

"Maybe a month ago. They made me write down and memorize her name, and then burn the paper."

"Which is why you remembered her name wrong. You said *Tsokol* initially."

"Am I in trouble for that?"

"No, not with me, and no one else knows. But I have to figure out who she is and what she's doing here. The men who paid you, do you know where they were from?"

"I would say England. We spoke in English and the one who did all the talking had one of those silly mustaches they wear. And he didn't speak either French or Spanish."

"Sometimes I think they set out to conquer the world just so they didn't have to learn foreign languages. So yes, that sounds like the British all right."

"You're still a policeman?"

I was surprised by the question. "Yes, of course."

"Good. I have worried about you and Nicola. With all that's happening, what I read about how they're treating the men especially."

"I'm too old to be of any use in their factories, but thank you for your concern." I glanced through the window, where Nicola was standing imperiously over the radio, arms crossed and glaring at me. "And Nicola sends her love."

"She is with you?"

"As ever. Anything else at all you can tell me about this imposter?"

"No, Henri. I'm sorry."

"That's fine, you've been very helpful. Be well, my friend. Oh, and Lucas?"

"Yes, Henri, I'm still here."

"If the Germans come asking about her, lie better."

He laughed again and I hung up the phone, sinking into one of the chairs across from Proulx's padded seat. I put my feet up on his desk and pondered what I'd just heard.

A lying imposter, but she's on my side?

Only one way to resolve that conundrum. I hopped up and went out into the squad room, where I switched off the radio and thanked everyone for their cooperation. Most ignored me, which was the norm, but Nicola followed me into my office.

"Henri, what was that about?"

"That was step one in discovering the identity of an imposter."

"An imposter?"

"Yes. Maybe even an assassin." Her eyes widened in either surprise or disbelief but, for me, that theory was back on the table. Maybe even right in the middle of it.

CHAPTER TWENTY-FOUR

I wanted so badly to confront Natalia, to find out who she really was and what she was doing, but I'd just gotten to the Préfecture and had a job to finish up before I could go anywhere. I traipsed back to the cells to find Darroze still sitting on his bed, but now belching contentedly. A half-empty bottle of wine sat on the floor and the discarded wrappings for what I assumed to be cheese and some meat delicacy lay on the floor.

"Now you know," I said. "I'm a man of my word. Any of that cheese left?"

His eyes slid to his pillow, so I assumed what he'd not shoved down his gullet was poorly hidden there. I left it alone, and he reached for the pencil and paper, which was on the table by his bed.

Merci, he wrote.

"You owe me a second name."

He sighed, then wrote: *You won't like it.*

"Doesn't matter whether I like it or not," I told him. "I just need the truth."

Better cell? he wrote.

"We're working on it. Stop wasting my time, Darroze. I already told you, it's in your interest for me to find out who killed Guy Remillon." I leaned over him and stared into his eyes. "Unless it was you."

He shook his head and quickly wrote something down. *The princess.*

"Mimi?" I asked, wanting to confirm. As if there was another princess living somewhere in the building. He nodded. "Why did you dump the gun in the rubbish bin?" I asked.

Not me, was his written reply.

Another Natalia Tsokos lie? I wondered.

"Why did you report Mimi?"

He hesitated, before writing: *Two suspicions. One: black market. Two: when you put me in better cell.*

I didn't know if we even had better cells, but I nodded and said, "Fine. But tell me first, then you get your cell."

He crossed his arms again, slowly shaking his head. I wanted so badly to slap his petulant, snitching face—not because it'd get an answer from him, just because he was annoying the hell out of me. I refrained, fairly certain that loosening his jawbone in a literal way would inevitably tighten it metaphorically, and I needed to know what he thought Mimi had done. I could ask her myself, of course, but my friends and family had been lying to me a little more than usual as of late, so before I confronted her I wanted to have as much information as possible.

I left Darroze where he was and found Tremblay. "Do we happen to have anywhere nicer we can put him after all?"

"Not really. Maybe some of the cells are less drafty than others, but it's not like any of them come with room service and silk sheets."

"Which is what that *connard* is asking for."

"Isn't he here for killing someone?" Tremblay asked. "If so, why are we not dusting him up, if it's information you need out of him?"

"I'm starting to think that the old-fashioned ways are not always the best. On top of that, his jaw is busted and if we pluck his fingernails out he won't be able to write, either."

Footsteps behind me made me turn, and I was surprised to see Daniel Moulin in front of me.

"Henri." He nodded at me and shook hands with Tremblay. "I heard what happened to Claire Raphael."

"How much did you hear?"

"Enough. Too much. That you tried to help her."

"Until the last part." I didn't know if Nicola had told him I'd dumped her body in the Seine like so much trash, but I assumed so.

"By then, she was dead." He shrugged, and we both ignored Tremblay's confused looks back and forth between us.

"She most certainly was." I turned to the young *flic*. "Go into Darroze's cell and take away everything you just gave him. Tell him I'm finished negotiating, and he can rot in that cell for all I care."

"*Oui, monsieur.* Do you want me to give him a little—"

"No, Tremblay. Keep your hands off him, just take his luxuries. On your way out, leave him a clean piece of paper. Tell him it's from me."

"Yes, sir, will do."

"And check under his pillow, he's stashed the last of the cheese there."

Tremblay nodded and set off toward Darroze's cell, and I looked at Moulin.

"Something I can help you with?" I asked.

"The new girl at your building, Natalia Tsokos."

"What about her?"

"Some German soldiers came looking for her, about an hour ago."

"Why?"

"I don't know." He grimaced. "I did ask, but they have a rude way of letting you know to mind your own business."

"Did they arrest her?"

"No, that's why I'm here."

"Meaning?"

"Meaning she wasn't there. She was gone."

I cocked my head, confused. "Gone? Or do you mean she just was out?"

"I went into her apartment with the Germans. Well, behind them, after they left. The place was cleared out, none of her stuff was there."

"Nothing?"

"Honestly, Henri, absolutely nothing. I didn't know what to make of it; well, of either thing. Why the Germans wanted to talk to her and why she's disappeared."

"Those things normally go together."

"Maybe she knew they were coming?"

"She helped me out of a jam yesterday, which involved aiming a gun at a senior Nazi." I shrugged. "We had an agreement to let the incident slide, on both sides, maybe he didn't and maybe she guessed he wouldn't."

"Which Nazi?"

"Zoeller, the one seeing Claire Raphael."

"You think maybe he came back to clean up loose ends?"

"I certainly hope not." I smiled mirthlessly. "I'm a very loose end indeed."

"Maybe he trusts you to keep your side of the bargain, but not her."

"That doesn't sound right, somehow." I shook my head, thinking. *But why else would the Germans come looking, why else would she run? Could Lucas somehow have warned her that I knew she was an imposter?* This seemed as good a time as any to tell Daniel. "You know, she's not who she said she was."

"I don't understand."

"She showed up at the building, claiming to be the niece of Lucas Nomikos. A fake letter of introduction from him, and no other proof of who she really was. We just took her word for it and gave her his old apartment."

"How do you know this?"

"I spoke to Lucas directly."

"Good Lord, Henri, that was a bold move. The chief getting the bill for that?"

"He won't mind, a worthy expense."

"So, what does this mean?" His brow crinkled in thought as he tried to piece it together.

"I honestly don't know. I can't fathom why she'd lie to us if she was . . ." I lowered my voice, even though we were the only ones down there and listening, "on our side. Against the Germans. But she does indeed appear to be very much on our side, against the Germans."

"Do you want me to try and find her?"

"What I want is to solve the murder of Guy Remillon." I waved my arms, annoyed. "Every time I try, some new pile of horseshit gets dropped in the road in front of me. Like this."

"How can I help?"

"I don't know, to be honest."

"Darroze isn't confessing?"

"Definitely not. And his defense just got stronger."

"Meaning?"

"Meaning, Natalia is the one who reported him as hiding the gun. She's no longer here to testify, and even if she were I'm not sure how credible she is given her lies about who she really is. Which we don't even know."

"What else do you have on him?"

"Darroze? Well, he was out of breath from taking the trash out, he admitted doing that to me. But maybe it was just the trash, and not a gun. I also found a piece of paper burned in his grate, it looks like a directive from the Germans to investigate."

"I'm not following."

"I think Remillon was carrying that piece of paper when he was shot."

"Ah, I see," Moulin said. "The question being, how would Darroze have it? The only way would be him taking it from the body after he'd shot Remillon."

"Exactly."

"Good evidence."

"Not exactly definitive in my book," I mused.

"Other than a confession, what else is there to do?"

"You think Darroze is guilty?" I asked.

"I don't know, but the way I see it, if he's not, then who is? Even if it's Zoeller, you can count me out when it comes time to slapping handcuffs on him. That's a death sentence, for sure, and I mean for you, not him."

"One thing is bothering me." I stroked my chin in thought, and realized I was a day or two behind shaving. "There were two of those papers, authorizations to investigate or whatever they were."

"I don't understand . . ."

"I found one in Darroze's apartment, in the grate, and the other one was taken by that SS creep, Hahn."

"Still not following," Moulin said, looking slightly irritated.

"First, it means, obviously, Remillon had two targets. Second, it means that whoever killed him intentionally took one of the orders and left the other."

"Darroze, it was in his grate."

"Or someone put it there. Someone who had a key to his apartment. To all our apartments."

"Natalia? That's crazy."

"Why? It's true, she does. Did."

"What's her motive for killing Remillon?"

"I don't know yet. But she shows up the morning he's killed— you think that's a coincidence? I'm not sure I believe in those anymore."

"The word was invented for a reason, Henri. And what better to lead a detective down the wrong path than a coincidence he can't explain and doesn't want to believe in?"

"Another thing bothers me about her."

Moulin gave me a sly grin. "You're like the kid who wants to punch the pretty girl to get her attention. She didn't kill Remillon, Henri. She just got here, had no reason to."

A wave of cold fear swept over me as a thought that had been bouncing merrily around my head settled deep into my brain and flowered.

"She took me to a restaurant and afterward we collected some papers. We were supposed to take them to a bookshop, that's what she said."

"What are you talking about?"

"But carrying papers like that, having them in your home, that's as dangerous as harboring a fugitive."

"You're not making sense."

"She said we were supposed to deliver them to a bookshop. Some bookshops have printing presses for their own imprints, things publishers don't want to publish en masse. Poetry, short stories, things like that." Moulin was out of words, he just looked at me quizzically. "Whatever those papers were, they were intended to be reprinted."

"And so what if they were?"

"She brought them to our building, putting herself in danger by merely having them. Why would she do that instead of taking them where she said they were going?"

"I don't know." He sighed, apparently resigned to not understanding. "But I suspect you're about to tell me."

"There's no reason in the world to do so." I met his eye. "I don't think she was ever planning to take those papers anywhere. She took them there because that's precisely where she wanted them."

"But why?"

"For the same reason Mimi had a stash of those damn broadsheets in her apartment. Natalia is the one printing it. That's why she came to France, to start that damned newspaper, and somehow she's persuaded Mimi to help her. Or at least cover for her."

"Why would Mimi risk her neck like that, for a stranger?"

"Because she thinks she's invincible. Her money and name have always gotten her what she's wanted, she never suffered for a thing and can't imagine what being in danger is actually like. And because it's exciting and she gets to fight back in a way she never could otherwise."

"Meaning?"

"Meaning I think part of her resents being a woman, being limited by the things that limit women."

"You think she wants to carry a gun and bayonet against the enemy?"

The image made me smile. "I guarantee she's imagined it."

"But wait." Moulin's brow furrowed. "If you're right, that means . . ."

"Yes," I said grimly. "It means that somewhere in our building there's a printing press. And if the Germans find it, we're dead. And not metaphorically, Daniel; very literally dead."

CHAPTER TWENTY-FIVE

Dark was settling over the city's rooftops as I stepped out of the Préfecture to walk home. The wind had dropped and the air sat eerily still around me, picking up as I crossed Pont Neuf and wound through the streets to rue Jacob. Outside my building I stopped to smoke; the cold felt good on my face and I knew it'd feel even better as I warmed my lungs. And I wanted to think.

I'd never been so disconnected from a murder investigation, and while it was partly my fault for judging my victim, I had to acknowledge the outside distractions, too, the ones that in the old days would have been an annoyance but now put lives in danger. People lying to me about what they saw, Nicola being involved somehow with those damn newspapers, and now Natalia Tsokos, that pretty and sweet-seeming addition to the building, being not at all who she claimed to be.

And what about Daniel? Such a good cop, a clever man, and as close to my sister as anyone. Closer to her than I was, these days. Which meant . . . was he being honest with me? More to the point, was he being duped by Nicola, too? I'd thought about quizzing him inside, but if he didn't know I didn't want to open that can of worms between them.

I suddenly longed for the world as it was, harsh and bloody at times, but without the twists and turns, the lies and deceptions that I was sinking neck-deep into. I took a long drag and watched as a dog ambled down the street toward me. Some sort of Scottish terrier, wooly and small, and he seemed to drift from one side of the street to the other like a drunk. About fifty yards from me he stopped and sat, staring at me and panting, waiting for me to do something.

He wasn't the only one waiting. But first I had to find that damned printing press. I turned to go into the building but stopped when I bumped into Moulin coming out.

"Henri, there you are. I forgot to tell you, what with all that's going on. Guy Remillon's mother was at the Préfecture this morning. She wants to talk to you."

"Why didn't someone tell me while I was there?"

"Durand said he looked for you but couldn't find you. She was being difficult so I think they got her out of there as soon as possible. Sorry for not telling you before, it slipped my mind." He glanced at his watch. "She lives right around the corner, I can go with you if you like."

"No, I prefer these kinds of meetings be one-on-one. It's not easy to talk information out of someone like that if there are two cops in the room staring at her."

"I've heard you say that before," he said with a smile. "Just trying to help."

"Thanks. I'll go now, get it over with. Do you know her address?"

Moulin pulled a notebook out of his pocket and flipped through the pages. "Here. Apartment 4 at 36 rue Perronet."

"That is close," I said. "Good." I patted my jacket pocket to make sure I had my own notebook. "Why don't you look for that damn printing press in the building. Don't do anything with it, it'd be too heavy for one man to move anyway. Just . . . cover it up or something. No one will come looking tonight but I want it found and gone by daylight tomorrow, whatever it takes."

"Absolutely; yes, sir."

I smiled as I walked away. Two minutes ago I was wondering if I could trust Moulin, and here I was giving him an assignment that, should he be on the wrong side of things, could cost me my life. And most likely my fingernails immediately before that. I shuddered and kept walking, a simple left and then right taking me to Madame Remillon's building. It was much like mine, but was smaller and dirtier when I stepped into the lobby. Without a fake but industrious concierge it was bound to be, I mused.

I took the stairs to the third floor and apartment 4. I gave her front door my police knock, which is to say fast, hard raps so she'd know I wasn't some causal passerby or neighbor wanting a favor. I waited and was about to knock again when I heard the door unlock from inside, and it cracked open to show half the face of a woman who looked to be in her seventies.

"Madame Remillon?" I asked.

"Who are you?"

"My name is Henri Lefort, and I'm investigating the murder of your son."

She stared at me for a moment then opened the door to let me in. She didn't actually say, *Come in*, but she opened the door and walked back into her apartment, so I followed. She led me into a sitting room that was adorned the way you'd expect a seventy-year-old to furnish it. Heavy curtains blocking the waning light of the day, books and trinkets filling the shelves, and more pictures on the walls than I could count. A quick look told me she was a religious woman.

"Please, sit." She settled into a high-backed armchair that was positioned opposite a rock-hard sofa that I lowered myself onto gingerly. She wore a black wool sweater, a heavy tweed skirt, and fingerless wool gloves. The room was cold, so I could see why. I rubbed my hands to stave off the chill, which came from more than just the room's temperature.

"Thank you, and my condolences on your loss," I began.

"Why didn't you come before today? Is it normal to wait three days to visit the nearest relative of a murder victim?"

"These days there's no such thing as normal. But I apologize for not coming earlier. I promise I've been hard at work on the case."

"The case." She snorted derisively. "That's all it is to you."

"No, I assure you—"

"Was he killed because he worked for *them*?"

"And by *them*, who do you mean?"

"You know perfectly well." Her bony fingers tangled with each other in her lap. "Please don't treat me like a fool, monsieur . . ."

"Lefort. Detective Lefort," I reminded her.

"Lefort, yes." She took a deep breath. "Well, was he?"

"I'm not sure who killed him or why," I said. "But it's possible that someone didn't like him working with the Germans."

She laughed quietly. "No Frenchman works *with* the Germans, Detective. You work for them, or against them."

"You may be right about that. Do you know why he chose to work for them?"

"Survival. At least that's what he said. He lost his job at the bank and we had no way to buy food. He's . . . he wasn't a very sociable person, he didn't have many friends, so finding another job was difficult for him."

"Did he try, or just sign up immediately with the Germans?" I heard the judgment in my tone, but not in time to tamp it down.

"He tried, for about two weeks."

"Did he go to them, or did they find him?"

"I think . . . he knew someone doing it. Easy money, he said. I think he liked the power." She shook her head. "That wasn't how we raised him."

"His father, is he . . . ?" I looked around as if he might be hiding behind a curtain or chair.

"No idea. He wanted Guy to be in the arts, an actor. To take after him."

"He was an actor?" The thing about conversations with strangers is they tended to lead you to unexpected places. And this place, this apartment, did not smack of the arts.

"He wanted to be. A performer of some sort, anyway."

I gleaned from her not knowing where he was and her use of the past tense that his thespian desires had led him away from this funereal home.

"When did you last see him?"

"Is this relevant somehow to my son's death?" she asked, a little sharply, I thought. "Is my former husband a suspect?"

"We never rule anyone out, Madame Remillon, but I can't say that he is. I was just curious. Forgive me if I was too forward."

"If you must know, the man was last seen, not by me mind you, at a traveling circus in Clamart."

"I see."

"I always wondered what that did to Guy," she said wistfully.

"How old was he?"

"Nine, almost ten."

"Ah, a tender age. Old enough to know, too young to understand."

"My husband of fifteen years left me to join a traveling circus, Detective. Something I couldn't begin to comprehend, let alone explain to Guy."

"Indeed, of course not. Did you know what he was working on for the Germans?"

"Only generally." Her face twisted with distaste. "People would write complaints and he would look into them."

"What kind of complaints?"

"If you don't even know that by now, Detective, I don't hold out much hope of you finding his killer."

I smiled. "You are a clever woman, and don't worry, I know what you're talking about, of course."

"Do you think that's what got him killed?"

"I think it's highly likely, yes. But let me ask you, can you think of any other reason?"

"Like what?"

"I don't know. But I don't want to blinker myself; just assume it's because of the *corbeaux*."

"Is that what they call them?"

"The letters, yes. The people who send them are *indics* or *mouches.*"

"Worse than, if you ask me," she said bitterly.

"I tend to agree."

"Which means you don't approve of my son's new profession."

"Madame Remillon, I investigate the murders of drug dealers, whores, thieves, and even murderers. I do so without judgment and without prejudice." I didn't add *until now and your son*, despite the temptation. At least the other criminals could still be patriots.

"No." She shook her head slowly.

"I'm sorry, no what?"

"No, I can't think of any other reason why someone would wish to harm him. Have you ruled out robbery?"

"His wallet and other effects were still on him, so we don't think it was robbery."

"I warned him, you know." She was clutching at her dress, still shaking her head. "I told him nothing good would come of this. But he insisted. He said he didn't know how else to put food on the table, to take care of me. Well, he's not taking care of me at all now, is he?"

"No, and I'm sorry for that." I cleared my throat. "May I look in his room?"

"Hmm?" She was lost in thought for a moment. "Yes, of course. His is the small room at the back of the apartment, end of the hall. Help yourself."

"Thank you." I rose and found my way to the hall and walked down to the door to his room, which was closed. I turned the handle and reached inside to turn on the light. I was surprised to find myself in what could have been the small room of a teenager. And a young one, at that. The single bed was made up, either by him or his mother, and on the stand beside it were three tattered books. Fiction, all three, and for young adults. On the walls were posters of Marseille footballer Jules Dewaquez, who I recognized thanks to his mustache, and the actress Renée Adorée. I was a little surprised uptight Madame Remillon allowed such a thing, but the actress looked demure, with the sauciness of her bare shoulder mitigated somewhat by the flowery bonnet on her head, and the somewhat sad countenance she wore beneath it.

I started looking through a chest of drawers but found only clothes, then turned to his desk, which was also made for a child. It was covered in books and postcards, ones he'd apparently bought, because they'd not been written on nor mailed. I wondered if he'd been a collector, but stopped wondering when it didn't seem to help with anything. The desk drawers were filled with old school assignments, terrible crayon drawings, and the usual clutter you find when a man, or woman, doesn't like to throw things away. I was hoping for a diary, or maybe something from the Germans that would lead me in the right direction, but closed the bottom drawer without finding anything. I'd expected to find something related to the work he was doing for the Germans and, when I didn't, I wondered if that meant he had an office or other space elsewhere. I went back to the living room, where Madame Remillon sat staring into the cold, unlit fireplace.

"Would you like me to get that going?" I asked.

"There's no wood."

"Right, of course."

"Did you find anything?"

"Nothing useful, no."

She gave me a little smile. "Would you tell me if you did?"

I smiled back. "I might. That all depends on what it was. But I really didn't."

"You are a Christian, Detective?"

"Non, madame."

"Why not?"

I'd been asked that before and the question itself puzzled me. It's as if being a believer was man's default position. Not just any believer, but specifically a believer in the god of the person doing the asking.

I chose my words carefully, wanting to be honest without being insulting. "If there's a god allowing all this to happen, all this murder and mayhem, then I'm not sure He deserves my devotion and praise."

"We can't know His purpose," she chided. "We can't presume to understand the reasons for the things He does."

"If He exists, you may be right. But if you believe He's all-powerful and omniscient, seems to me He can achieve whatever He wants without all the bloodshed."

"That bloodshed is caused by man, Detective. Man, who the Lord has seen fit to give free will. If we abuse that, then He's not to blame, we are."

"I was in Notre Dame a few weeks ago. A man next to me was doing small circles where he stood, looking up and around him, marveling at the beauty and majesty of what has to be Paris's finest church. He told me how grateful he was to God for guiding the hands of the architects, builders, and craftsmen in constructing such a divine place."

"I'm sure he was right about that," Madame Remillon said firmly.

"I'm not saying he wasn't. It's a nice thing to believe. But I just wonder, why does your god get credit for all the good things in the world, and none of the blame for the bad things?" I lifted my hat and gave her a small bow. "But there's so much I don't understand, maybe that's just one more thing. Thank you for your time and, again, my condolences."

She rose and followed me to the door in silence, and when I stepped out she said, "You'll tell me if you find the person who killed Guy?"

"I will, I promise."

"And please tell me if you give up on finding him. I need to know that, too."

"I have never given up on a case yet, Madame, and I have no intention of doing so now."

"But if you do."

"I will tell you myself, and explain why."

"Thank you." She began to shut the door, but hesitated. "Tell me, if you don't believe in God, what do you believe in?"

I thought for a second. "Someone told me recently that hope is about all we have left to believe in. I'm hanging on to that."

"I see." She pursed her lips in thought. "Might I suggest you give God another try, Detective? You can find Him in your heart; I truly believe He's in there waiting for you. And if you do, then you will have both Him and hope to believe in. These days, it seems to me that two things to believe in might count for a lot."

And that, right there, is why I avoid debates with religious people—they are so damn hard to prove wrong.

CHAPTER TWENTY-SIX

January 4, 1941

The next morning I headed back to the Préfecture with two tasks in mind. The first was to get some answers from Darroze. I didn't normally have to interrogate a suspect this many times, but his intransigence, his busted jaw, and me hitting a wall in the investigation made an exception of him.

On the way down the stone steps to our jails I passed Daniel Moulin.

"Morning, boss." He saluted casually, which was more formal than I needed.

"Can I assume from not seeing you last night you didn't . . ." I lowered my voice, "you didn't find a printing press in the building."

"I looked, everywhere. And no, nothing."

"The invisible but ever-busy printing press, eh?" I shook my head. "I wish I knew what the hell was going on in my own world. Anyway, what are you doing here?"

"Just dropping off a human package."

"Anything interesting?"

"Not really. Drunk asshole sitting on the balustrade of Pont Neuf, as likely to fall forward as backward, so I thought I'd save him from a watery grave."

"No doubt he's grateful."

"Hardly." Moulin chortled. "Naked is what he is, bloody idiot."

"That must have been a sight."

"An eyeful indeed. What are you doing here?"

"Darroze."

"He still denying everything?"

"And I'm trying really hard not to believe him."

"You have doubts?"

"A few. What I don't have is a motive."

"Have you ever solved a case where there is no motive?"

"Never. When someone commits murder, there's always a reason. It doesn't have to make sense to you or me, or anyone else in the world. It just has to make sense to them in the moment."

"Anything I can do to help?"

"Invent a truth serum?"

He smiled. "Seems like we'd all be out of work pretty quickly if that happened."

"The lawyers and judges would." I patted him on the arm and continued down the stairs. "We'd still have to catch the bastards."

To my relief, Darroze was able to talk, albeit more of a

mumble than actual speech. But I could understand him, which meant we could dispense with the notepad and pencil.

"Why am I still here?" he grumbled when I sat on the wooden stool opposite him. He was on the concrete bed, a few thin blankets under him for padding, and he looked pale and wan.

"Because you're not playing along and I don't like you," I said matter-of-factly.

"Do you still think I killed that man?"

"Did you?"

"No. Why would I?"

"That's what I can't figure out. Plus, it's more your style to tell tales and let someone else do your dirty work."

"You think I had someone else kill him?"

"You're not clever enough." I shook my head slowly. "Are you still denying you hid the gun in a rubbish bin?"

"Yes, of course I am. I didn't do that. I don't have a gun, I've never had one."

"They're not hard to get hold of these days."

"I wouldn't know."

"Yesterday you told me you wrote two notes about Mimi."

"The princess? No, just one note."

"Fine, one snitching letter with two complaints." I leaned forward, trying to keep my cool. "Don't play games with me, Darroze. I'm at the end of my tether."

"You said you'd get me out of this cell."

"I'm not doing deals with you. I tried being nice, I brought you food that most people haven't seen in six months. I haven't laid a finger on you, either, though god knows I'm tempted."

"Why should I help if there's nothing in it for me?"

"I can't figure out why you're more interested in a comfortable cell than me proving you're innocent by finding out who really killed Guy Remillon." I sat back and crossed my arms. "Which suggests to me, you're the one who killed him and you're just looking for a comfortable landing zone."

"I didn't."

"What else did you say about Mimi?"

He looked at me in a way I'd seen a hundred, maybe a thousand times before. He was deciding whether or not to tell me the truth. Maybe deciding whether to tell me anything at all, but I could almost hear his brain at work.

"Fine, I suppose you're right. I didn't kill that *mec* so I need you to find out who did and get me out of here."

"I don't work for you."

"Yeah, you do. You work for the people of the city and I'm one of them."

"Not while you're in here, you're not."

"You sure you want the truth?"

"Positive," I said. "Why wouldn't I?"

He smirked. "You think you're so clever, but you're blind as a bat."

"How so?"

"The two complaints against your precious Mimi were proper and justified. She's involved in the black market."

"She buys food for herself and her friends, no one gives a damn about that, Darroze."

"I do. The Germans do." He was angry now and pain flashed in his eyes as he spoke through his clenched jaw. "It's always the same with you people—"

"What people?"

"You. Her. Police. Rich people. Don't give a damn about the

rules, about everyone else. You use your power and money to get what you want and everyone else can go to hell."

"Did you snitch on her because she didn't buy you some carrots, for god's sake?"

"She's never done anything for me!"

"And why should she?" I was almost shouting. "You live in the building but all you do is complain about this, and moan about that. What have you ever contributed to anyone?"

"I keep myself to myself, no harm in that."

"Stop stalling, you miserable little shit. What did you tell the Germans about her?"

"The newspapers."

"You said she was the one printing those newspapers?" I asked, incredulous.

"Maybe not printing, but involved. Distributing."

"Based on what?"

"I saw her carrying a bundle of them. That proves she's involved."

I uncrossed my arms but resisted the temptation to squeeze his neck.

"You know what they'll do, don't you?" I said through gritted teeth.

"Who? Who will do what?"

"I told you what your snitching did to the Millers."

"You said they were probably tortured, but you don't know that." He was defiant. "You were just guessing about that. Trying to intimidate me."

"They tortured me, Darroze. Stripped me naked and submerged me in ice water until I thought my heart would give out. You know why?"

This seemed to surprise him. "They did?"

"They most certainly did."

"Why?"

"Because one Nazi thought maybe perhaps I might possibly know something about those newspapers."

"But . . . that wasn't my fault."

"No, but if they torture Mimi, it *will* be your fault."

"She's the one breaking the law, not me. If she doesn't want to get in trouble she shouldn't break the law."

"The law—" I cut myself off.

"And, if you must know, I was planning to move into that apartment, right before she did."

"What are you talking about?"

"She just swans in without caring what other people, residents already in the building, want. Acts like she owns the place."

"Did you . . ." A sharp pain arrowed through my brain as a few pieces of this particular puzzle fell into place. "Did you write those *corbeaux* so you could take her apartment?"

"It's not *hers*."

"Is that why you gave up the Millers, too?" When he didn't reply, or even look at me, I knew I was right. "Why didn't you move in once they were gone?"

He fiddled with the blanket under him. "Their plumbing was worse than mine. I didn't . . . realize that at first."

"Darroze." I kept my voice as calm and quiet as I could. "You're having people in our building killed because you want an apartment with better plumbing. Did I get that right?"

"If people are breaking the law, that's on them, not me," he protested through clenched jaws.

"You'd have Mimi exterminated by those Nazi bastards for good pipes."

"She wasn't the only one breaking the law with those newspapers, you know."

"Oh? Someone else's name make it into your little missive to the Germans?"

"Yes, actually." He was defensive, angry, as if he'd convinced himself he really was on the right side of this.

"Who?"

"Is she a cousin or something? Girlfriend?"

It took a moment, and then my stomach dropped when I realized who he meant.

"You put Nicola's name in your complaint?"

"I had to, she was with—"

He didn't finish his sentence, and likely wouldn't finish one for another month or two, thanks to my right fist. I hit him where GiGi did previously, square in the jaw, only I'm fairly certain I hit harder. Darroze's head twisted on his neck with the force of it, and he crumpled sideways onto his concrete bed. I stood over him for a moment, fighting the urge to finish him off with my bare hands, and I eventually consoled myself with the knowledge that an unconscious, broken-jawed Darroze was good enough work for the moment.

My mind was working overtime as I stepped out of his cell, tracing the steps in my head that Darroze had taken to snitch on Mimi and Nicola. He'd written the notes, either mailed or delivered them by hand, and someone here in the Préfecture had processed them and, one way or another, they'd found their way into Remillon's traitorous hands. He'd been murdered before he could investigate and report back, and both *corbeaux* had been taken from his body. One was taken well after the murder by that creep Ernst Hahn, and the other, I had to assume, was taken by the killer. That was the one that I'd found in Darroze's apartment, burned to a crisp.

But if Darroze himself had not burned it, and as much as I detested the bastard, I saw no reason why he would kill Remillon and burn his own complaint, then who did? Now Mimi and Nicola both had a reason to kill Remillon, but only if they'd known about the complaint, and how would they? Whoever had done this had access to Darroze's apartment, I reasoned, which seemed to reduce the number of suspects to two: myself and the key-bearing concierge, Natalia Tsokos.

My musings were interrupted as I passed the cell closest to the desk where Pierre Tremblay sat, back on guard duty. The viewing portal was open and the inmate had his face pressed to it, looking out.

"Hey, you!" he called out. "Detective . . . *merde*, I don't remember your name, but I know you." He slurred just about every word, and I was not in the mood to deal with him.

"Yeah?" I replied, but kept walking. "I put cuffs on you at some point in your life?"

"What? No, of course not. I did you a goddamn favor, and this is how you repay me?"

I stopped in my tracks, and then took two steps back. I couldn't see his whole face but of the bit I could see, there was something familiar.

"What's your name?" I asked.

"Duggan. Christophe Duggan." A blast of sickly-sweet breath rolled out of the portal, making me take a step back.

"Duggan . . ." The name rang a bell but I still couldn't place him. "I don't understand, who are you and why are you here?"

"Because apparently *flics* from Montmartre don't get the benefit of the doubt when they lose their way for a moment."

"You . . . you were the naked, drunk man on the bridge?"

"Mais non," he huffed, outraged. "I was not naked, I had on a perfectly good pair of shoes. Although it's true, I was very drunk." He belched and I took another step back. "Still am, if you must know."

I stared at the opening in his cell door, my mind processing the import of him being there.

What the hell is going on? I asked myself, but I came up with no good answers.

I turned to Tremblay. "I have two jobs for you. Get a doctor down here to see Darroze, he reinjured his jaw somehow."

"Yes, sir."

"But first, get Duggan here some clothes, something hot and nonalcoholic to drink, and a comfortable place to sober up. But don't let him out of your sight."

CHAPTER TWENTY-SEVEN

I was starting to think I might be getting close to solving the case. I just needed the oddly spinning pieces of the puzzle to, well, stop spinning and fall into place. In the meantime, I needed to know if anyone other than Darroze and Remillon suspected Nicola and Mimi of printing, or even just distributing, those newsletters. Obviously I didn't believe they were printing them, and even if there was a press in our building I was sure it was there temporarily, not to be used but hidden until it found a permanent home. However, I could imagine a world in which those two idealistic women could be talked into dropping off copies around the neighborhood.

"Idiots. Bloody idiots," I muttered on my way upstairs. I was headed to the office where Noel Petit was in charge of the damned *corbeaux* that came in. The first three people I asked for directions claimed ignorance of the newly created division, either because they'd never heard of it or wished they hadn't. The fourth person directed me to the southwest corner of the fourth floor, which had once been used as an evidence room. I hurried through the door and found myself standing in front of Gregoire Vacher, the young *flic* from the farcical raid where we'd found Nicola hiding in a trunk.

"Detective Lefort," he said, standing to attention.

"Calm down, lad. Keep your seat."

"Yes, sir." He sat just as hurriedly. "Sir, what happened with the woman we found locked in the trunk?"

"What do you mean?" I knew exactly what he meant, but I was entirely unclear what he knew and if his interest was merely casual, or more focused.

"It's just that I checked the jail records and she was never brought in. Didn't you arrest her?"

"Oh, her." I thought quickly. "The strangest thing, Vacher. Turns out she'd gone into the building seeking food and come across the people responsible for those newsletters."

"Oh, really?" He looked dubious. "She told you that?"

"Yes, indeed. She said they talked about shooting her, but instead locked her in the trunk." I shook my head solemnly. "Sure enough, she'd have suffocated in there. You noticed it was locked from the outside, I assume?"

"Err, yes, sir. The latch, that's right."

"Indeed. We saved her life, poor thing was terrified."

"You're sure she wasn't part of it? Maybe accidentally locked herself in the trunk while hiding?"

"Have you ever accidentally locked yourself in a trunk, Vacher?"

"No, sir."

"Well, then. There you go."

"It just seems odd that—"

"Vacher, listen to yourself," I interrupted. "You're suggesting she's both the mastermind of the illicit newspaper operation, and simultaneously stupid enough to lock herself inside a trunk."

"Well, when you put it like that, sir."

"I do. And as far as she's concerned that matter is closed." I looked around. Apart from Vacher behind a desk, the room was lined with filing cabinets. "You're working for Noel Petit."

"Yes, sir."

"Volunteer, did we?"

"Most definitely not, sir."

"Glad to hear it. Now then, I have questions."

"I've only just started, sir, but will answer if I can."

"Right, first of all I'm looking for the list of apartments that are abandoned. The one we share with the Germans, somehow."

"It's more of a book than a list, sir."

"Where is it and how does it work?"

"Here." He tapped a thick ledger in front of him. "The addresses are added as they come in, to the back. Every night a German runner comes and copies the new addresses, so we both have the same list."

"Who makes the entries?"

"I do, or any *flic* who comes across an abandoned place. You wouldn't know this as a detective, but we're now trained to ask when we're at a building, make a note of it."

"I see." I flipped the book open and started looking through the addresses. "This would be easier for me if it was organized by arrondissement."

"I don't think it was designed for you, sir."

I glanced to see if he was being rude or just mildly insolent. I decided the latter, so I didn't clip his ear.

"Aha, found it."

"Found what, sir?"

"Never you mind." I studied the entry, then showed it to Vacher. "Your writing?"

"No, sir." His eyes narrowed. "I remember that one. Odd."

"How so?"

"First time an apartment owner has come in to register their own address. Nice place, too."

"Describe the person."

I paid close attention and committed the description to memory, which wasn't hard. When he was done, I thanked him and asked my next question.

"So, how does this treacherous little operation of Noel Petit's run?"

He looked down, obviously shamed by my choice of words. But I was past caring about people's feelings; I could get back to that once I'd gotten myself some answers.

"Well, sir. Wherever the complaints or pieces of information are addressed, to the police or the Germans, they are redirected to us here. We review them and we do one of four things, depending on how substantive they seem."

"Go on."

"If it's just someone complaining about a neighbor, we stamp the complaint *No Action* and file it away."

"In one of these." I gestured with my arms to the metal cabinets surrounding us.

"Correct, sir. Or, if the allegation is serious but doesn't have

supporting evidence or information, we assign it to a volunteer investigator. He or she goes out and asks both the reporter and the subject of the complaint questions."

"He or she?"

"There's a dearth of men, sir. We have women volunteers, too."

I grimaced at the thought. "So they ask questions, and what, write up a report?"

"Exactly. If the complaint is significant enough and appears substantiated then either we or the Germans make further inquiries."

"With ice baths and hot pliers."

"Sir?"

"Never mind. That's two of the four courses of action."

"Oh, yes. The other two are either sending actual police officers to investigate or notifying the Germans right away so they can act."

"I see. And the vile French men and women who do your bidding, they're given written orders by the Germans?"

"It's called a . . ." His face scrunched up as he worked to remember the German name, "Untersuchung Genehmigung. I'm fairly sure that's right. It means an Investigation Authorization."

I pictured the paper I'd found in Darroze's grate. The words that hadn't been burned away were *Untersuchung gen—*.

"Are there copies of these authorizations?"

"Copies?"

"Yes. Do you make and keep copies of these pieces of paper?"

He thought for a moment. "We don't. Usually the investigator brings the original back and it becomes part of their report. But I don't know if the Germans do, I don't see why they would."

"Let's hope not."

"Sir?"

"Nothing. If you did keep copies they'd be . . . ?"

"In the cabinets. They're organized alphabetically, three letters per cabinet, one per drawer. Last name of the subject."

I went over to one and opened it. "*G*, *H*, and *I*. Which means, this one must be *A*, *B*, and *C*." I stepped to my left and yanked the second drawer open. "Ah yes, the *B*s." There were only ten folders, and none of them belonged to a Bonaparte. "What if more than one person is named in the complaint?"

"I don't know. Maybe then they make a copy and add it to both?"

I found the *P* drawer and went through the folders, relieved not to find Nicola's name. I straightened when, behind me, a door opened. I looked over my shoulder and saw the figure of Noel Petit step out.

"What's happening out here?" He looked back and forth between me and Vacher.

"Just doing some policework," I said vaguely.

"You don't get to take any of those files." He pointed at the cabinet next to me. "The Germans were very clear about that."

"I'm sure they were. Clarity is a gift they possess." I slid the *P* drawer shut. "I think I'm done here."

"Good, then you can help me with something."

"Me? Help you?" That seemed highly unappealing, and while he outranked me I was more than willing to pick up an insubordination charge to avoid helping his frightful division do their dirty work.

"I need a man who can shoot straight." I assumed he was referring to my killing a robber with one shot the previous year, an event that had made the newspapers because Princess Marie Bonaparte's life had been saved. And the man I shot had just killed a policeman. I tried not to feel flattered, because I was pretty sure Petit and I had very different ideas about the kinds of people who deserved to be shot.

"I don't do firing squads," I said. "I'm allergic to them."

"What?" He looked irritated at my glibness. I got that look a lot. "No, nothing like that. We have a raid planned in an hour, assuming we can get enough men together. The Germans are providing four soldiers but I've not been impressed by the ones they've been sending so far."

"Terrible shots, are they?"

"Not that. They don't speak French, so how the hell am I supposed to communicate with them?"

"Imagine invading a country where you can't speak the language." I shook my head sadly. "Maybe we can ask them to go back to Germany and invade once they've learned French."

"What the hell are you talking about?"

"To be honest, I'm surprised you don't speak German."

"Surprised I—"

"Yes, why would you volunteer for an anti-French and pro-German role when you don't speak German?"

He stiffened at the insult. "You do not understand what we do here."

"Oh, I think I do. You take information from rats and use it to ruin the lives of already-oppressed citizens. Maybe have them killed. That sound about right?"

"I'm not arguing with you, Lefort." A nasty glint appeared in his eye. "But I am seconding you for my raid."

"I'm busy. Murder investigation, sorry."

"You can go back to that this afternoon. Your victim will still be dead."

"You'll need to clear this with my chief, Louis Proulx."

"I will. Either before or after, whenever I decide to do so."

"As much as I'd love to assist, I don't speak German either and my aim is rusty. Take Vacher here, I'm sure he's practiced more recently than me."

"He's already on the team. And so are you, Lefort."

"Sir, I have a suspect in the cells below I need to question, and several other leads that can't wait. If you want to delay your raid for a day, maybe a week . . . a year, I'd be happy to get clearance and join you. Today I cannot."

Petit turned red with anger. "You listen here, you insubordinate *connard*. Unless you want your badge permanently removed you will do as I say."

"Sir, you do not have the authority to—"

"Oh, you're quite right, I don't." A smirk spread over his face. "But the people I work with every day most certainly do. They have the authority to take your badge, Lefort, and so much more than that. You want me to call them and get them involved?"

"Seems like that'd be a strange conversation seeing as you don't speak German."

"Some of them speak French, damn it!"

I realized, maybe too late to save myself, that I was pushing buttons when I should have been backpedaling.

"Let me go talk to Chief Proulx," I said, my tone much more conciliatory.

"No need, I'll do it myself." He pointed at me. "And you will report in one hour to Place Furstenberg."

"Place Furstenberg," I repeated, and my blood ran cold at the name.

"Yes, you know where that is, do you not?"

"Yes, I do." I most definitely did—it was less than a hundred yards from my building.

"Good. We'll stage there, go over the plan, and move quickly to the target building from there."

"May I ask? The target building is . . ."

"In rue Jacob. Illegal newspaper operating out of there, we've been reliably informed."

CHAPTER TWENTY-EIGHT

This bizarre sequence of events seemed to exemplify life in Paris these days. On the one hand, the authorities believed they had discovered the printing site of a newspaper, despite the efforts of clever people to keep it secret. Their next move, then, was to add to the raid team a man with the deepest conflict of interest and who, from their view, might himself be involved with the illegal operation. It wasn't just that the right hand didn't know what the left hand was doing, it was that the right thought there was no left hand. Or the right hand was trying to empty the pocket that the left hand had already . . . well, the idea is clear enough.

Hand metaphors aside, I had precisely one hour to drop what I was doing and stop the people dearest to me from being arrested, tortured, deported, and killed. So, I saluted the weasel called Noel Petit, exited his offices, and made a beeline for the homicide squad room. When I got there, my heart sank—Nicola was nowhere in sight.

I stuck my head into Chief Proulx's office. "Have you seen Nicola this morning?"

"She was here a while back."

"Well, she's not here now."

"What a marvelous detective you are, Henri. Did you figure that out all by yourself?"

"Chief, I don't have time for this. You have no idea where she is?"

"I have no idea where anyone is." Chief Proulx threw his hands up in exasperation. "I have no idea where the hell you disappear to. Albert Durand has been in and out like this place is a hotel. GiGi all but lives on avenue Kléber now."

"Noel Petit has me taking part in a raid in an hour. I need to find Nicola before then."

"Why, is she the target of the raid?" He said it while laughing, but then saw my face. "*Merde*, Henri, I was joking. Surely not?"

"The less you know the better. I'll see you later."

I all but ran down the stairs and out of the Préfecture, and once I hit the pavement I strode determinedly toward and then across Pont Saint-Michel, toward my building. But when I turned onto rue de Seine I came to a sudden halt.

"No passage!" Three uniformed Germans had blocked the entrance to my street with a portable wooden barrier and some rusty barbed wire.

"Police. I'm police." I showed them my credentials, which was greeted with deepening frowns and shakes of the head. I'd learned months ago those didn't carry the sway they used to; not with our unfriendly invaders, anyway. I tried several more times to persuade these apes to let me through, and even thought about hurdling their barrier and making a run for it. But I'd seen that maneuver too many times during the first war with these bastards, and while just one of them might have missed me enough times for me to make it to safety, three Nazis shooting at my back made the odds of a dash for it unsavory. And even if I did make it in one piece, I'd be trapped inside their cordon, and with no good explanation for giving them the slip.

I wound my way to Place Furstenberg, my mind racing. If I'd known more about what Mimi and Nicola were up to, I might have been able to help. Was there a printing press in the building? If there was, and I knew where, I could volunteer to clear that space and, shockingly, not find anything there. But everyone had been playing the game of Better Not to Know, including me, and now the darkness they'd kept me in looked set to consign the only people I cared about to a very untimely, and ugly, demise.

I smoked a cigarette, and then another, and when I looked at my watch I saw it'd decided to start working again. I set the right time thanks to some hand gestures with two Krauts guarding this entrance to rue Jacob. And then, right on time of course, our four burly uniformed escorts arrived with Gregoire Vacher, a uniformed *flic* I didn't recognize, and Noel Petit himself. He was deep in discussion with the largest of the Germans, who, as it turned out, did in fact speak French. I listened in to the plan.

"The street has been blocked off for an hour." Petit turned to the big German. "Warner, right?"

"*Oui*," he said gruffly. My guess was he didn't like taking orders from diminutive Frenchmen, a sentiment I shared.

"Right, good. So, we all go in together, I don't expect any

armed resistance. Warner, have two of your men secure the front and back so no one can get in or leave the building. Understood?"

The big man grunted and nodded.

"Then we'll split into teams of two and go apartment to apartment. Get everyone out onto the stairs and search. Any evidence of that damned newsletter, be it machinery or copies of it, you let me know. We start at the bottom and work our way up. Squeeze the place. Got it?"

Everyone nodded and mumbled, including me. I was still trying to figure a way to either stop the raid or place myself in pole position to find, or not, whatever evidence there might be. I could assign myself Mimi's apartment, but surely with the burning of the copies she'd had, there'd be nothing inside. Was she stupid enough, arrogant enough, to run such an operation out of her own apartment? Maybe the basement? Or Natalia's now-empty rooms?

And at some point I had to let Petit know I was raiding my own building; not doing so would be suspicious all by itself. I figured I'd wait until we got to the front door, and act out a mixture of shock, surprise, and outrage on the way in.

The guards stood aside as our posse clumped past their barrier and started down rue Jacob. I moved up beside Petit as we got close.

"You're making me nervous, boss."

"How so?" Petit asked.

"That building on the right is mine. It's not the target, right?"

"That one?" He pointed. "That's our target, yes."

"Well, this will be a waste of time."

"Seriously, you live there?" He stopped so we all stopped.

"I do. And if there were any shenanigans afoot inside I'm pretty sure I'd know about them."

"Well, apparently not," he said curtly, and started walking again. I scurried to keep up.

"Do you have a name for the tipster?" I asked.

"It came from an Eric . . . maybe Ernst Hamm, or something like that. One of those black-suited Nazis. He said there was a written complaint but somehow the written form got lost."

Somehow. "Hahn, yes, I'm familiar with him. Nasty piece of work."

The big German flashed a scowl at me, and Petit didn't reply. The entrance to my building loomed larger and larger and Petit barely paused outside before steaming into the lobby with us in tow. Immediately, Warner rapped out an order to two of his colleagues, one of whom went to the back door, the other setting up at the doors we'd just come through. Not for the first time, I felt violated. My home, my sanctuary was yet again being trespassed upon by men with bad intentions.

"Lefort." Petit waved me over. "You have a basement?"

"A cellar, yes, but I don't know if anyone uses it. I've not been down there in years."

"Perfect hiding spot, then."

"Or too fucking obvious, but I'll go check."

"No." He put a steadying hand on my chest. "Still not sure I can trust you. I'll look myself."

"If you don't trust me to search, what the hell am I doing here?"

"That's yet to be decided." Petit turned on his heel and followed Vacher to the back of the building and the stairs to the cellar.

"You want us to wait or what?" I asked testily.

"Do the ground-floor apartments," Petit said over his shoulder. "Then wait."

I resisted the urge to make an unprofessional gesture at his retreating back. Instead I turned to Warner.

"There are two apartments per floor. Down here is the concierge's and an empty one. I'll clear the concierge, you take the empty. It should be unlocked." That was thanks to the Germans, who'd mandated empty apartments remain unlocked in case they wanted to billet troops there. They'd found it too much trouble to kick in doors and then replace the broken jambs and locks, so from their perspective the rule made sense. Unfortunately, it also made sense for homeless drifters and drug users looking for a place to crash. We'd kept them out of our building purely by vigilance and dumb luck.

Warner nodded and gestured to his comrade. I turned to the *flic*.

"Your name?"

"Maurice Lavigne, monsieur."

"You're with me, Lavigne." We let ourselves into what had been Lucas and then Natalia's rooms, and I half expected to see her inside, or some sign of her. But she had indeed cleared out.

"Here, monsieur. On the floor, looks like bloodstains."

"Old ones. And we're not here to solve actual crimes, Lavigne, we're here because of newspapers."

"Yes, sir." I could have sworn he stifled a smirk, which made me like the kid.

We swept through the place and I felt a sense of relief at the emptiness. Back in the lobby, I could hear Petit and Vacher returning.

"Spiders and rats," Petit said. "Some old bottles I thought about pinching, but since this is your place, I left them for you."

"Very kind. Nothing in the concierge's apartment."

Warner and his partner came out of the empty apartment. "Nothing in there. Nice enough place, might relocate myself."

"I wouldn't, the plumbing in this neighborhood is terrible," I said. Bad enough Germans kept visiting the building; I sure as hell didn't need one living here.

"A little far from where I want to be anyway," Warner said gruffly.

As we started up the stairs, the acid in my stomach burned hotter. We cleared the second-floor apartments, one of which was empty, and the other housed an elderly couple, Monsieur and Madame Toulard, who were always glued to each other and wouldn't even say hello on the stairs.

Together, the posse of four Frenchmen and two Germans headed to the third floor. We'd barely started up when, above us, the sound of footsteps caused Warner and Petit to draw their guns. I was as surprised as they were to see a man in police uniform stopping on the landing in front of Gerald Darroze's apartment.

"Daniel Moulin, isn't it?" Petit asked.

"Oui, monsieur." Moulin nodded and then looked blankly at me. *"Bonjour, Détective Lefort."*

"Moulin, how are you?"

"Very well, sir. May I ask what's happening here?"

"I'm in charge," Petit said officiously. "We're searching the building for evidence of illegal newspaper printing."

"This building?" Moulin seemed genuinely surprised.

"Don't tell me you live here, too." Petit sounded exasperated.

"No, sir. Just checking on a crime scene, making sure it's undisturbed." He gestured to Darroze's apartment, where police tape was now plastered back and forth across the front door.

Who did that and when? I wondered, but knew better than

to ask. A second later I realized. Moulin had done it, and more likely than not behind Darroze's door was the very evidence Petit was looking for.

"And it's my crime scene, Petit," I said, figuring I needed to stop playing dumb and start taking charge. Or at least help steer the ship that Moulin was piloting.

"How is there a crime scene in your building that you're in charge of?" he asked, incredulous.

"That's a question for Chief Proulx," I said. "He decided that since I didn't hear or see anything related to the crime, I was clear to investigate. Especially given our dearth of manpower right now."

Petit looked at me suspiciously. "And the crime was homicide, since you're on it?"

"Correct. A man shot outside the building and the owner of this apartment is in custody."

Moulin jumped in. "And it's closed off because we've not been able to go through his things, see what connects him to the crime."

"Closed off since when?" Petit asked.

"Oh, since the man was arrested," Moulin lied glibly.

"But the murder was outside?" Petit moved toward the door.

"Yes," I said. "But we're sure inside there will be evidence as to why."

"When did this happen?"

"The early morning of December 31, New Year's Eve."

"And why haven't you been through his place yet? That was days ago."

"Partly a manpower issue," I said. "People keep seconding me to take part in pointless raids."

"Don't be insolent, Lefort. Take down this tape, I'm going inside."

"I'd prefer you not to, sir," I said, not budging. "Not only will that upset my crime scene, but the door's locked."

"Your crime scene is outside," Petit said. "Warner, kick the door in."

"Jesus, Petit, at least let me clear the place, so I can look out for evidence of my murder." It was worth a shot, and Moulin tried to back me up.

"I think that would be best, sir," he said. "The fewer boots through there the better."

Petit thought while Warner applied the heel of his to the door, which gave way with a loud crack.

"No, I still don't trust that you're on the up-and-up," Petit said to me, then turned to Moulin. "And you appearing on scene like a ghost doesn't fill me with confidence. You two check the other apartment on this floor, I'm going into this one."

"But sir," Moulin began, only to be cut off by the warning finger of an impatient Petit.

I threw Moulin a worried look. It was a clever way to keep the apartment secure, and would have worked nine times out of ten. But Petit was turning out to be the most suspicious bastard I'd ever met, and if he did find something inside it would now be obvious Moulin was trying to hide it.

"Come on, Detective," Moulin said, taking me by the arm and steering me to Claire Raphael's old apartment. Vacher started to follow.

"We've got this," I told the young *flic*. "Wait here and make sure Petit isn't jumped or doesn't break his neck looking into an empty toilet."

"Yes, sir."

Claire's front door was unlocked and we went right in, me behind Moulin, who closed it behind us.

"What's in Darroze's apartment?" I whispered.

"Dust and mice," Moulin said with a grin. "A bit of protesting too much did the trick, looks like."

"You meant for him to go in there."

"And us to go in here. Where we won't find anything at all."

I jumped at a woman's voice behind me.

"Oh, Daniel. He'll find a little something."

I swung around and my mouth fell open in surprise.

"Hi, Henri," she said, batting her eyes as flirtatiously as anyone ever did. "Delightful to see you again."

"Jesus, Natalia, what the hell . . . ?" I didn't even know what to ask at that point.

"Oh, don't be mad, handsome." She nudged me with her hip. "At least I didn't ask you to help me move."

CHAPTER TWENTY-NINE

"You two, both of you"—I kept my voice a low growl, but I knew its angry tenor came across as clear as a bell—"have a whole lot of explaining to do."

"Henri, for now we just have to clear this place and let Petit know all is well." Moulin put a calming hand on my arm, but it didn't do the trick. "Right, well, I'll have a look around so we can truthfully say we did. Be right back."

"You moved out of the downstairs place and into here?" I asked Natalia.

"Yes. I know it sounds cold and cruel, but there's more room up here and I want—"

"I don't care about that," I interrupted. "But I want to know who you are. And no lies, no half-truths, I want to know what's going on."

"Oh, Henri, you're so adorable when you're strict." She gave me that wide-eyed smile that I found hard to resist. "I'm Natalia Tsokos."

"Maybe that's your name, but you're no relation of Lucas Nomikos."

"I'm not?"

"We have this great modern invention called a telephone that allowed me to speak to him directly. And he's a terrible liar, even though he tried for a minute."

"Hmm, yes." Natalia frowned. "I did have my doubts; he seemed very honest."

"Unlike some people."

"Get off your high horse, Detective," she said, but playfully. "Natalia Tsokos is my real name. Pretty much everything I said about myself was true."

"But you needed to move in here without suspicion, without too many questions."

"And Lucas was supposed to provide that. Oh well."

"So? Why are you here?"

"The same reason the authorities are going through the building."

"The newspapers?"

"I have training in producing and distributing them. So yes."

"I figured. But why here, exactly?"

"Let's just say someone in the building reached out to people who know me, wanting to do something for the cause."

"Oh my lord." I groaned, a little too loudly. "It was Mimi, wasn't it?"

"No comment," she said with a small smile.

"You should have told me. She should have told me."

"She wanted to keep you out of it, protect you."

"And how is that working out?" I said grimly.

"Not as planned, I admit."

"So where is it?"

"Where is what?"

"Don't act dumb. The evidence those people," I pointed to the door, "are looking for."

"In pieces in the bathroom. Lots of pieces."

I groaned, this time just inwardly. "Then let's hope Daniel's sleight of hand is convincing."

"You called?" Moulin reappeared.

"We're done here." I turned to Natalia. "You need to get out of here in case Petit wants to look around. Without you in here we can explain how Claire has disappeared, blame those machine pieces on her."

"But my things are in here," Natalia protested.

"Then if he does come in, let's hope he doesn't look at them too closely." I thought for a moment. "If he takes our word for it, I'll knock twice on the door and you slip out as we head upstairs. If he doesn't, you're still the concierge and you're trying to figure out where Claire went. Got it?"

"Yes, sir." Natalia saluted, a little cocky in the moment, I thought.

"Let's go," I said to Moulin. He followed me to the apartment door and when we stepped out, Petit and Vacher were exiting Darroze's place.

"Anything?" I asked.

"No, you?"

I had a choice to make, and a split second to make it. I could say we found the parts and blame Claire, absolutely. But, even if the Germans believed that, they might find Natalia's belongings in there and, even if they didn't, there was a high probability that everyone in the building would be punished. And the Nazis were not into slapping wrists.

"All clear." My heart raced as I said the words. I could have blamed Claire for the machine parts, but who would Petit blame for saying *All clear* when it wasn't? Me.

"Right, next floor." He waved the Germans and two *flics* ahead of him, and for a moment he paused. "Which floor do you live on, Lefort?"

"Top one. And no printing presses are running up there without me knowing."

"Unless you're running them."

"Not possible."

"How's that?" Petit had one foot on the stairs but stopped again.

"I'm a terrible speller, no one would read a word I printed."

He acknowledged the joke with a brisk nod of his head, then carried on upstairs. I leaned against the jamb by the door and gave it a couple of gentle knocks. Then I steered Moulin ahead of me to the staircase and started up behind Petit. Behind us, I heard the door open quietly and prayed that neither Petit nor any of his goons would look back. They didn't, but as I watched them intently my heart ticked faster.

Merde. There are still two goons downstairs. German ones at that.

I turned and started back down, a flight of stairs behind Natalia. I hurried but also tried to be quiet, while trying to make it look like I wasn't doing either. I didn't dare call out to her, so I just went as fast as I could, which was less fast than her dainty feet carried her. I thought if I caught up with her I could slap handcuffs on her and escort her past the Germans, just like she and I had discussed previously, a pretend arrest. But she was too far ahead, and I didn't want the Germans helping with the process, as they wouldn't understand my French and might take her themselves.

"Natalia," I called out as I hit the landing above the ground floor. "Wait."

She'd reached the lobby and one of the Germans was moving toward her. I realized I had my handcuffs in my hands, and they could both see that.

"*Halt!*" he commanded, and I noticed for the first time how young he was. Eighteen or nineteen at most.

"No, it's all right," I called down. "You can let her go."

But he either didn't hear or didn't understand, instead looking afraid and drawing his pistol. Natalia slowed and then looked up at me, confusion in her eyes. The young German held up one hand, telling her to stop again, and maybe it was the alarm in the German's eyes, maybe the fear in mine but, for whatever reason, she herself panicked.

"I have to go, I have to go," she said, and ducked under the German's arm.

"*Halt!*" he said again, and raised his pistol.

I shouted. "No, wait. *Nicht schießen! Nicht—*"

Natalia was almost at the front doors of the building and the German was no more than ten yards from her when he ignored my pleas and fired, just once. The sound of the shot split the air and echoed around the lobby, and the bullet itself picked up Natalia's small body and threw her into the door. She hit it face-first, and then slid to the floor where she lay motionless on her side.

I raced down the final set of stairs and past the young man who'd shot her, a look of surprise on his face as if he'd not meant to. I skidded to a stop where she lay, kneeling to touch her, to see where she'd been hit. My fingers felt the blood that soaked the back of her coat, and I turned her over carefully. She was wheezing, struggling for breath, and I knew at least one lung had been penetrated.

"Natalia, just hold on," I said, trying not to sound terrified. "We'll get a doctor here, you're going to be all right." I looked up at the German, who still stood there like a statue, just staring. My brain struggled to find the words, so I said them in French first. "Call a doctor. *Rufen Sie einen . . . einen Arzt!*"

But he just stood there, a child holding a gun, eyes wide and disbelieving as Natalia's blood soaked my hands and, with a gentle cough and a moan that I barely heard, the light went out of her eyes forever.

CHAPTER THIRTY

Apartment doors flew open and feet clattered down the stairs toward us, but I saw and heard them through a fog of rage that, oddly, spurred on my mind but slowed my body. I stood and turned toward the young German who'd shot Natalia and, as I took a step forward, he dropped his gun on the tiled floor. His eyes were wide and his face as white as a sheet, and in a moment he rushed past me, slamming into the door that Natalia's body wasn't blocking and all but threw himself into the street outside.

I looked down at Natalia, her face drawn and still, and her eyes still open but utterly lifeless. A hundred times, maybe a thousand, I'd stared into the face of death, which I knew not to be a state of rest or any other platitude. Death was a pitiless moment in time, a stopped heartbeat that turned a living, breathing, loving, brave human being into a corpse. Natalia, here and so alive a minute ago, was now long gone, and my heart was shattered by the pain of it.

Daniel Moulin appeared from behind me, kneeling by her side and doing what every cop does when he comes across someone who's just been shot—he felt for her pulse and when he found none, he paused for a moment and then gently closed her eyes.

"What the hell happened?" he asked, and I thought I heard an accusation in there.

"She didn't stop," I said weakly. "We were telling her to wait, to stop, and she panicked. She got scared and panicked and ran for the door."

The lobby was filling up, with the Germans there for the search and pretty much everyone who still lived in the building.

"Who shot her?" Moulin asked.

"A kid. He's just a kid." I gestured to the door. "He's outside, probably puking."

Amid the hubbub, Petit started to shout questions and instructions but I ignored him and stepped outside. The young German was on the other side of rue Jacob, squatting on his haunches with his helmet on the pavement in front of him. I was right, he'd puked into the gutter and now was staring at the ground, deep inside his own head.

They say there's a first time for everything, but that doesn't usually include killing people, especially pretty young girls. But as I well knew, war turns life's usual matrices upside down and inside out, including the general presumption that we can live out our days without taking another's life.

I walked over to him, careful not to get too close. "You speak French?" I asked.

He turned his head slowly, and I watched as his eyes refocused to see me. "*Oui*. I am studying French literature at university. I was."

"Which one?"

"Berlin." He turned his gaze back to the pavement. "I was a student. Now I am a murderer."

"A murderer? No, not that."

"She's dead." A plea lingered in his eyes, a hope that maybe, somehow, he was wrong.

"She is. And you did shoot her. But I'm not sure it was murder." I'd gone from wanting to throttle this kid to seeing him the way I'd seen so many in the 1914 war. Which is to say, a uniform, a rank, and a gun are all signs you're in the army, but you don't really know you're at war until you do your patriotic duty and kill someone. A disturbing handful took pride in that moment but most were like this kid, and fucking hated themselves for it. Time and more kills dulled that self-hatred, but only by blunting one's very soul: a poor solution to an awful problem.

"I didn't know what to do." He was shaking his head. "I didn't know. She shouldn't have done that."

"I know."

"Why did she try and run away?" He looked up at me again, eyes pleading for an answer that would satisfy him.

"She was scared. Like you, she was young and didn't know what to do."

"I didn't want to hurt her. I never meant for . . ." His voice trailed off and he was back to examining the ground.

Behind me, the doors to our building opened and Warner stepped out.

"Hey, soldier. Come here."

"Give him a minute," I said. "He's not used to . . . this."

Warner sighed and walked slowly over to us. "What happened?" He asked me and not the kid, for which I was grateful.

"Everyone panicked. The girl was scared and wanted to leave, he didn't want her to. It just happened, and very quickly."

"I see." He looked down at his comrade. "You're not in the shit, if that's what you're worried about. If she tried to run you're allowed to shoot her."

"I'm guessing that's not his main concern right now," I said. "Jesus, how young do you enlist them?"

"He's at least eighteen. A man."

"Sixteen," the soldier corrected. "I lied on my application."

"That so?" Warner reached down and grabbed the kid's shoulder. He hauled him to his feet, then stooped and picked up his helmet, which he shoved roughly into his junior's hands. "Bet you're wishing right now you hadn't, eh?" He chuckled at his own wit and, with his hand on the youngster's shoulder still, started to direct him down rue Jacob toward the blockade.

After a few steps the kid twisted around and I saw tears streaking his face. "Tell her I'm sorry. Please, tell her I'm sorry."

I watched as they made their way to the end of the street and turned the corner. I was about to head back into the building when both doors opened and Petit and his search team exited. He came over to me, and appeared rattled.

"We're done here, obviously." He shook his head slowly. "Did he have to shoot her?"

"They never have to," I said. "They just decide to. It's like a goddamned instinct now. If it's any consolation, the kid is devastated."

"Not as devastated as her." He jabbed a finger toward the

building. "For heaven's sake, I don't even know what to do now. Is there an investigation when a German shoots one of us, or not?"

"It's like the fairground. They get to take potshots at us, and the worst that happens is they don't get a stuffed animal. Except he didn't miss, so he probably will."

"I hope it makes him feel better," he said sarcastically, then looked at me. "You knew her?"

"I did."

"Well?"

"Well enough to know she didn't deserve that."

"You two weren't—"

"No, we weren't," I said hurriedly, without really knowing why. "Look, if you want I'll take care of everything here. She has some friends I need to tell, who can maybe help with the burial." Tears pricked my eyes as I said the words, and I looked away. "What a waste."

"You don't think she was really into anything illegal, do you?" he asked. "Is that why she tried to run?"

"Petit, for crying out loud. She was scared. She was young. She just wanted out of there, that's all."

"Yes, of course." He straightened and gestured for his team to follow him. "I suppose I'll include her death in my report, but if you can take care of . . . everything, that would be very helpful. You know, I'd feel a lot better if we'd found something in there. Damn shame."

I wasn't sure if the *Damn shame* applied to Natalia's death or the raid coming up empty but I didn't care to ask. The sooner he and his goons left my street, the happier I would be. As they walked away, Daniel Moulin stepped out. We met in the middle of the quiet street.

"I don't know what to say," he began. "They said she hit the German and tried to escape?"

"She didn't hit anyone. She got scared and ran. Does Mimi know?"

"She came out of her apartment and saw Natalia's body, so yes."

"We need to move it."

"I did. I put her inside her old apartment."

"Thank you."

"What do we do now?" he asked. "And do we do it as police or friends?"

"There's someone I need to tell. A friend, I think he is."

"Who?"

"Come with me and find out."

• • •

We used our credentials to get on the Métro, and sat in silence as the train clanked and rattled beneath the city streets. The carriage was busy but we found seats when an older couple got up and waited by the door to exit. I watched them, their gentle gestures and soft touches to hand, back, and elbow, all just part of their being together, instinctual moments of comfort and care.

They stepped off in unison at the next stop, taking away my distraction—I was acutely aware that the last time I'd ridden a train was with Natalia. I remembered the way she stood up to the old man harassing her, how she'd not needed me to step in, but I'd done it anyway. Despite the dozens, no hundreds, of people I'd known who'd been killed in this war and the last, her death was threatening to overwhelm me. Moulin seemed to sense this.

"Henri. Are you all right?"

"Honestly, I don't know. She's one more in a long list, I know that."

"It's not just a list, though. Some matter more than others."

"So it seems."

"And you and she had . . . something. A chemistry or some sort of connection. I don't know."

"You think?" I was surprised. I liked that he'd said that; I thought people had said stuff like that just to irritate me.

"I do." He sat back as the train doors opened again. "This damned war."

"Yeah." We sat there in silence as the train shunted itself up to speed. A minute or two later, I reminded myself, as much as him, "And I still have a case to solve."

"True, but somehow that doesn't seem so important right now."

"Funny you should say that."

"What do you mean?"

"This is us." The train slowed and we got to our feet. When it jolted to a stop I yanked the door open and we stepped onto the dusty, crowded platform. "This way."

"You never said where we were going."

"It's kind of a secret."

"I'm good at keeping those."

"I know."

"Henri, why are you being so cryptic all of a sudden?" He hurried to keep up with me as we climbed the stairs and stepped out of the Métro into the light. "And what did you mean earlier when you said—"

"Just keep up, Daniel," I said, not slowing down.

We took two wrong turns before I found the right street and the unmarked house. I reached for the door handle and Daniel said, "You're not even going to knock?"

"Do you knock when you go into a restaurant?" I asked, and pushed the door open. "Take off your shoes."

Moulin rocked back on his heels as the smell of cooking washed over us.

"My god, what is this place?"

The room was empty; I assumed we'd just missed whatever crowd showed up for the lunch hours.

"Natalia brought me here."

"Like a . . . date?"

"No, not a date," I said brusquely. "Business."

"What business, yours or hers?" He fell silent as Amit appeared in the archway.

"Monsieur Henri, please take a seat." He gestured to the whole room, letting us know we could sit where we wanted.

"Amit, we can't stay. I'm here with news. I don't know who needs to know, who to tell, but I'm assuming you do?"

He looked at me for a moment, and then his steady gaze waved as he realized we only knew one person in common.

"Natalia?" he asked in whisper. "Arrested, or . . . ?"

"Not arrested, and perhaps we should be thankful for that. She was shot an hour ago. I'm sorry, but she's dead."

"You are sure?" The eternal question when people hear such news.

"Yes. I was there, I saw it."

He looked down, and his whole body went still. He stayed like that for what felt like an age, before finally taking a deep breath.

"Where is she now?"

"She's at my building."

"There are people who would like to . . . see her. Take care of her. Is that possible?"

"Can I ask who?"

"Better you don't. Friends and some family is all you should know."

"Thank you, yes, I think that would be good. Have them come to my building, I'll write the address down. And thank them for me, I honestly didn't know what to do."

"Ah, Monsieur Henri." He gave me a soft smile. "You came here, which means you knew exactly what to do."

I smiled, and pulled out my notebook to write down my address. I tore off the paper and handed it to him.

"Thank you, Monsieur Henri."

"I want to ask you so many questions."

"About Natalia?" He smiled again. "That is your job, and also your nature. But we both know you should not, and that even if you do I will not be able to tell you anything."

"She was as good a person as she seemed?"

"Oh, no, not at all." He shook his head, then looked up. "Much, much better. She is with the angels now, where she has always belonged."

We put our shoes back on, and I closed the door gently behind me. We began walking back to the Métro station and were both silent for a while, but then Moulin glanced over.

"So, back to the investigation?"

"You mean Monsieur Remillon's murder?"

"Right, unless you're satisfied Darroze did it."

"No, no. It wasn't Darroze at all."

"Really? How can you be so sure?"

"Simple." I stopped and faced him. "Because I know who actually killed Guy Remillon."

"You do?" His eyebrows arched in surprise. "Well, good. Who?"

"Ah, the great reveal, always a fun moment." I started walking again, and he quickly fell in beside me. "It's normally the end of the story for a detective, isn't it?"

"I don't know, I suppose so."

"Not this time, though, dear boy. No, this time I have even more questions than I did before I figured out who killed him."

"Henri, what the hell are you talking about? Who was it?"

"Well, now, I shall tell you." I put a friendly arm around his shoulders. "It was you, Daniel. You killed Guy Remillon."

CHAPTER THIRTY-ONE

We ducked into a new bar, which was an attractive rarity all by itself. It was called Chez Maman, and when we stepped inside we saw freshly painted walls and what looked like brand-new tables and chairs spread throughout the room. The bar itself was at the back of the space, and tending was a woman in her twenties with bright orange hair. We were the only customers, which is probably why she was leaning over a book and smoking a cigarette.

I pointed Moulin to a seat in the corner farthest from the bar and went to get us something strong.

"Almost," the bartender said, holding up a hand to stop me talking while she finished her paragraph. "Right, all done. What can I get you gentlemen?"

"I'll start with an explanation as to how the heck you've managed to open a new bar right now."

"I can't go into details, but it is related to a nasty incident at the One-Two-Two. You know what that is?"

I nodded; I'd been inside the famous brothel myself not so long ago. Not for the usual reason, but on a case.

"Let's just say the incident involved a drunk, horny, and very senior German official who forgot to read the rules about hurting the girls."

"You worked there?"

"And now I own this place. Moving up in the world, you might say."

"Congratulations. My name is Henri."

"Call me Maman."

"I will. And we'll take two whiskeys, if you have any."

"I have everything, for now anyway. My apologetic German benefactor is ensuring my opening months are fruitful and unmolested." She took a drag on her cigarette. "Which is a pretty ironic way of phrasing that. I even have a telephone if you know anyone else who has one to receive a call."

That gave me an idea. "I do. I'll be quick, I promise."

"At the end of the bar, help yourself. And two whiskeys coming up."

I could see Moulin watching me as I placed the call, and kept it short and sweet like I said I would. I hung up and carried the drinks to our table.

"You calling the uniforms to come get me?" Moulin asked with a rueful smile.

"You're not denying it?"

He took a sip. "I'm not admitting it, either."

"Probably a wise decision."

"What makes you think it was me?"

"The lies, Daniel. It's almost always the lies." I sniffed my own glass and took the smallest sip. "I didn't realize until you brought that drunk to the cells."

"The one from the bridge."

"The one who supposedly housed you in Montmartre and let you go. And yet you didn't recognize him."

"Maybe I was just really drunk, too drunk to remember faces."

"Except he let you go because you'd sobered up."

"Ah."

"I had an idea after that and checked the list of abandoned homes in Paris, the ones destined for our friendly invaders."

"And what did you find?"

"I found an entry for your apartment, which was somewhat at odds with your story. The *flic*'s signature next to the entry was illegible but I imagine that was on purpose, and, if we bothered to check, the handwriting will match yours."

"And why would I do such a thing?"

"So you would have a reason to move into our building. Help Mimi with her little newspaper scheme."

"How devious of me. If true."

"Agreed. And it is."

"And why did I shoot Guy Remillon?"

"That's the most straightforward piece of the puzzle. He was looking into Mimi's activities. The black market stuff, but also the printing press."

"Solid motive."

"What I couldn't figure out is how you knew when he was coming. You arranged for some poor sap to play you in Montmartre—I'm curious who that was by the way—so you must have known when Remillon was making his visit."

He looked at me over his glass before replying. "Where are we headed with this?"

"Do you mean, are you going to be enjoying the attentions of a firing squad in the near future?"

"Do I get to choose that over the guillotine?"

I lit a cigarette and took a long draw. "You know something about me that could destroy my career. Yet you've not brought it up at all."

"You really think I'd use that against you? Blackmail you into silence?" He looked genuinely offended. Then again, I was finding out he was a pretty damn good liar. "I made you a promise about keeping that secret, Henri, and whatever you decide to do, I intend to honor it."

"Very decent of you." I took another sip of whiskey. "And to answer your last question, neither."

"Neither?"

"Firing squad nor guillotine. Neither of them are in your future."

"You're not turning me in?"

"Without an admission I don't have definitive proof. Even if you did confess, I'm not sure I'd believe it because it'd come from a man who's lied to me already on this case. Plus, I have two very different descriptions of the killer and you only match one of them." I sat back. "And on top of all that, there's the burned evidence I found in Darroze's apartment, the same man seen stashing the murder weapon. And I can't disprove that statement now that the person who made it is gone."

"Natalia."

"Right. Just laying my cards on the table."

"There's something you need to know about her." Moulin took a swallow of his drink. "Since we're laying out our cards."

"Tell me."

"She wasn't scared. At the end. That's not why she ran."

"What do you mean?"

"There are things in Mimi's apartment, things the search party would have found. Natalia knew that."

"You're saying she caused a distraction, that distraction, on purpose."

"Yes. She knew we'd all be in great danger if they searched Mimi's place, and she knew that if she made enough of a fuss downstairs the search could be derailed."

"My god, she made a fuss, all right." A wave of sadness swept over me. Guilt, too, for not seeing Natalia's bravery at the time.

"That woman was never scared of anyone or anything," Moulin said. "She told me she jabbed a gun in the ribs of a Nazi."

"She did, and not just any Nazi." I raised my glass. "Here's to a brave and wonderful soul. Natalia."

Moulin raised his. "Natalia." We drained our glasses and Moulin chuckled. "She really did like you, did you know that?"

"Be quiet."

"I'm serious. And I know you noticed her flirting with you."

"She did, but I assumed she did that with everyone."

"Not with me."

"That's because you're low-ranking and particularly ugly."

"Must be." He shook his head sadly. "This damned war, taking someone like that from us."

"Now you know why I'm not turning you in."

"Meaning?"

"It's not like it used to be, when we had good guys on one side and bad guys on the other. It's just not that simple anymore." I stubbed out my cigarette and lit another one. "Does she know?"

"Nicola? No."

"Just Mimi, then. And she's also good at keeping secrets."

"She is. Another one?"

"Why not."

Moulin went to the bar and brought back two more whiskeys. "Better make this the last, I'm used to watered-down booze, and this isn't."

"Good point. That's why I stick to Mimi's wine."

"*Santé.*" We clinked glasses and drank. Moulin cleared his throat. "You said before, you couldn't figure out how . . . the alleged killer knew Remillon would be at the building when he was."

"Not at first, but then it became obvious."

"How so?"

"When I was at Petit's new department I saw that they keep the list of abandoned apartments near where they receive and file the *corbeaux.*"

"Ah, yes, that they do."

"So, someone who went in to log an abandoned apartment might, without any difficulty at all, be able to look through incoming complaints and find one relating to themselves or, perhaps, a friend."

"Yes, I see how they might indeed be able to do that." Moulin nodded over his glass.

"And if a French or German official had assigned it for investigation on a certain date and time, well, they'd see that, too."

Moulin nodded. "I heard they sometimes notate the authorizations that way."

"And so this hypothetical person could know exactly when someone like Guy Remillon would be paying a visit."

"I would say that your hypothesis holds water."

"Unlike me." I stood. "Don't go anywhere and don't touch my drink."

I found my way to the bathroom, my head lighter than I thought it would be. Maman was serving the good stuff, and as long as she did, I'd be making the trip here.

When I walked back into the bar I saw Nicola in my seat. Her hands were clasped in her lap and she was white as a ghost. Moulin leaned forward toward her and was talking earnestly. I hung back until he spotted me. He said something else, and Nicola took his hands and smiled softly at him. Moulin smiled back, then stood and waved me over.

"She drank your whiskey, not me," he said.

"She probably needed it more than I did."

"I wondered who you'd called, feared the worst."

"I figured she didn't know, thought you'd want to tell her yourself."

"You are a wise and kind man, Henri."

"Very rarely." I put out my hand. "One secret apiece, let's try and keep it to that, yes?"

"Agreed." He shook my hand. "I need to get back to work, I'm very low level and can get in trouble for disappearing for hours at a time."

"Not to mention drinking on the job."

He laughed and stooped to kiss Nicola's forehead, and she and I watched him leave.

"Sorry for finishing your drink," she said as I sat down opposite her.

"Too early in the day for me anyway. Are you all right?"

"What does that mean these days?" She twirled her finger around the top of the glass. "But yes. He told me—"

"Stop. I don't want to hear it."

"Ah, yes. You're Detective Lefort as well as Henri, my brother. Sometimes I forget." She cocked her head and looked at me. "Part of me is surprised you're letting Daniel off the hook. But then part of me isn't. I suppose things aren't black-and-white like they used to be."

"I think they might be, though. You just have to look at it differently."

"Meaning?"

"Killing has always been illegal, and still is."

"Except when it isn't."

"Exactly. The question remains the same: Was my reason good enough to let me escape the guillotine? It's just that the bag of reasons got fuller since the Krauts arrived."

"So how do you resolve the case?"

"I have yet to decide. You have a suggestion?"

"I mean, either you tell Proulx you can't solve it, which doesn't sound like you. Or . . ."

"Or Darroze swings for it?"

"Right. That's the safer option; you know the Germans aren't going to like someone getting away with killing one of their minions."

She was right, and I'd already thought of that. If I declared the case unsolved, or unsolvable, the Germans might decide that reprisals were in order. They couldn't just allow one of their servants to be murdered in the street, not without *someone* paying the price. Several someones, even. And I had a notion of who they may be, given the Germans' penchant for executing those closest to whatever insult they'd been served. In other words, Natalia had saved the residents of my building once, and now Darroze might have to do it a second time.

"I've never condemned an innocent man before," I said.

"That you know of."

"True, but the knowing it, that's what doesn't sit well."

"You said he's innocent. Is he really?"

"Of this crime, yes." I thought about it. "But of others, worse ones? Absolutely not. He single-handedly condemned the Millers to death, and did his damnedest to condemn Mimi as well."

"He has blood on his hands, for sure," Nicola agreed. "Just not for Remillon."

"So this would be karma instead of justice." I lit a cigarette and ignored Nicola's frown of disapproval. "I can live with that."

"Are you sure?"

"He chose his side. He made his choices. And look, I'm not going to fake evidence or make up any lies to send him to the gallows."

"I thought it was the guillotine."

"Whichever. My point is that I'm not going to do any more than I have, and if the powers that be decide he's guilty, then this is his own doing."

"Not all his own doing," Nicola prodded.

"I'll live with myself. The rules have changed, and if a man is willing to condemn his neighbors to death for buying wine and cheese, or just for being English, then he's a danger to everyone around him. And if he's released, that means us. As far as I'm concerned, he attempted to murder Mimi, and that's barely an exaggeration. No, he's reaping the consequences of trying to take advantage of the German occupation, sacrificing others for his own selfish needs. I'll shed no tears for him."

"I won't either. I'm just sad for him, that he's that way. I can't understand why someone would be so callous."

"He told me your name was on one of his *corbeaux*."

Her eyes grew wide. "Are you serious?"

"I am."

"What did he say about me?"

"Well, honestly, I don't know." I thought back with satisfaction to the moment he told me. "I hit him in the jaw before he could give me details."

"Good for you." She sat back and smiled at me. "My sweet protective brother."

"For me, maybe that was the final nail in his coffin."

"What do you mean?"

"That he tried to sacrifice you." Tears stung my eyes, and I looked away. "I can't have that."

"Oh, Henri." Nicola put a hand on my arm and gave it a gentle squeeze. "You'd have to make your own coffee in the mornings."

I managed a smile. "See, I told you he was a monster."

"I'm not arguing. Shall we go?"

"In a moment. I want a promise from you first."

"Anything."

"No more secrets. Not to protect me or for any other reason. If we're going to make it through this damned war, then we need to stick together. And that means no secrets, even if you think I won't like it."

"Agreed. I hated not telling you things, truly. So I promise, no secrets."

"Good. Now let's go see Mimi."

"Why Mimi?"

"I plan to extract the same promise from her."

"I think she'll be on board."

"Good. So tell me, what's in the building that shouldn't be?"

She grimaced. "A dismantled press and too many copies of the newsletter."

"We need all of it gone. If the Germans realize their search was interrupted, they could come back."

"Sure, Henri, but the problem is always the same. Where?" She wagged a finger. "And don't tell me the river, we're not giving up."

"The river was my first suggestion." I recognized that look of determination. She wasn't giving up and I didn't want to force her to lie to me. "But I think I have a better one, if you insist on staying in the newspaper business."

"I do insist. What's your idea?"

"The Croix-Rouge."

"I don't understand."

"The Métro station. It's close to us, but not too close, and has been closed for more than a year. Almost two. No one goes there, and if they did, you'd hear them coming and have several escape routes."

She clasped her hands together in delight. "My goodness, Henri, it's perfect. You're a genius."

"Only when I drink good whiskey."

She laughed. "I bet Mimi could get you some."

"I bet she could." I stood, too quickly, and had to steady myself. "Come on then, escort your genius brother home. We now have two things to discuss with her."

ABOUT THE AUTHOR

Nick Berard

Mark Pryor is a former newspaper reporter and felony prosecutor, originally from England but now working as a criminal defense attorney in Austin, Texas. He is the author of the Hugo Marston mystery series, set in Paris, London, and Barcelona. Mark is also the author of the psychological thriller *Hollow Man* and its sequel, *Dominic*. As a prosecutor, he appeared on CBS News's *48 Hours* and Discovery Channel's *Investigation Discovery: Cold Blood*.